HARD SHADOWS

J.B. TURNER

HARD SHADOWS

A **JON REZNICK** THRILLER

Published by Thomas & Mercer, Seattle

www.apub.com

Amazon, the Amazon logo, and Thomas & Mercer are trademarks of Amazon.com, Inc., or its affiliates.

EU Product Safety Contact:
Amazon Media EU S.à r.l.
38, avenue John F. Kennedy, L-1855 Luxembourg
amazonpublishing-gpsr@amazon.com

ISBN-13: 9781662527401
eISBN: 9781662527418

Cover design by @blacksheep-uk.com
Cover image: © Tim Robinson / ArcAngel; © Volodymyr TVERDOKHLIB, © Kevin Cass, © Kamenetskiy Konstanti / Shutterstock

Printed in the United States of America

HARD SHADOWS

One

FRENCH QUARTER, NEW ORLEANS

The bar was on lower Decatur.

Jon Reznick headed there, in the back of a cab, watching the scenery pass through a rain-streaked window. Neon-lit reflections in the standing water on the streets. The wipers sluicing the driving rain from the windshield. A crack of thunder as they headed past Bourbon Street, where a group of kids danced and splashed in the puddles like they hadn't a care in the world. The driver began to make idle chat about the storm hitting the city, how long it would last, how bad it would get, how much worse he had seen. But Reznick was miles away.

The driver turned his head rather than use the rearview mirror. "You picked some crazy night to go out for a drink, pal," he said. "You meetin' a girl or something?"

Reznick's mood was low. He sat in silence. In the distance, bolts of lightning streaked through the sky, illuminating the French Quarter.

The cab hung a right onto Decatur and pulled up sharply outside The Abbey.

The taxi driver turned around fully. "That's us, buddy."

Reznick handed over a fifty-dollar bill. Told the driver he didn't need change.

"Appreciate that, man. Take care. Summer brings the crazies out. It don't matter if the weather is stormy or not, the crazies are always out there. Don't forget what I'm telling you. It's dangerous."

"I'll keep that in mind." Reznick stepped out of the taxi, slamming the door shut behind him.

The sultry night air was thick like glue, but the rain cooled Reznick's skin. The pungent aroma of weed wafted from a group of guys standing outside a bar across the street.

He headed inside The Abbey, glad to get out of the downpour.

It was as cold as an icebox, the jagged new wave music an assault on his senses.

Reznick sat down at the bar. He ordered a Scotch and a Pabst Blue Ribbon. He took in the dark and dingy interior—the black decor, Christmas lights still flashing in a corner. The floor was buckled and worn, sticky from generations of spilled booze.

The Abbey was cash only, open twenty-four hours a day, and catered to serious drinkers.

Reznick immediately relaxed in this environment. He had visited the bar numerous times before, whenever he was in the city, usually with hardened ex-Delta buddies looking to kick back for a few days once a year. The jukebox began to play "Rockaway Beach" by The Ramones. It was loud. Ridiculously loud. But the other customers didn't seem to be listening to the music.

A Black guy wearing shades and a pork pie hat was drinking a Bud Light, playing a slot machine. A huge, red-faced white guy, sweat beading on his forehead, wearing a Vikings T- shirt and khaki shorts, was shouting loudly to anyone who would listen that he was an air traffic controller. A friend of his, with a Vikings hat on, was doing push-ups at the end of the bar.

The news channel on one of the TVs had footage of a growing American naval build-up in the southern Caribbean. Another screen was showing a report of a random stabbing in the nearby neighborhood of Tremé. No one seemed to be watching the TVs apart from Reznick. He sipped his cold beer. He felt as if he needed it.

A seventy-something Creole woman—teeth clenched, eyes bloodshot, beer-stained T-shirt, spilling the contents of an overflowing plastic cup of orange booze—began regaling an old-timer wearing a Ted Nugent tee about the time she had gotten stoned smoking grass while high on acid with Dennis Hopper at a funeral in Taos, New Mexico. The guy laughed so hard he fell off his barstool, lying crumpled on the wet floor.

It was that kind of place.

The bartender looked at Reznick, shaking his head. "You believe this shit?"

Reznick downed his shot, pushed the glass forward. The bartender poured another. "Never a dull moment."

"Three nights ago, a guy pissed his pants dancing to a video of Madonna on TV. I mean, what the actual fuck?"

Reznick said nothing.

"So, where you from, man?"

"Up north."

"That's a big place when you're in New Orleans. How far up north? New York?"

"Way up north. Maine."

"Shit, you're a long way from home, man. That's practically Canada."

Reznick nodded into his cold beer. He felt drained, lost in his own thoughts. He had been visiting an old friend of his from his Delta days, Ray LeBlanc. His buddy was dying slowly, painfully, in the hospital. Riddled with cancer. In his lungs. In his blood. Emaciated. Terrible.

That evening, Reznick had said his goodbyes to Ray. A man he had never seen cry in his life had cried in front of him. The doctors said he only had days left, pumped full of morphine. Reznick had spent hours at his dying friend's bedside. He had hugged his weak body tight, said a silent prayer, then left the University Medical Center. He hadn't looked back. His mood was as black as the New Orleans night.

Reznick hadn't been in The Big Easy for years. Maybe it was the summer storm currently lashing the city, but it seemed a lot quieter than usual. The jukebox began to play "Yellow Moon," a pulsating, bluesy, swamp reggae track. The Creole woman got up to dance, swaying, eyes closed, grooving to the hypnotic sound of the music.

The bartender pushed another shot of Scotch toward him.

Reznick handed him a fifty-dollar bill. "Get yourself one. Keep them coming."

"Thanks, man. Don't mind if I do."

Reznick looked around at the drink-soaked boozers inside the bar. "Seems like they're having a good time."

"Damn straight. This is the place for it. Open every goddamn hour of the year."

Reznick sipped his Scotch.

"You like the city?" The bartender ran a rag over a puddle on the bar.

"Just how I remember it."

The bartender opened a cold beer and leaned in as if in a conspiratorial manner. "You've got to be careful; keep your eyes open."

"Oh yeah?"

"Three weeks ago, cop was shot right outside. Right in the fucking head. I mean, come on, what the hell? Every cop in the city was swarming this street for days afterwards, you couldn't spit without hitting one."

Reznick knocked back his shot, enjoying the warm, burning sensation in his gut. He took a large gulp of his beer. He wasn't in the mood for discussing crime, weather, or much of anything for that matter.

"I was one of the folks that carried him into the ambulance. Believe it or not, he survived."

"He survived?"

"Yeah, he did."

"Someone must've been looking out for him."

"Damn straight. Shot in the fucking head, point blank. You know who it was? It was the M3 crew. You heard of them?"

Reznick shook his head and studied the bottles behind the bar as an old Johnny Cash song began to play. The bartender, skilled enough at his job to sense Reznick wanted to drink alone, headed to the other end of the bar. He wiped down the bar top some more before serving a bearded man three double vodka and Cokes on the rocks.

Reznick finished his beer. He thought for a moment, then signaled the bartender and ordered another, along with a large Scotch.

He stayed and drank in the bar for a couple of hours. The booze wasn't lifting his mood, unable to shake the images from his head of his dying friend.

Reznick felt waves of tiredness wash over him. He had been up before dawn back in Rockland, Maine, to catch a flight down to New York. Then a three-hour layover, before a bumpy Delta flight to New Orleans.

Reznick glanced up at the news footage on the TVs.

The bartender returned, leaning against the bar. "You want another?"

Reznick ordered a large plastic cup of bourbon and Coke on the rocks. He handed the guy another fifty-dollar bill. He walked out of the bar, plastic cup of booze in hand. A blues song played full blast. An old Willie Dixon tune.

He headed out into the stormy night. Down Decatur and across to Latrobe Park, adjacent to an old church. He looked up at the rain pouring from the heavens. Reznick felt empty, thinking of Ray and his impending death. He stood there, drenched—maybe in penance, maybe just for the hell of it.

Reznick saw a spectral figure lying curled up on a park bench. It was a panhandler, swathed in plastic bags and sodden cardboard. He moved closer. The man's face was weather-beaten and sun-blistered, an unlit cigarette hanging limp from the corner of his mouth. Beyond the man, at the far end of the small park, Reznick spotted a couple of junkies, soaked to the skin, smoking from a glass pipe.

The warm rain lashed his face and hair.

Reznick sipped the strong bourbon, crunching on the ice, thinking of the old days. Thinking of Ray. A strong, tanned Cajun boy who took no shit. A phenomenal warrior.

It was hard to think of Ray being unable to fight the cancer that was eating him alive. At the hospital, his sad, blue eyes had looked scared. Ray had never looked scared before. Ever. But as Ray faced his end, fear clearly haunted him.

Reznick had held his friend's bony hand as Ray's sister wept softly in the corner. He closed his eyes for a few moments now, said a silent prayer for Ray. He was soaked to the skin. He knocked back the rest of the icy bourbon, throwing the empty plastic cup into an overflowing trash can.

He'd had enough.

The following morning, Reznick's cell phone was vibrating on his bedside table, rousing him from sleep.

His head was pounding, and his throat felt dry as sandpaper. He groaned, reached over, and picked up his phone, half expecting it to be Trevelle Williams, his hacker pal. But it wasn't, it was a number he didn't recognize.

"Yeah?" Reznick said, gruffly.

A man's voice stated, "I'm looking to speak to a Mr. Jon Reznick?"

Reznick sat up in bed, getting his bearings. His head hurt bad, like a drill behind his eyes after the booze and pent-up emotion from the day before. "Who's this?"

"My name is Lawrence Morgan. I'm a partner at a law firm in Washington, DC. I've been asked by a client of mine to contact a Jon Reznick. Is that you?"

Reznick turned on his bedside light and squinted against the glow. "How did you get this number?"

"Your number was given to him, in the strictest confidence, by a friend of yours. I can explain all that. Are you Jon Reznick?"

"Do you mind telling me what this is about?"

"I represent a client who knows a lot about you. My client has indicated he would like to meet you."

"Meet me? What about?"

"Truth be told, my client doesn't know who to turn to."

Reznick wondered why the guy was being so cryptic. "Your client? What's his name? You need to give me some details."

"Those will be forthcoming. But first he requested that you meet him in person."

"*He requested.* What the hell is this? I've got no idea who or what you're talking about. You need to give me more. What does he want to talk about?"

"I'm not at liberty to divulge that information."

"I don't know what the hell you're talking about. And I don't really care. Who's this friend of mine who gave you my number? Stop wasting my time—I've got a plane to catch in three hours."

"My client . . . he knows all about you."

"There you go again."

"My client has contacts in the highest echelons in the intelligence community. Does the name Martha Meyerstein ring a bell?"

Reznick's senses switched on just hearing her name. He had worked closely with former FBI Assistant Director Martha Meyerstein over the years on numerous classified investigations. She had retired from the Feds and, last he heard, she was lecturing on national security at a university in Washington. But he was intrigued that she would hand over his number to someone. "You've got my attention. Go on."

"Would you agree to meet with my client?"

"Not really." Reznick checked his watch. He wanted to shower before going to the airport. He felt irritable, having to deal with a weird call from a stranger first thing in the morning. "Look, I'm going to hang up now."

"Please don't. My client is waiting for you."

Reznick sighed. "Martha's name bought you exactly this much more of my time. Now it's run out. What exactly does this person, whoever they are, want to talk about?"

"My client said to mention Gideon. That might give you a geographical idea as to what this is about."

Reznick sobered up with a prickle. He knew exactly what *Gideon* meant. It was related to a failed CIA-backed coup in Venezuela in 2020.

"That's what he has authorized me to share. So far. Please understand, I have to be careful what I say." A silence stretched between them. "I can reveal my client's identity if you agree to meet him. I promise, he is a man of great intelligence and integrity. But he believes you and only you can help him. He feels that he can trust you."

Reznick closed his eyes, his mind focused on catching his flight home. He wondered if Meyerstein had shared details of his roles in previous, classified investigations, and if that's what had piqued this mystery man's interest in him.

"Can you meet my client today?"

"Today? What's the hurry?"

"I've been told he has secret information he's been privy to. He stressed the urgency. Time is of the essence as far as he is concerned, Jon. He knows what you do. I've spoken to his father as well. He says there are plans in place."

"What plans?"

"My client can tell you all about it in person. I'll send you his contact details. Then I'll leave the rest up to you."

Reznick was now intrigued by this bizarre call. "So, he got my number from Meyerstein?"

"Correct. He knows Meyerstein well. I believe she has talked fondly about you and your résumé, what you can do. Your skill set."

Reznick closed his eyes for a moment.

"Will you see him?" Morgan said.

"I must be crazy. But what the hell, I'll see him."

"I'll be in touch."

Reznick ended the call. He wondered if this was an approach from the CIA to do some work overseas. But he pushed those thoughts to one side for the moment, then got up, showered, shaved, and put on some fresh clothes. He quickly packed his overnight bag, grabbed his airline tickets and his phone. He headed down to the lobby and checked out.

A cab picked him up outside.

Reznick got into the back seat and the car pulled away through the streets of New Orleans. Nothing but blue skies overhead; the storm had passed in the night. His cell phone pinged. He checked it. A text message from Lawrence Morgan.

My client is Stephen Leahy. He is a patient at Lakeland Psychiatric Hospital in Maryland. He has an incredible story to tell.

Two

The lines snaked around the departure terminal of Louis Armstrong New Orleans International Airport as far as the eye could see.

Reznick hated waiting in line. He decided to head to a coffee shop and order a strong black coffee. He had countless questions after the surreal call from the lawyer. So he turned, as he inevitably did when he wanted answers, to Trevelle Williams, ex-NSA cybersecurity genius. Trevelle had helped Reznick on countless assignments inside and outside of the FBI. And he had never let Reznick down.

Reznick found a stool in a quiet corner as he sipped his coffee.

Trevelle's phone rang four times before he answered. "Morning, Jon, how you feeling today? Rough night?"

"Had better mornings, that's for sure."

"Drinking down in New Orleans is bad for your health, man, let me tell you. But I'm assuming you don't want to discuss your night in the French Quarter."

"I need your help."

"What do you need?"

"Check out the name Stephen Leahy: L-E-A-H-Y. I got a call this morning."

"From Leahy?"

"No, his lawyer. I was told Stephen Leahy wants to see me, and he has contacts at the highest levels within the intelligence community."

"Who told you this? The lawyer?"

"Correct. Lawyer's name is Lawrence Morgan. Said his client was a in Lakeland Psychiatric Hospital in Maryland. And he wants to see me there."

"The client is a psychiatric patient? I don't like the sound of that."

"Strange for sure."

"Leave it to me. I'll check it out."

Reznick ended the call. He drank his coffee as he read a message on his phone from his daughter, Lauren, who was in Jakarta, working for the CIA. She had previously talked of leaving the Agency, but she had changed her mind after a month off back in the States. She was an analyst and had been offered a civilian job back in DC. However, the CIA had given her a nice raise and more time off, and she had signed a new contract.

He was immensely proud of his daughter, his only child. But he missed her. Badly.

Reznick was already contemplating forgetting about the trip to Maryland. He headed to the boarding gate for the flight to New York, and then up to Maine.

His cell phone rang.

"Jon, it's Trevelle. So the attorney, Lawrence Morgan, is a big-shot lawyer in DC. Has represented several senators, high-profile clients in the arts. Very expensive. So he's real, bona fide."

"Okay. What about Stephen Leahy? Does he even exist?"

He heard the sound of tapping on Trevelle's keyboard back at his base on Captiva Island, Florida.

"Okay, we are up and running for the day! So, Stephen Leahy—wow! He absolutely exists."

"What do you mean, *wow?*"

"I mean wow! He absolutely does exist and then some. He's at the CIA Directorate of Operations, no less."

Reznick took a few moments to process this information. "So why is his lawyer saying he's in a psychiatric hospital in Maryland? That makes no sense."

"I'm looking at mentions of Leahy in electronic communications, various datasets. Give me a minute . . . So, Stephen Leahy is the Deputy Director of the CIA for Operations. He's top dog. He's had a wide reach over the years. Counterintelligence, counterespionage, he's been all over the Agency. He's legit."

Something didn't add up. "Dig a little deeper. I'm starting to wonder if this is all some sort of bizarre hoax."

There was the sound of more frantic tapping. "I'm looking at the names of the patients within the hospital. And he's not there."

Reznick was relieved that Trevelle had saved him a wasted journey. "It sounded too far-fetched to be true. So it's a hoax. The call was bullshit."

"Well, there's certainly no one by the name of Stephen Leahy in that hospital."

Reznick heard the announcement that his flight to New York was beginning to board.

"Are you still there, Jon?"

"Yeah, I'm still here."

"The lawyer called you first thing this morning?"

"First thing, yeah."

"The question is, why would a reputable lawyer say a top CIA officer was his client and was being held in a psychiatric hospital when he's not?"

Reznick grew concerned that his cell phone number, despite being wrapped up in military-level encryption, had been hacked. "Who the hell knows?"

"What are you thinking?"

"I'm thinking about what gate my flight to New York is leaving from."

"What else?"

Reznick tried to puzzle out why he had received the call from the lawyer if the information was false. It didn't make any sense. "So there's no record of Stephen Leahy at that hospital? You've checked and double-checked?"

"Absolutely. There's no trace of him there."

"Unless . . ."

"Unless what, Jon?"

Reznick headed toward the line at the boarding desk. "Bear with me . . . Unless it is true, but they want to ensure his privacy, so he was admitted under a different name."

"Interesting." The sound of more tapping. "Hold on . . ."

"What are you doing?" Reznick asked.

"I've pulled up Leahy's date of birth. Wondering if they might have admitted him that way. Fake name, correct date of birth."

Reznick popped a Dexedrine pill, crunching it hard. The amphetamines would hit his system in no time at all, giving him the boost he would need to get through whatever was coming next.

"And . . . boom! We're in!"

"What have you got?"

"Toby Breslin, exact same date of birth as Stephen Leahy, is a patient there."

Reznick made a mental note of the name. He wondered what the hell was going on.

"You're intrigued, aren't you, Jon?"

"I don't know. Maybe it's really him and the guy's had a full-on breakdown. And maybe the Agency doesn't want people to know. Hence the false name."

"I can hear the cogs in your head turning, Jon. You're going, aren't you."

Reznick's mind was racing. He was curious. More than curious. Besides, what did he have to lose? "Fuck it."

"What are you going to do?"

"I'm going to see what this is all about."

Three

The psychiatric hospital was situated just off a highway, concealed from view behind towering pines and tall oaks, dissolving into the woods that fringed and concealed the facility.

Reznick wondered what he was going to find as he turned off onto a winding country road in his BMW convertible rental car, blue skies overhead. Here he was, against his better judgment, in the middle of rural Maryland, preparing to visit a CIA intelligence chief he had never met or even spoken to. A man who might be a patient there, maybe under a false name, if Trevelle's hunch was correct.

Reznick pulled up to the visitors' parking area outside the hospital. He locked the car and walked through the automatic glass entrance doors. He immediately came to a desk, where a thickset security man sat, a walkie-talkie on his belt.

"Can I help you, sir?" the man said.

"Good afternoon. I'm here to visit Toby Breslin."

"And you are, sir?"

"I'm an old friend of his," Reznick lied. He offered his fake ID giving the name James Levy.

The man eyed him with suspicion. "You don't mind if I pat you down for weapons, drugs, phones?"

Reznick handed over his cell phone and keys, rather reluctantly. He had left his Beretta locked in the glove compartment of the car. He raised his arms to be checked by the guard.

The man patted down all the angles expertly. "This all seems in order, Mr. Levy. We'll give you your phone and keys back at the end of your visit if that's okay?"

"Of course, thanks."

A second, burly-looking security officer approached, a set of keys rattling at his belt. "Follow me, sir."

Reznick followed the guard down a series of corridors with bars on the windows and doors, cameras watching their every move.

"You a close friend of Toby's?"

Reznick nodded. "We go way back," he lied. "Twenty, thirty years."

"Always been a perfect gentleman to me."

"That sounds like him."

The guy escorted Reznick down to a nurses' station. "Visitor for Mr. Breslin. This is James Levy, old friend. He's clean."

The nurse checked her watch. "You made it just in time. No visitors after three p.m.," she said. "So unfortunately . . . fifteen, maybe sixteen minutes at best for you. Is that okay?"

"That's fine. How is he?"

"Toby? Good as gold. Quiet. But he appears amenable. We're checking on his progress at intervals, monitoring him closely."

"Does he get many visitors?"

The nurse shook her head. "Afraid not. You're the first."

"Why is that?"

"I don't know. But I guess that's just the way it is, right? Some families or friends don't want to accept the stigma of mental health issues."

Reznick shrugged. "I guess so."

The nurse escorted him to a room at the end of a long corridor. She turned to face Reznick. "Your friend has got the best room. Biggest, anyway." She checked her watch again. "He's placid. But you're on the clock. Fourteen minutes. Sorry. We're quite strict on that. We have hidden cameras to make sure Toby is safe, just so you know."

Reznick nodded.

The nurse unlocked the door, pushed it open. "I'll be outside if you need anything," she said. "He's not violent. So he'll be fine."

Reznick walked into the room and was greeted by the smell of cigarette smoke and the sound of a large air-conditioning unit growling high up on the wall.

A gray-haired man sat on an easy chair, legs crossed, smoking a filterless cigarette as if lost in a dream. He wore a white linen shirt, chinos, and boat shoes. He reached forward languidly to a wooden table with an overflowing ashtray; there was a brown leather chair on the other side. He tapped his cigarette, some of the ash drifting down to the table, before bringing it back to his lips.

The man didn't acknowledge Reznick's presence for a few moments. He just looked out through the barred window to the lake across the hospital grounds.

Reznick approached, clearing his throat so the guy would know he was there.

The man slowly turned around, cigarette in hand, and smiled. "Ah, there you are . . . I didn't think you'd come. Take a seat please." He indicated the brown leather chair.

Reznick sat down opposite the old man and began to study him. Lined face, gray pallor, watery blue eyes, nicotine-stained fingers on his right hand. There was a fug of blue smoke in the room. "That habit will kill you."

"We're all going to die. One thing that's not in dispute, right? Only the Lord knows when he's going to take us."

Reznick said nothing to that. "So why am I here?"

"Why are any of us here?"

Reznick sensed this wasn't going to be easy. "I'm not into existential philosophy."

"Do you believe in God, or do you believe in free will?"

"I trust in God."

The man laughed. "As do I. I believe we operate in a moral universe. Right and wrong. I don't believe in a nihilistic universe. You know who didn't either?"

Reznick shook his head.

"Dostoyevsky."

"I haven't read him."

"You should. He said, 'If God does not exist, then everything is permitted.' Just imagine such a world. An amoral universe. Doesn't bear thinking about."

Reznick wondered if this guy was for real. He needed to get the conversation back to business. "I've come a long way to see you. I was contacted by your lawyer. At least he said he was your lawyer."

"I would have contacted you myself, Jon. I was going to do just that, after speaking to your friend Ms. Meyerstein in DC. She gave me your number. I briefly spoke to my lawyer, passed it on to him in case anything happened to me. Within an hour I was under arrest and driven here. I have no access to a cell phone. I can't send letters. I can receive visitors. But I believe that will stop next week. You got here just in time."

"Why would they stop visits? Are you suicidal?"

The man tittered, dragging hard on his cigarette. He watched the smoke rise to the ceiling. "You'll have to ask them that."

"I'm asking you."

"The hospital, rightly, thought it was inhumane, against my rights, to refuse me visitors. That's what they told me. But I believe the powers that be are about to get a court order denying me that right."

"How do you know?"

"I know how they operate. If you know that I'm here as Toby Breslin then you know something of how they operate as well. Anyway, I'm grateful you came. I'm impressed you managed to realize I was being kept under an alias. And no, I'm not suicidal, despite everything."

"Let's start with some basics. Who are you?"

The man nodded. "You already know my name, Jon. My real name. You can call me that if you want."

"What do you want from me, Stephen?"

Leahy tilted his head back and closed his eyes. "What does anyone in America want?"

Reznick shrugged. "Listen, I've travelled a long way to be here. I'm grouchy at the best of times. And I'm not in the mood to play games. So you need to start answering my questions now."

"I haven't got long, they say. Riddled with cancer. And they also say I'm batshit crazy."

"Are you?"

Leahy snorted and shook his head, leaning forward to stub out his cigarette. "I'm not. Interestingly, two psychiatrists paid by the CIA say I am. Delusional apparently. Say I'm a risk to myself. You'll have to figure out who's telling the truth. Me or them?"

"You're not making a convincing case for me to hang around much longer. Why did you want to speak to me? I was told about your intelligence background. And that you have a story to tell. Let's talk about that."

Leahy picked up the packet of Gitanes from the table and lit up another, blowing the smoke out through the side of his mouth. "I believe you killed a friend of mine. The best friend of my father. William Crenshaw. Former counterintelligence head at the CIA."

Reznick stared at the man sitting before him, wreathed in smoke. The revelation that Leahy had known Crenshaw crashed through his head like a concrete block.

"I am who you think I am. Stephen Leahy of the Central Intelligence Agency. Here's an interesting fact. Crenshaw was also my godfather. I checked your file when I heard Crenshaw had been killed. I read the way you went about tracking and finally neutralizing him in the Middle East. Fascinating. You took along a very resourceful Scot, if I'm not mistaken."

"Mac," Reznick provided.

"That's what I read. Mac, ex-SAS. He came along for the ride. Crenshaw didn't stand a chance, even with the Russians protecting him."

Reznick nodded.

"Quite a combination. Lethal. And before you ask, I'm glad you killed him. Crenshaw was a traitor. The worst sort."

Reznick shifted in his seat. "So now we're getting somewhere. Question is, Stephen, getting back to my original point, why exactly am I here? I feel like we're going around in circles."

Leahy closed his eyes for a few moments in silent contemplation. "The Agency is different than when Crenshaw was around. I acknowledge that. I'm talking mid-sixties to mid-seventies. When my father was in the CIA, same time as Crenshaw, it was the old boys' network."

"Your father was in the Agency?"

"Look it up, Jon. His name is Michael Leahy. Retired fifteen years ago, down in Florida."

Reznick realized Stephen was heading off the beaten track of the conversation. He wondered if that was deliberate.

"The DC set with James Angleton and all those others was paranoid, interventionist, rabidly anti-communist. Angleton said he coined the phrase *wilderness of mirrors* to describe the work of the intelligence agencies. He was alleged to have told everyone that he made up that phrase. But he was full of shit. It's actually from a poem by T. S. Eliot. Like I said, he was crazy, saw spies and threats everywhere, even amongst his colleagues."

Reznick let Leahy riff on his reminiscences of the CIA from days gone by.

"Angleton was viewed as clinically mad by his colleagues. Which is interesting in light of what's happened to me. Some believed Angeleton lost his mind when it was revealed that his friend Kim Philby was a Soviet spy. Bit of a mindfuck, right? But I can tell you, I'm perfectly sane, thank you very much."

Leahy tilted his head to one side in a thoughtful manner. "So, the CIA is a different beast these days, or so it seems. But . . . scratch beneath the surface, and there are echoes of the same tired Cold War mindset lingering. Attitudes forged by men like Dulles, guys like that. You know what I'm talking about?"

"I'm aware."

"You see, Jon, those elements, for better or worse, haven't gone away. That same mindset is as entrenched and intractable as ever. It's a zero-sum game. America on one side, Russia and China on the other. It's a dangerous, dangerous mindset. If they lose, we win. And vice versa."

"I understand."

"And you know where this leads? Proxy wars, killings, and spheres of influence. It's dangerous, it's corrosive. Pax Americana, the international order we created, the relative peace we have enjoyed since the end of the Second World War, that's gone. But this time for good. This is no longer a unipolar world, America at the forefront. And this greatly alarms and keeps the people within the CIA and the Pentagon awake at night. Instead of embracing our alliances or refashioning their responses, they double down."

Reznick sighed.

"Am I boring you?"

"Is there a point to all this? I'm not here for a geopolitical masterclass, fascinating though it may be. Let's back up. Why the hell are you here? Tell me more about that."

"Simple. They say I'm crazy."

"And are you?"

Leahy nonchalantly blew blue smoke rings toward the open window. "No more paranoid than the next man who has worked at the CIA for thirty-five years."

"You're painting an interesting picture. The problem is, I still have no idea why I'm here. Why did I come all this way? What do you want to tell me?"

"You're here because I want to warn you."

"Warn me?"

"Plans are afoot. Very advanced plans. Remember what I said about the Cold War mindset?"

Reznick nodded.

"Well, Pentagon planners—with the CIA's seal of approval—are coordinating a false flag attack on foreign soil. The problem is the collateral damage will include the deaths of many Americans."

Reznick sat in stony silence.

Leahy chuckled corrosively. "Don't believe me? I don't blame you, it's far-fetched, I know. But I promise you, it's going down. There's going to be a war down in Latin America like you wouldn't believe."

Reznick got up from his seat and walked toward the door. If he hadn't been convinced of it before this conversation, in the past thirty seconds it had dawned on him that maybe Leahy actually was batshit crazy. "I've heard enough. There's nothing I can do about whatever it is you're talking about."

"Jon?"

Reznick turned around. "What?"

"Have you heard about the Monroe Doctrine?"

Reznick looked steadily at Leahy.

"It outlined, in some detail, that the Western Hemisphere, including Latin America, was off limits for European powers: France, Britain."

"Where are you going with this?"

"But then there was the Roosevelt Corollary. That, in effect, updated that doctrine. And it laid out the American position. It said, basically, any bad shit happens down in Latin America, and we've got the right and authority to intervene, for national security. Interventions. American military invasion, by another name."

Reznick was getting bored again with the political history lesson. "Are you finished or are you going to put some meat on the bone?"

"I've laid out the framework for their thinking. It has already started, Jon. The groundwork. A narco-cartel boat was blown out of the water recently in the Caribbean. You see that?"

"Something on the TV news about that, yeah."

"It's America feeling its way in. The skirmishes have started. Shaping the public narrative. And there have been numerous bombings of drug cartel compounds across Latin America. Ideally, they'd like a soft putsch, convincing the generals down there to overthrow the president of a failed state."

Reznick had read about how all on board the cartel boat had been killed. He had also seen TV coverage showing US planes bombing drug manufacturing sites across South America.

"You with me? But if that fails, then it's game on. This is just the warm-up. They're laying the groundwork for what's to come if the generals don't succeed in their military coup. The real stuff will start in Guyana. I want someone to know before it's too late."

Reznick frowned. "You're telling me America is going to attack Guyana?"

A smile crept across Leahy's scaly face. "I don't blame you for not believing me. It's crazy, right? Outlandish at the very least. Operation Gideon might have failed, but I'm telling you, as the Lord is my witness, this operation in Guyana won't fail. They say I'm insane? You ain't seen nothing yet. But I've got to hand it to them. Their plans may be diabolical, but they're also brilliant. A young man at the Pentagon drew up the blueprint."

"Listen, I'm out. A whole bunch of hypothetical scenarios—"

"Wait a minute, Jon. I'm begging you. A few more moments of your time. That's all I ask. My name is Stephen Leahy. I exist, as you can see. I work for the Agency. But they want to bury me, Jon. Silence me forever. Ask yourself why they would want to do that."

Reznick stared down at the tragic, chain-smoking man.

"I'm pouring my heart out to you. The least you can do is give me a few fucking moments of your time."

Reznick cleared his throat. "What do you want from me?"

"Just listen. I know you're a good man. A patriot. The first part of the operation—not these skirmishes that have been ongoing for the last year—is to blow up American-owned oil terminals and rigs in Guyana."

"Why the hell would we do that?"

Leahy shook his head, almost disappointed. "I'll tell you why, Jon. I was—in fact I still am, technically—the Deputy Director of the CIA for Operations, until I was ousted in a coup by people I thought were my friends. I gave my life to the Agency. And so did my father before me. That's why I know about all of this."

Reznick observed the haunted look in Leahy's tired eyes.

"I spent most of my career abroad. Several tours as chief of station. Beirut. Beijing. Mexico City. Baghdad. I didn't see my children grow up. I was working. All the time. It was something I've always regretted, not seeing them enough."

Reznick felt a strange compassion for the brilliant stranger in front of him. Perhaps he was being played by this highly intelligent man. A man who had operated in the shadows for decades. But for some reason, Reznick felt compelled to stay to hear the full story. "Tell me more about Guyana. Give me details."

"What do you want to know?"

"Whatever you can tell me. What's the ultimate goal?"

Leahy looked pleased, suddenly satisfied. "Very astute, Jon. Quite simply, Guyana will be the pretext for a major military intervention by America, perhaps the biggest and most disastrous since Iraq. You were there, weren't you?"

"Yes, I was."

"So was I. It was a shitshow on acid. Hundreds of thousands of deaths. Anyway, the regime change is not planned for Guyana. The war will not be directed at Guyana. The bombings of American-owned oil rigs in Guyana will be blamed on the Venezuelan government. The war will ultimately target its neighbor, Venezuela. You got me?"

Reznick could see the twisted logic. The socialist regime, a thorn in the side of American presidents for decades. Illegitimate in the eyes of most US politicians.

"Regime change time again, and everything that entails! Listen closely. They'll be claiming it's a war against narco-terrorism funded by Venezuela. And America is going to pin the blame at the door of the Cartel of the Suns."

"What's that?"

"A narco-cartel, run by high-ranking Venezuelan military officers. So that will be a pretext to destroy the drug gangs in Venezuela supposedly flooding America with fentanyl-laced cocaine. The problem is that most fentanyl is produced in Mexico, not Venezuela. And most cocaine comes from Colombia. Go figure."

Reznick said nothing.

"You look shocked. But that's where it will happen. The plans are already in place. It's a pretext for war. A war like you wouldn't believe. It'll set Latin America on fire. You think the CIA coups in Guatemala, Honduras, and all the rest were a fucking generational mess? You ain't seen nothing yet. Remember the zero-sum game I mentioned? This is it. America kicks the shit out of a Russian and Chinese geopolitical ally—Venezuela. See the big picture now?"

Reznick walked back over to Leahy and sat down again. He knew he should have just walked out when Leahy started to sound as if he had disappeared into a conspiracy theory black hole. But some part of what Leahy was saying seemed to contain more than a kernel of truth. The plans Leahy had outlined, in a military sense, were strangely believable in their twisted logic.

"The American empire is dying. This is the final throw of the dice. To impose its will, to secure the vast natural resources of South America. Do you know how many years of proven oil and gas reserves exist in Venezuela?"

Reznick shook his head.

"One thousand years. The world's largest proven oil reserves. Think about that. You understand now why we're desperate to get in there? But there's also the chance to destroy Russian and Chinese influence in Venezuela and the Western Hemisphere for good."

"It's a lot to take in. And it's certainly quite a tale."

"It's no tale. As the Lord is my witness, Jon, this will happen. I saw the fucking plans. I read them from cover to cover. Written by Brigadier General Michael Johnson. It was too late, there was nothing I could do. I was the only person to object. The only one. The Pentagon is taking the lead. With the CIA in the loop. That's how it works. That's how it's always worked. You get it now?"

Reznick eyed the door again, then looked around the room for a clock. The nurse had said fourteen minutes, and it felt like he had been there for twice that already. And Leahy still hadn't come to the crux of the matter. Why had be gone to all this trouble to tell Reznick?

But Leahy was on a roll now. "I've been neutralized. I objected, and you know what happened next? They claimed they found drugs in my desk. Well, it's a fucking lie. They have a timetable. The plans are already underway, Jon."

"What if I said this sounds more like some far-fetched fantasy of yours?"

Leahy's blue eyes sparkled. "It does, doesn't it? I know it does. But you need to understand they're all in on this. Latin America will be in fucking flames for decades. You and me, we know how this ends."

Reznick knew all about false flags. Covert military operations—bombings and killings blamed on another government as a pretext for war, in this case Venezuela.

"And it's got a codename. Yellow Rain. From the chemical that was dropped on Cambodia. Their private joke, I guess."

Reznick rubbed his hands over his face, exasperated at not only what he was hearing but Leahy's tone of absolute certainty.

Leahy went quiet for a few moments. "It's brilliant when you think about it. Demonic in its brilliance. But I'm telling you the goddamn truth. How would I know about you killing William Crenshaw? Only someone with the highest-level CIA or Pentagon clearance could access that."

"What if I said that many might consider your actions, revealing classified plans, to be an act of treason?"

"Call it whatever you want. My conscience is telling me this is wrong. This is evil."

"What's your legal position, Stephen?"

"Theoretically, I can be offered some level of protection under the Intelligence Community Whistleblower Protection Act."

"How's that going?"

"I think you can see that, Jon."

Reznick pinched the bridge of his nose as he contemplated what he had just been told. "You can be locked up for what you're telling me."

Leahy nodded. "I'm well aware of that. But toppling the government of Venezuela by killing hundreds of Americans in Guyana is an outrage. Monstrous. Not many tears will be spilled over the Venezuelan regime. America believes it's an illegitimate government, the recent elections falsified. I don't disagree with that assessment. Widespread intimidation by supporters of the ruling party, widespread fraud. It's already in a state of collapse. But America is running with the narrative that military narco-cartels are operating across Venezuela with impunity, spreading drugs and misery to America. And maybe it's based on truth, to a marginal extent. But I'm telling you, the Guyana plans I have seen mean many American lives are going to be lost. The CIA have tried color revolutions in Venezuela, but to no avail. This time? It's not going to end well."

Reznick leaned forward in his seat, hands clasped. "Stephen, why are you talking to me about this? Why me? Why not Meyerstein?"

"I want someone to know. And I want someone who knows how black-ops and the CIA works. The system. I've been disappeared, Jon. I believe I have a moral imperative to act. I have a sense of duty. I believe you do too. I don't trust many people. But what Meyerstein told me about you, I feel like I can trust you. You know the world I'm talking about."

Reznick's gaze bored into Leahy's tired, defeated eyes.

"This is important. They're going to pin this on the government in Caracas. And before you say it, I'm not an apologist for the Venezuelan regime. But this is wrong. It's a pretext for war. The bombing of the rigs will spark bloodletting on the streets of

Guyana, directed by CIA operatives on the ground, and then on to Venezuela. Don't you fucking get it? Can't you see it?"

Reznick sat in silence, processing the deluge of information he had just received.

"I spoke to Martha shortly before they brought me here. I feared they were going to come for me. I asked her if there was anyone she would trust. She gave me your name. Jon, listen to me very carefully, this is going to happen. People need to know."

Reznick noted that Leahy was repeating the apocalyptic warnings over and over again, like a metronome. "Can I be blunt?"

"I wouldn't expect anything else."

"What if I said I thought you'd made this up? Maybe to get some attention? Maybe as a little game?"

"I would say I don't blame you for thinking that, Jon. Look at where I am, after all. They give me antipsychotics. I pretend to take them. But I'm of sound mind. I fear for America. I fear for my family. I fear for you."

"I think you need to talk to someone else."

"Don't you get it? There's no one else I can speak to. And I can't keep this to myself. The plans are in motion."

"I'm not the kind of man who could stop this even if I wanted to. I'm just a regular guy."

"Jon, please don't bail on me. I've got no one else."

Reznick sighed. "Okay, let's assume these plans exist. Where's the proof?"

"Where do you think? Special access program files, locked away deep in the Pentagon."

"So there are no copies to verify anything you're saying?"

"There were. I showed them to my father. He's a smart guy. Three days after I learned of the operation I headed down to his house in Boca. I'd managed to copy some of the plans onto a micro-SD card to show him. The day after that, I met up with Meyerstein in DC. She gave me your number. She told me you were the one person she would trust with her life. Then I sent my lawyer your number, through encrypted mail. Lawrence Morgan is the family lawyer as well as a close friend. You see, I feared they would come for me. And I wanted someone to reach out to you if I disappeared, so to speak. I'm glad I did."

"What's your father's name again?"

"Michael. Michael Leahy. Remember, former CIA?"

Reznick closed his eyes for a moment, overwhelmed. He was getting a bad feeling about this. "You do realize that what you did was absolutely against the law, right?"

"I didn't know who else to turn to. My father worked in counterintelligence with Crenshaw for decades and I wanted his advice."

"Why not contact the Office of the Inspector General if you had concerns?"

"I tried to do it the right way. Within hours: I was ignored. Eugene Buckley, that's his name. He assured me he would deal with it personally. I never heard from him again."

Reznick had heard just about enough. "The Inspector General ignored your concerns? Why would he do that? That doesn't make sense."

"I know it doesn't."

"So you leaked this classified intel, if it even exists, to your father, a retired intelligence operative?"

"Correct."

Reznick shook his head.

"What else was I supposed to do? The Inspector General, Buckley, never got back to me. I also sent three more encrypted emails to Buckley outlining my concerns over the next two days. Nothing!"

"Come on, Stephen, we both know that's a very serious breach of national security protocols."

"I had no choice."

"We all have a choice."

"I felt like I had no one to talk to about this. So, I reached out to my father. Then, the following day in DC, I reached out to our family lawyer, Lawrence Morgan. And I assume when my father found out that I'd been brought here to this hospital the night after I'd seen him in Florida, he too reached out to Morgan. Can I be frank?"

"Please."

"I think they're going to kill me. I believe they will kill me. I don't think I'll get out of here alive."

"Why do you think that?"

Leahy tapped his forefinger against his temple. "I know . . . And if I wind up dead, trust me, it won't be because I took my own life. Don't forget that."

"Can I speak to your father to see if he can verify what you've said?"

Leahy cocked his head, eyes hooded, black as coal. "No, you can't speak to my father."

His tone had seemed to change now. Icier.

"Why not?"

"I learned yesterday morning that my father drowned while out deep-sea fishing. This allegedly happened three days ago. A freak wave or something. You see what I'm dealing with?"

Reznick was starting to question if all this could really be true.

"One final thing, Jon. If you decide to pursue this—know this. You will be a marked man. They will come for you. Just like they came for me."

Four

When Reznick left the psychiatric hospital, after picking up his cell phone and car keys, once again patted down by the security guard, his mind felt as if it was in a state of flux, which was ironic given where he'd just left. He asked himself what the hell had just happened. It was like an assault on the senses, the bizarre time he had spent with Leahy. A highly learned, articulate, and charismatic man.

He honestly didn't know what to make of it all. Maybe it was a performance and Leahy just enjoyed spinning conspiracy yarns. Leahy had come across as smart, analytical, and more than a bit anxious and paranoid. But a small part of Reznick also wondered why the hell he would reach out to a total stranger to share classified information? He wasn't sure he believed the reason Leahy had given.

Reznick got back in the convertible and drove away, relieved to be out of there. He had no way of knowing if he was being played by an intelligence officer who had been in the game too long. A man who was washed up. Damaged.

But what if Leahy was actually telling the truth? It would be a terrifying truth. If Reznick took his words at face value, maybe

Leahy really did simply want the world to know about this false flag operation.

The more Reznick thought about what he had been told, the less sure he was about Leahy. He had sensed the fear in Leahy's voice as the man had revealed these classified plans he claimed to vehemently object to. The supposed collateral damage. Hundreds of Americans killed. That bothered Reznick more than any of the rest of it. It had clearly bothered Leahy too. Reznick knew all too well, as Leahy did, what the CIA was all about. But killing innocent American citizens abroad . . . no question, that had piqued his interest.

Maybe that had been Leahy's plan all along—to draw Reznick into his paranoid world of intrigue and deception, reeling him in like a fish. But why would Leahy go to such lengths, reach out to Meyerstein, just to contact Reznick? If this was a trap, what was the endgame? The whole thing was overwhelming.

Reznick decided to head straight to Washington, DC, instead of returning to Maine. He changed lanes and accelerated before calling Trevelle, relaying the gist of his conversation with Leahy.

"Sounds like a nutjob," Trevelle said.

Reznick was surprised at his friend's immediate dismissal. "Maybe. I don't know."

"You don't actually believe this guy, do you, Jon? He's in a psychiatric hospital for a reason, right?"

"What he told me about very specific covert plans seemed, at least to me, to have a grain of truth about it. A semblance of credibility. This guy knows what he's talking about."

"He could also be weaving a ton of bullshit intelligence disinformation so you gobble it up."

"But why? For what purpose?"

"Maybe he wants attention, people to visit him, I don't know."

Reznick drove on as he considered what Trevelle was saying. "It's a possibility. But then why go to all the trouble to reach out to Meyerstein?"

"It's pure chance that she gave out your name and number."

"Maybe she believes him. Trusts him. She's known him for years apparently."

"Jon, they don't put people away for no reason."

"Here's the thing—and this is just my take on the situation and what I saw—for someone who is supposed to be showing signs of paranoid hallucinations, he seemed very composed, very assured."

"That doesn't mean anything."

Reznick sped along the highway, surprised by the lack of traffic. He was torn on whether he should head to the airport and get a flight back to Maine, or head into the city. He wondered if he should reach out to Martha Meyerstein. But there was so much about his meeting with Leahy that was still gnawing at him.

"What can you tell me about Stephen Leahy's father?" he asked Trevelle.

"Why?"

"He mentioned something interesting about his father. I want to find out what he did before he retired. Just to see if it matches up with what Leahy told me."

"Give me a minute."

"No problem."

He heard frantic tapping as Trevelle searched open-source, civilian, and military databases across the United States to confirm if what Stephen Leahy had said stood up to scrutiny. "This just got a whole lot more interesting. Are you listening?"

"What've you got?"

"Michael Leahy, retired and highly decorated senior CIA counterintelligence officer, died three days ago. Boating accident. Drowned."

"Source?"

"*Miami Herald*. He had retired down to Boca Raton."

"Interesting."

"That match what Stephen Leahy said?"

"To the letter. Stephen said he had reached out to his father about this secret CIA plan. And now Stephen's in a psychiatric hospital and his dad is dead. Could be a coincidence. But it seems off."

Trevelle groaned. "Jon, I got a bad, bad feeling about this. None of it makes much sense. It's just plain weird."

"The messenger is weird, but the plan . . . I don't know, Trevelle. It rings true."

"Jon, some might say that this is some conspiracy bullshit—sorry for being blunt."

Reznick drove on, processing Trevelle's understandable skepticism. "I hear you."

"Do you?"

"It's crazy, I know. I get that. But . . ."

"But what? I don't understand why he even contacted you. What does this have to do with you? Unless it's to lure someone from Meyerstein's world into his paranoid, delusional orbit."

"It's way out of left field, I get that. I can't ignore that."

"Why the hell would you even care about this guy? Why are you concerned?"

"What if he's telling the truth? Martha Meyerstein is one of the smartest and most level-headed people you will ever meet. And she's known this guy for a long time."

"Okay, let's imagine he's telling the truth. Talk through what he said."

"The level of detail he had about the plans was incredible. And the quiet, assured manner with which he delivered the message. None of it resembled the ramblings of a delusional psychiatric patient. I've seen quite a few of the Delta crew, or Navy SEALs, who suffered breakdowns after Iraq. This guy was nothing like that."

"Tell me again about these plans."

"Stephen Leahy was very, very worked up about a special access program and the plans that had been drawn up. Plans he had seen."

"*Claims* to have seen," Trevelle amended.

"Okay, claims to have seen. Plans he claims to have read. Pentagon plans. Highly classified."

Reznick glanced in his rearview mirror as a black Suburban pulled up tight behind him.

"Secret plans," continued Trevelle. "And that is what the Agency and the Pentagon do."

"Agreed."

"And then there's the death of the father. Stephen being taken to a psychiatric hospital under a false name."

"You're coming around?"

"Just feeling it out. Why did Meyerstein give him your name?"

"Shortly before he was hospitalized, he reached out to her, asking for someone he could trust. Implicitly trust. She gave him my name and number. He sensed they were coming for him and he sent my number, securely, to the family lawyer, Lawrence Morgan, just in case. And then that lawyer reached out to me. Morgan used to represent Michael Leahy too."

"Do you feel obligated to this guy because he reached out to Martha Meyerstein? Is that what this is all about?"

"No. I don't know . . . The plans, he was very focused on them. Very, very specific. He even gave the codename of the operation. Yellow Rain. Special access program, no doubt. Maybe an unacknowledged SAP. I'm assuming just disclosing the existence of the plans is illegal. And if he's telling the truth, he's passing on highly classified government secrets."

"So what now?"

"Here's my problem. What if this guy is actually telling the goddamn truth? What if what he says comes to pass and I knew about it and ignored it?"

"What's it to you? You go looking into this, if it is legitimate, you're going to wind up in deep, deep trouble. A whole lot of trouble."

"You want me to turn a blind eye to this?"

"I don't want you to turn a blind eye to anything.

Reznick drove on, changing lanes, checking his rearview mirror for the Suburban. Nowhere in sight.

"What if this guy is manipulating you. It's the nature of intelligence operatives, right?"

"I don't dispute that. My question is: is he or is he not telling the truth?"

Reznick saw a sign for DC and switched lanes.

"What if I just put out some feelers? Speak to a few people. See if there's any merit in what Leahy is saying. Maybe speak to Meyerstein. Maybe Leahy's lawyer. Nothing more than that."

"So you're heading to DC?"

"I am."

"Jon, I'm saying this as a friend. Be careful."

Reznick laughed softly. The traffic was getting heavier as he approached the outskirts of DC. "You worry too much, man. I'll be in touch."

He glanced in the rearview mirror. The black Suburban was right behind him again.

Five

With Trevelle's words still ringing in Reznick's ears, and a few minutes after the black Suburban tailing him once more disappeared from sight, Jon arrived in steamy, downtown Washington, DC. He pulled up outside the Sofitel hotel and left the rental with the valet, then checked in with a false ID under the name Frank Sopel. He was mindful that, if Leahy was being monitored at the hospital, he needed to try to stay anonymous in the city.

Trevelle always organized that side of things, allowing Reznick to move around the country—and abroad—as and when he liked, without attracting too much attention. He had twenty, maybe twenty-five separate IDs or passports in the hidden safe in his basement at his home back in Rockland. Trevelle used an American guy, a top document forger, who now lived in Marseille. Reznick knew it was illegal, but his work over the years had necessitated him entering and leaving countries undetected, and false identities were a standard trick of the trade. Plus, as he'd learned in the past, if foreign security knew you were using a fake ID, that was the least of your problems.

Reznick went up to his room. He was starving after the flight and his trip to the hospital and the drive to DC. After ordering room service, he felt into a fitful sleep.

The following morning, he showered and freshened up before heading out again. It was a blistering August day in DC, the heat merciless. Within minutes, his T-shirt was stuck to his sweaty skin. He stepped into Zeke's Coffee on 15th Street NW. He sat down in a corner booth and sipped his coffee, eating a chocolate chip cookie. He checked his messages. His daughter had sent a photo of herself, also drinking a cup of coffee, outside a café in Kota Tua, Jakarta's Old Town. He sent her a love heart emoji and the words *miss you*.

Reznick checked his watch, left a twenty-dollar bill with the check, and left. He walked over to the offices of Morgan, Wieser & Murray, on 7th Street NW. He walked into the lobby and checked the marble slab inside the doors listing the dozens of companies based in the building. The law firm was the sole tenant on the eighth floor.

Reznick rode the elevator up and headed through the firm's marble entrance hall toward an impressive, highly polished glass desk.

The young woman behind the desk smiled. "Morning, can I help you sir?"

"Yes, you can. I'm looking to speak to Mr. Morgan. Lawrence Morgan."

"Are you a client?"

"No, I'm not."

The woman winced. "I'm sorry, sir," she said, as if reciting a well-rehearsed spiel, "Mr. Morgan is tied up in meetings today."

"Tell him Jon Reznick is at reception. He'll know what it's about."

"I'm sorry, sir—"

"Give him a buzz. He called me recently. Urgent business."

The receptionist winced. "This is not how we operate, sir. You need an appointment, and even then, you must be a client of the firm."

Reznick remained pleasant although she was stretching his patience. "Just call him. Tell him it's urgent. It's about a client of his."

The young woman picked up the phone and sighed. "Mr. Morgan, I'm so sorry to bother you, sir . . . Yes, I understand you shouldn't be disturbed. But I have a gentleman with me, a Mr. Jon Reznick, who wants to speak to you about a client of yours . . . Yes, he said it's urgent." The receptionist nodded as she listened to her boss. "I know, sir, he doesn't have an appointment, but he's insistent." She put down the phone and smiled. "You're in luck. He's in his office." She pointed down a long, carpeted hallway. "All the way down, last door on the right."

"Appreciate your time," Reznick said. He strode along the hallway and approached the office. He knocked twice, and went in.

A burly besuited man sitting behind his desk peered over half-moon spectacles. "Jon, come in."

"Thanks."

"Bit unorthodox, but glad to meet you. Lawrence Morgan, managing partner. Did you see Stephen?"

Reznick nodded. "I did. That's why I'm here. I've got some questions."

The lawyer gestured to a leather seat opposite his desk. "I'm surprised you went."

Reznick sat down. "So was I. I didn't know if what you'd told me was real."

"Let's get down to business, Jon. What do you want to know? If I'm being frank, I didn't expect you to turn up at my office. It is a bit irregular."

"So are the circumstances your client has found himself in."

Morgan shrugged. "Fair point: it's a sin. I'm working on it—around the clock, doing whatever I can to get to the bottom of this. So, how can I help?"

"Your client is being detained within the psychiatric hospital, as you said. And I learned a lot during my visit."

"I'm glad." Morgan opened a legal pad and began to scribble down some notes. "I'd like to hear all about it."

"I can talk about the visit, sure. But what I'd really like to talk about is your understanding of Stephen Leahy."

"There is a thing called client confidentiality."

"I'm well aware of that. But I made the long trip to see your client as you requested. And I'm hoping you can answer a few questions for me."

"What do you want to know?"

"How long have you known him?"

"Stephen? The better part of twenty years. I've represented him for the last ten years. But I have also been his father's lawyer for decades."

"Michael Leahy?"

"Yes, I was Michael's personal attorney for four decades. I hadn't heard from him in a couple of years. But when he called me, he sounded like a broken man—telling me Stephen had been committed to a psychiatric hospital. He wanted my help."

"Interesting. Let me ask you something. Stephen told me that Michael died in the last few days."

Morgan watched him, his face like stone. "It's devastating."

"It was a boating accident, according to the *Miami Herald*."

"Yes, that's right."

"I guess accidents happen."

Morgan gave a rueful smirk.

"You don't think so?"

"I work in the law. I represent clients. I use my language with great care and attention. But I'm not speaking as a lawyer now. I'm speaking as an old friend of Michael's. The whole thing stinks."

"How come?"

"When Michael came to me and told me that Stephen had been committed to a psychiatric hospital, he was in a bad way. Shaking, incredulous. The news nearly killed him. Paranoid delusions and hallucinations, they said. As a father of three sons, it would be enough to break me. It's impossible to understand how he must have felt. I was flabbergasted when I heard. But then Michael drowning in a boating accident? Within a week of his son being committed? Come on."

Reznick nodded. "Was there any chance that he might have taken his life, heartbroken about what had happened to his son?"

"Not a chance."

"How can you be so sure?"

"He was a Christian. Devout. He would never do anything like that."

"I'm guessing we can't rule out a simple accident, a bit of bad luck, bad weather?"

Morgan shrugged. "I guess we can't totally discount it. But Michael was a highly experienced sailor. He often sailed his yacht out to the Bahamas. He loved it there, as did Stephen and his mother. Fifty nautical miles to the Bahamas from Florida. He had done it a hundred times before. He knew what he was doing at sea. And he was risk-averse. A squall or storm, and he wouldn't set out."

Reznick was getting a better understanding of the closeness of the Leahy family. "Sounds like quite a close-knit family."

"They absolutely were. Tell me more about this visit to Stephen. I'm intrigued. He is my client after all. How's he holding up?"

"I thought you would already know that, Lawrence, being his attorney."

"Regrettably, apart from Stephen's brief call and message with your details before he was committed, I haven't spoken to him. The hospital won't let me see him. And I only found out he was in hospital from his father."

Reznick was taken aback at that revelation. "Legal representation is a right under the law, no?"

"It's just another worrying aspect of this story. How was he?"

"Did you know that he's being kept at the hospital under the name Toby Breslin?"

Morgan scribbled down the name on his legal pad. "I didn't know that. Now that is interesting."

"I thought so. Just in case they deny that Stephen is being kept there. They're using the same date of birth. That's how I figured it out."

Morgan rubbed his hands together. "Very astute of you, Jon. That is intriguing. Worrying too."

Reznick nodded.

"What was Stephen's demeanor like? Was he pleased to see you?"

Reznick shrugged. "What can I tell you? He's an interesting man. Very complex. Highly intelligent."

"He is."

"He was eager to share details of secret military plans. Classified stuff. That's why he wanted to speak to me."

"Do you believe him? About these military plans?"

"I don't know, if I'm being honest," Reznick said.

"Is that why you're here?"

"In a way, yes. I didn't know where else to go. Thought it was as good a place as any to start: his lawyer. If nothing else, to let you know how he is."

Lawrence took off his glasses, laying them carefully on the legal pad. "I would have advised Stephen not to share classified information with you. Which is obviously illegal."

"It is. But he did it anyway. Maybe he's past caring."

"I think it's quite the opposite, Jon. He cares greatly about this country and what he believes to be ethical. But like his father, he is not uncritical of the actions of the Agency. What was his frame of mind?"

"Fine. Highly articulate. Stephen was very much in control of the conversation. He wasn't ranting and raving. I thought he came across as eloquent and composed. In many ways, he was steering the conversation in the direction he wanted it to go."

"That's the Stephen I know. He's all these things. Would it surprise you to learn that I've been trying to get two independent psychiatrists to visit him at the hospital to interview him?"

"I didn't know that."

"But my request for an independent medical evaluation for my client has been refused. Multiple times."

"On what grounds?"

"National security."

Reznick thought that strange. And he wondered how a lawyer could be denied access to his client. The right to counsel was protected by the Constitution.

"I also received a letter from the Pentagon, copying in the Director of the CIA. Addressed to me at this office. Hand-delivered and signed for."

Reznick shifted in his seat. "Very interesting. What have they got to hide?"

"I think they're trying to intimidate not only me, but Stephen as well. Create a sense of helplessness, that kind of thing. Cut him off from contact."

"What can you do about it?"

"It's going to be an uphill struggle. I'm preparing a case to sue the American government. The CIA. Stephen's treatment has been outrageous on multiple levels."

Reznick shifted in his seat.

"Do you mind me asking the details of what he told you? You're under no obligation. I would just like as much information as possible."

Reznick nodded. "Stephen first gave me a geopolitical masterclass. He eventually cut to the chase. He mentioned a highly classified, covert foreign operation. He wants people to know about it."

Morgan nodded. "That's how I understood the situation from Michael Leahy."

"Problem is, I don't know if it's some paranoid fantasy, or if it's reality."

"It is definitely not a paranoid fantasy."

"How can you be so sure?"

Morgan cleared his throat. "When Michael Leahy sat in the very seat you're sitting in now, less than a week ago, he confirmed exactly the same."

"Was he repeating what Stephen told him?"

Morgan shook his head. "Michael had been shown an excerpt, a snippet of the classified document. I wouldn't have advised Michael or Stephen to take that course of action. But there it is. And it was Michael Leahy who passed me not only the name and location of the psychiatric hospital, but also details of the plans. Which, in itself, is problematic for me. Stephen had voiced his grave concerns to his father about the entire operation. Stephen was the sole voice in the CIA and the Pentagon to object. The only one. Think about that. He told his father that he wrote them a detailed memo, outlining how, in his opinion, not only were the plans illegal, but the country would be walking into a quagmire that could bog down the military for decades. It wasn't just about human lives—American lives—though that's part of it. He laid out the rationale that it was all fundamentally flawed in intelligence and military terms as well as legally. The memo, according to Michael, was measured, cogent, and strongly argued, couched in legal terminology, citing case law."

"Let's be super clear, Lawrence. If there are government plans in place and they are carried out, and those plans kill hundreds of innocent Americans abroad, as per these plans, that would be illegal?"

"One hundred percent. Let's start with basics. Title 18 of the United States Code, the main criminal code of the US federal government. USC 1119, the Foreign Murder Statute. You know what that says?"

Reznick shook his head.

Morgan opened a book on his desk, flicked through pages. "Here it is," he said tapping a page. "I'm going to read this out loud so there's no ambiguity. *A person who, being a national of the United States, kills or attempts to kill a national of the United States while such national is outside the United States but within the jurisdiction of another country shall be punished.*"

"Does that law apply to those on the ground, whether they be CIA operators or private security firms acting on our behalf?"

"If you have signoff on that, from the United States Secretary of Defense for one, the Director of the CIA another, and the people they kill are innocent, not terrorists, they would be liable, unquestionably."

"What about the President?"

Morgan gave him a wry expression. "The President, in my eyes, would be immune from criminal prosecution for what would be deemed officially sanctioned acts."

Reznick mulled that over for a few moments. "So let me get this straight. Whatever way you cut this, it's illegal."

Morgan nodded.

"And a subsequent administration could come in and prosecute those in the Pentagon, and Langley who signed off on it, but not the President?"

The lawyer nodded. "And it's why, according to Michael Leahy, Stephen was so vehemently against the plans. Morally, it's wrong. But also legally it's wrong. He wanted no part in it. I think he became alarmed at the potential unforeseen consequences of this secret black-ops mission. We all know that America conducts classified operations across the world: Afghanistan, Syria, Iraq, probably a dozen or so other places we won't ever find out about. But because it would be American lives at risk as part of the collateral damage, in Stephen's eyes this would have been unconscionable."

"I don't want to labor the point. But I will. Michael Leahy . . . he said that Stephen definitely showed him an excerpt of the plans?"

Lawrence nodded. "I've known Michael for a long, long time. He was as solid as they come. But when he sat there, right where you're sitting now, he was shaking like a child. This was a tough career intelligence officer. A former US Marine who served in Korea. He gave me an inkling of what these plans were about. No specifics. But categorically, he did *not* share a copy with me. He believed, as I do now, that the highest echelons of the intelligence community were trying to crush not only Stephen, but Stephen's credibility, because he so vehemently objected to the plans. So they needed to get him out of the way. Hence why he has been effectively detained against his will in a psychiatric hospital."

Reznick leaned forward. "There's something else you might want to know. Stephen told me that drugs were planted in his desk."

Morgan scribbled that down on his legal pad. "I did not know that. That's outrageous. Did he say what kind of substances?"

Reznick shook his head. "The problem you have is that you have no psychiatric proof that Stephen is or isn't crazy."

Lawrence tutted to himself. "That is the crux of the matter. And they've prevented me, his lawyer, from getting independent psychiatrists to check him out. But the Fourteenth Amendment of the Constitution is quite clear. If an individual has been committed to a psychiatric hospital involuntarily, the person has a right to legal representation. Knowing that, doesn't it all strike you as strange?"

Reznick nodded.

"When I called to visit Stephen in the hospital, my request was denied. But what you're telling me is that he is, in fact, being held under a false name. Why would that be?"

"They want to shut him away. Out of sight, out of mind."

Morgan nodded. "It's a very chilling situation . . . but I'd like to thank you for giving your time to see Stephen, Mr. Reznick. You were under no obligation. I know he wanted to speak to you. Someone who knows both the military and intelligence fields."

"I'm not sure there's anything more I can do even if I wanted to."

Morgan shrugged. "What can any of us do? I've been told he is a threat to himself. But I have yet to see any evidence. I'm hearing it third-hand, if proof even exists at all. It's only hearsay at this point. I want access to Stephen's medical notes. I want to interview him, talk to him. But this has been repeatedly denied. That you managed to make contact is all the more remarkable."

Reznick nodded. He felt helpless and frustrated. But Reznick knew he was only scratching the surface.

Morgan leaned back in his seat, a sardonic grin crossing his face. "I know it's a lot to take in, Jon. What are your thoughts?"

"The most telling thing is the extraordinary measures being taken to stop you speaking face-to-face with Stephen, and refusing an independent medical examination of your client. It's a clear sign that they not only want to keep Stephen out of sight until this—whatever it is—is over, but they want to lock the story down. Lock it down tight. But . . . there are cracks appearing."

"Very perceptive."

"What are your thoughts?"

"Jon, I've been a lawyer for the best part of forty years. I've represented errant politicians, tech billionaires, media stars, you name it. All kinds of interesting, successful people. But this case, more than any other, feels . . . I can only describe it as sinister."

"I get it."

"My firm is trying to access Michael Leahy's health records. That request has also been denied by the Pentagon on national security grounds."

"Are they able to do that?"

"Never heard of that in my life. I simply want to know if Michael was on any medications, maybe had an illness that might have caused him to lose his balance, fall in the water. His widow, Catherine, says she feels like she's losing her mind."

From what Morgan had shared, it seemed as if the US government really was intent on silencing a senior CIA officer by committing him to a psychiatric hospital and withholding his right to representation. Extraordinary measures. Reznick reflected on the chain of events that had led to this point, unable to shake off a growing sense of foreboding. He was beginning to believe that Stephen Leahy was telling the truth.

"Catherine's son has been taken to a psychiatric hospital, apparently in the grip of hallucinations which somehow no one who knew him saw any evidence of. Then her husband died in a freaking boating accident a few days after Michael visited my office. And you know what else she told me?"

"What?"

"She was visited by the legal counsel for the CIA along with some FBI special agents. They had a warrant to search her home. Took all the laptops, iPads, mobile phones. Every device belonging to her husband and her."

"Looking for evidence of a copy of the plans Stephen told his father about? Maybe collusion? Maybe evidence of sharing classified intelligence?"

Morgan snorted. "Know what the CIA lawyer warned her? He told her that if she said anything to anyone about her son, she would face charges for possible violations of the Espionage Act."

"She can't talk about her son? To anyone? Are you serious?"

"Again, citing national security. Talk about draconian. He warned Catherine that if she did speak to anyone about this, she would be arrested. They were really turning the screw. On a vulnerable widow."

"And that was after her husband died?"

"The body wasn't even cold."

Six

It was at that moment, standing in the lobby after his meeting with Lawrence Morgan, that Reznick saw it clearly. The visit by the CIA and Feds to Catherine Leahy's home in Boca Raton, warning her not to share classified top-secret intel, indicated there was real fear that this story was going to be leaked. Otherwise, why go to all that trouble? Why cite the Espionage Act?

Reznick left the glass office tower in downtown DC and walked out onto the sweltering street. He headed back to his hotel, deep in thought, trying to determine for himself if it was the CIA or the Pentagon who had ordered Leahy to be committed to the psychiatric hospital under a false name. Was this simply a ruse to throw anyone off the scent? Or the start of a process for disappearing the man entirely? Even Leahy's attorney had been unaware that he was being held under a different name.

Reznick felt conflicted. His rational side was telling him that none of this was his business. He was mindful that his daughter worked for the CIA. He didn't want any fallout from his interest in Leahy's case to jeopardize her career. Not in any way. But also, having served in the elite Delta Force and, before that, the Marines, and having also been a CIA black-ops contractor before working with the Feds in an unofficial capacity, he knew the critical importance of national security. He understood the consequences of highly classified secret plans being leaked. He also understood why the CIA and the Pentagon would want to lock down the story.

The problem was, despite his reservations about getting involved, he already was. Ultimately, he couldn't shake the feeling that these plans were real, illegal, and also, from his point of view—if what Stephen Leahy was saying was correct—morally wrong. He understood better than anyone that innocents died in wars. Inevitably there would be non-combatant casualties and deaths. But that didn't make it right.

Reznick had circumstantial evidence—Morgan's revelation about being denied access to his client, the refusal of a psychiatric evaluation, and the heavy-handed visit to Michael Leahy's widow all gave credence to what Stephen Leahy had said. The kicker was he had no concrete proof. Nothing. Only the word of a man who'd been committed to a psychiatric hospital. But if these plans were legitimate, American citizens in Guyana would be killed. And not only there, he realized, as he pulled on that thread. Americans would die in and around Caracas too, all for the overarching aim of overthrowing the Venezuelan government. Jon considered what was at stake: one thousand years of oil and gas, the world's largest proven oil reserves, not to mention untold rare earth minerals essential for computers, phones, and numerous other gadgets. He had read articles in *National Geographic* about the vast mineral wealth of Venezuela. It was in America's backyard. And Uncle Sam was casting his envious eyes over the bounties it contained.

Reznick needed to keep perspective. This was still all supposition. It would come down to him making a judgment. He still hadn't seen hard evidence of these plans for himself. He needed to know for sure before he could make a decision. He texted Trevelle to see what he could dig up.

Reznick returned to his hotel room and packed his overnight bag, already knowing what he was going to do. He wanted answers. Maybe he was being impetuous, but it was as if a switch had been flicked inside his brain.

He caught a cab to Ronald Reagan Washington Airport. It was out of character for him to act without a real strategy, not typical of his normal analytical behavior, his more considered approach. But something was stirring inside him. Was it his conscience? His moral code? Was he intrigued enough to be drawn back into the shadowy world he knew so well?

Was he being impulsive? Was it because he sensed something was off?

Maybe it was all of those things.

Or maybe it was just that he was being played. Maybe Stephen Leahy was playing some kind of elaborate intelligence game with his lawyer. With Reznick. But could this really be just misdirection and deception? And if so, why—and where did Reznick fit into that plan?

Reznick sat in the back of the cab and texted Trevelle to get the address of Catherine Leahy in Boca Raton. He was mindful that she probably wouldn't welcome his presence.

A few minutes later Reznick, received a text back. A phone number and address.

When his cab pulled up at the airport, Reznick headed through Reagan and into the terminal and called Trevelle. "Appreciate that, man."

Reznick updated Trevelle on the meeting with the lawyer.

"You're going to cold-call Michael Leahy's widow? A few days after the Agency did the same? I'm not sure this is a smart move or even ethical, Jon. I would advise against this."

"I hear what you're saying. I just have a few questions."

"Seriously? Jon, you need to think long and hard about this. I think you're going to cross a line heading down there. You're not a journalist, man. I think it's time to take a step back."

"I'm simply going to ask her a few questions—what's wrong with that? And then I'm out of there."

"This isn't like you. You're a fucking assassin. You're not a human rights activist."

"I know full well what I am." Reznick strode on, eyes on the gate numbers on the board. "But I'll tell you what else I am. I'm an American, first and foremost. This is about what is right and what is wrong."

"What if you're wrong? What if this is all just bullshit? What if you're being played?"

"I guess we'll find out soon enough."

Trevelle sighed, changing tack. "How did it go with this visit to the lawyer?"

"It was an eye-opener. I was told that Michael Leahy, the father, had been shown some of the special access program by his son. Michael confirmed that with Lawrence Morgan."

"Interesting."

"So I think it's real. The CIA were down there confiscating all the Leahys' electronic devices. But I'm curious if there might be a hard copy somewhere."

"Jon, I don't know. I wouldn't want to fuck with the CIA."

"Neither would I. But just think about it. Michael Leahy contacts his lawyer to talk about this, then winds up dead? Within days? I mean, come on . . . seriously?

"I see that, Jon. But there's nothing you can do."

"I'm running all this stuff around in my head. There are so many things that already don't add up."

"Jon, if the CIA have visited Catherine Leahy, they might be alerted to your presence if you turn up. Think about it. Just leave it alone."

"I just want to see if this trip leads to anything. Maybe Catherine Leahy can help. I just can't shake the feeling that her son is telling the truth."

"You can't go knocking on the doors of retired, albeit dead, CIA intelligence officers. I guarantee the NSA will be tracking you."

Reznick bought a plane ticket to West Palm Beach on his phone, and added it to his Apple Wallet as he headed to the gate.

"What's the endgame here, Jon? What's your exit strategy? Have you thought about that? Where the hell does this go? Your last assignment was working for the CIA to track down an American-born sniper in Mallorca working for the Iranians, right?"

"What's your point?"

"Jon, wake up! This will put you at odds with the highest echelons of the CIA and the Pentagon. You know better than anyone not to get in their way. This is not a game. It's a conflict of interest against the CIA. You're a contractor for them, goddamn it."

"I hear what you're saying. But I can't in good conscience just walk away."

"You're scratching away at this, Jon. It's like a scab you're scratching until it bleeds. Where's the analytical guy I know?"

Reznick joined the back of the long line, waiting to board. "I need to go."

"Jon, you're killing me."

Reznick walked away from the boarding line, lowering his voice. "I'll tell you what has gotten into me. I don't want to see innocent Americans killed as part of a covert intelligence operation. A pretext for war. Don't you get it?"

"I get it. But if this is all real, you couldn't stop this even if you wanted to."

"I never said I could. But I feel like I'm obligated to at least try to get to the bottom of it. If nothing else, to let people know what has happened to Stephen Leahy."

"And then what?"

Reznick closed his eyes, realizing he didn't have an answer.

It was a two-and-a-half-hour flight from DC to Palm Beach International Airport. Bag slung over his shoulder, Reznick headed through the terminal, picked up another rental car, and drove down the I-95 toward Boca Raton. He turned off the interstate and skirted the edges of the upscale town until he saw a sign for the gated community, The Bay.

Reznick pulled up at the gatehouse, wound down his window. "Hey buddy."

The guy inside the booth opened the glass partition. "Yeah, who are you here to see?"

"Name's Frank Sopel. I'm here to speak to Mrs. Catherine Leahy. I just met up with her late husband's lawyer in DC."

"Are you from her legal firm?"

"No."

"Is she expecting you?"

Reznick took off his shades. "I flew down specifically to speak to her. A private matter related to her late husband, Michael."

The guard shrugged. "I knew Mr. Leahy well. But I'm afraid you're not on the visitor list for today."

"I understand. Listen, it's a delicate matter. Can you call Mrs. Leahy?"

The guard rolled his eyes before picking up the phone. He was locked in a conversation for a minute or so—Reznick assumed he was speaking with Catherine Leahy. Then he turned around.

"You're in luck, buddy. Straight through the gate, sixth on the left, opposite the lake."

Reznick thanked the guard. He edged forward and the barrier lifted. He drove through, headed past the Mediterranean-style mansions with manicured lawns, water sprinklers spraying everywhere, cobalt blue skies overhead. He drove past a huge, sparkling lake which looked like the centerpiece of the community. Reaching the house the guard had directed him to, he pulled up on the driveway beside a Mercedes SUV, got out of the car, and walked up to the front door.

Reznick pressed the doorbell as he put his sunglasses in his jacket pocket. The door opened slowly to reveal a frail-looking woman, face gray and drawn, rheumy eyes bloodshot.

"Are you Catherine Leahy, ma'am?"

"Yes, I am. You're from the lawyer in DC?"

"Not exactly, ma'am," Reznick said. "I've come from a meeting with Lawrence Morgan. I'm sorry for your loss."

"But are you a lawyer?"

"No, I'm not. I'd like to talk to you about a couple things."

"Are you from the press? They've all been wanting interviews. But I don't want to talk. I've made that quite clear."

"I assure you I'm not from the press."

"So, who are you?"

"Lawrence Morgan contacted me yesterday. He told me about your son's predicament. He said that Stephen wanted to speak to me."

"Stephen? Do you know Stephen? Are you a friend of his?"

"Not personally. But Stephen wanted to meet me. We have a mutual friend who was in the FBI. So I met Stephen at the hospital."

Catherine Leahy looked over Reznick's shoulder, eyes darting from side to side. She placed her hand on her chest. "You spoke to him?"

"Yes."

"Why would he want to speak to you?"

"As I said, Stephen knows a close friend of mine who was in the FBI. I visited Stephen after she passed on my number."

The woman sighed. "Are you CIA?"

"No, ma'am, but I have worked on a consultancy basis for them in the past. But this is nothing to do with any CIA visit to your home recently."

"How is he?"

Reznick assumed she hadn't seen her son since he had been committed. "He seems okay. I have to say, he was quite agitated about some plans he was privy to. And what he said concerns me, too. Do you mind me asking if you've had the chance to visit him?"

Catherine folded her thin arms. "I was told not to visit him."

"You were told not to visit him? By who?"

Catherine gathered herself. "The General Counsel of the Central Intelligence Agency. I was scared when they all turned up at my door. My husband wasn't even in his grave and they were tearing through my family home like he was a criminal. My husband and my son served our country with distinction. I can't believe what's happening."

"I'm sorry to hear that. It must have been very difficult."

Catherine closed her eyes for a moment, reliving the trauma of the visit. "I was flustered; I didn't have my husband to help me. They made me sign a legal agreement. I said I wanted time to consult a lawyer, but they said there was no time. Said I could not under any circumstances visit my son. I was terrified. They said I might be sent to jail for a long time."

"I'm so sorry . . ."

"Tell me about Stephen."

"I saw him, Mrs. Leahy. And I spoke to him."

"I'm worried about him. How is he really?"

"I'm not a psychologist, but he seemed fine to me. Very composed. Very rational."

The woman laughed, tears in her eyes. "That's my Stephen—just like his father: cool, calm, smart. Thank you for letting me know he's okay."

"The problem is that he might appear to be okay, but his situation is dire."

"I don't understand why he's in hospital. I don't know what it's all about. Stephen won't even be able to attend his own father's funeral tomorrow."

Reznick felt terrible at the intrusion. "I'm so sorry for disturbing at a time like this."

"Why are you really here? I don't understand."

"I don't want to take up any more of your time. I believe your son, in his capacity as a senior CIA officer, might have passed on highly classified files or an excerpt of those files to your late husband. Maybe on a memory stick. I'm hoping that may be something I could have a look at."

The woman glanced over his shoulder again, watching a passing couple. Then she fixed her eyes back on Reznick. "I know what you're talking about. But I'm scared. I need you to go. Please, you need to get out of here. This is all too much."

"Mrs. Leahy, I don't mean to upset you. This is all related to what your son Stephen told me. He was talking about plans. Plans he didn't approve of. He has deep, ethical objections to them. Maybe he left the files here. Maybe there are paper copies. Maybe on a computer."

"They took all the computers: my laptop, my husband's iMac, my iPad. I don't even have a cell phone now."

"Ma'am, is there nothing that was left that you could show me?"

"Please, I'm asking you nicely, leave my property. Just go. They might be watching you."

Reznick turned around. His eyes scanned the lake. But there was no one around. He faced the anxious widow. "Who might be watching?"

"I don't know. Please, I'm afraid. They told me not to talk to anyone about Stephen."

Reznick could see how agitated the woman was getting. He pulled out a card with his name and cell phone number on it. "Who's *they*?"

"Please just go."

He handed over his card. "This is my number. No one will know you're speaking to me. Just text me. I promise this is a secure number."

The woman took the card. "Please go. They might be watching."

Seven

Reznick's face-to-face with a terrified Catherine Leahy was a turning point. Knowing the CIA General Counsel had gone to such extraordinary lengths to visit in person and silence her, Reznick could only conclude that the plans Stephen Leahy had outlined were real, and had not been contrived to manipulate him in some way. This was no wild fantasy from the mind of a lunatic.

Reznick drove out of the gated community and checked into an oceanfront room at the swanky Breakers hotel in nearby Palm Beach. He swam fifty lengths in the beautiful pool then ate dinner alone in his room as he recalled everything that had happened. He went to bed. But sleep wouldn't come, which was hardly surprising since he had been crunching on Dexedrine, drinking soda, and watching TV; the news showing a US gunboat in the South Caribbean destroying another alleged narco-cartel boat registered to Venezuela.

He got up at four a.m. and showered, before making the short drive to Palm Beach International Airport.

Reznick caught the first flight back to Reagan, more focused on what direction he should take. The conversation with Leahy's mother had left him feeling even more uneasy. Putting pressure on a newly widowed woman showed him the CIA were worried that any leaks needed to be plugged. They wanted to shut the story down, fast and for good. He understood the rationale.

Reznick tried to sleep on the plane, tilting his head back with some classical music playing in his AirPods, but it was no use. His mind was too active. Hour by hour, day by day, he was being drawn into a complex and disturbing series of interconnected events. He would be heading into uncharted waters if he proceeded with his one-man investigation. His instincts were telling him not to get involved in intelligence matters. He felt genuinely uncomfortable. But he believed in Leahy now, no matter how far-fetched the plans the man had outlined might seem.

Outside the airport in DC, he caught a cab back to his hotel. He had decided he needed to touch base with the person who had started it all. So he showered, changed, and messaged his friend: ex-FBI Assistant Director Martha Meyerstein.

Are you free to talk. I'm in town.

Reznick was curious what she made of this scenario. But he also wanted to relay to her what he had learned from his conversation with Stephen Leahy—about the plans he claimed to have tried to veto.

A few moments later Reznick's cell phone rang.

"Hey Jon," she said, the familiar Chicago accent still there even after decades in DC. "Long time, no hear."

Reznick beamed. "Nice to hear your voice again."

"Yours too, Jon."

"Listen, I'm in town, working on something. Can we meet up? Just for a little chat. I'm based downtown at the Sofitel."

"Well, Mr. Reznick, you're in luck," she joked.

"I am?"

"I'm free and I'm not far. How about we meet up in Lafayette Square at noon?"

That was only a block away from the hotel. "Sounds good. I'll see you then."

At half past eleven, Reznick headed to Zeke's Coffee. He felt in need of some sustenance. He bought a strong black Colombian coffee and a savory pastry. Then he walked casually over to Lafayette Square. He sat down on a bench in the shade of some broad oaks on the north side, drinking his coffee, wolfing down the pastry, watching the world go by. He could still make out the imposing sight of the White House through the verdant summer foliage.

Joggers, speed walkers, and yoga workout nuts all around. He wiped his mouth with the napkin, dropping it in the trash can beside him.

Reznick looked toward the redbrick National Courts Building on Madison Place NW, on the eastern side of the park. It wasn't difficult to see that Washington, DC, was not only the nation's capital; it was the seat of power, containing as it did the politicians, the institutions of state, government agencies, the White House, the State Department, the Treasury, the Pentagon just across the Potomac, the Department of Homeland Security, the FBI, the foreign embassies, and nongovernment organizations by the thousands. Power was all around. But more than anything this place was where the American government wielded power that could be felt around the world: economic, diplomatic, and, when required, military.

Reznick took a sip of the scalding coffee, enjoying the caffeine hit. A few minutes after noon, he spotted the immaculately groomed figure of Martha Meyerstein walking toward him, fashionable sunglasses on, impeccably attired as always.

Reznick stood up and kissed her on the cheek. "Nice to see you, Martha."

"Likewise." She sat down on the bench beside him. "Well, this is cozy."

Reznick looked pleased and peered off into the distance, her fresh lime and basil perfume lingering between them in the hot summer breeze. "Thanks for coming."

"Been a while, Jon," she said.

"Very true."

"You haven't changed."

Reznick smiled rakishly at her. "What can I tell you? You look good."

Meyerstein winced and shook her head. "Thanks, I'll take it. I don't feel too good."

"How's the lecturing game?"

"Not as exhausting as the FBI, that's for sure. Reasonable hours. Makes a refreshing change."

"You miss all the excitement?"

"That I could do without, trust me. On the other hand, I do occasionally miss the intensity of the work. And, yeah, I guess I miss working with you. Even the nail-biting bits. It was interesting, that's for sure."

Reznick sipped his coffee. "Listen, I hope you don't mind me intruding on your day. I know it's short notice."

"I'm happy to see you."

"I'm happy to see you, too. And I assume you know why I'm here?"

Meyerstein shook her head.

"Stephen Leahy. His lawyer reached out to me."

"His lawyer? Why didn't he speak to you directly?"

Reznick looked off into the far distance. He wondered whether she knew what had happened to Stephen Leahy. Maybe she was in the dark about him being admitted to a psychiatric facility, which would make the conversation uncomfortable.

"I don't know if you know this or not."

"Know what?"

"Stephen is being held in a psychiatric hospital in rural Maryland."

Meyerstein sat in stunned silence.

"I'm assuming you didn't know that."

"No, I did not. Are you sure? Stephen Leahy? The CIA's Stephen Leahy, right?"

"Right."

"That's . . . I find that hard to believe. And you know that for sure? That doesn't seem credible. Stephen?"

Reznick nodded. "It's credible."

"How do you know that he's in a hospital? Who told you?"

"I spoke to him face-to-face, inside the psychiatric hospital. That's how I know."

Meyerstein shook her head. "Talk me through this. It's a lot to take in."

"His lawyer in DC reached out to me when I was down in New Orleans a couple days ago. He said Stephen wanted to speak to me. I'd never met either guy before."

"Go on."

Reznick took a few minutes to carefully narrate the bizarre sequence of events from the moment he got the call from Lawrence Morgan.

"This is the craziest thing I've ever heard. But I shouldn't be surprised that you're in the middle of it."

"Stephen is being kept against his will. He's not crazy. Far from it."

"What was he so eager to talk to you about?"

"Military plans. Latin America. And that's where it all goes haywire. What he told me alarmed me. So much so that I wanted to talk to you about it. You gave him my number, after all. The whole thing is fucked up, Martha. It seems to be taking on a life of its own. I'm just trying to figure out where I should go from here. I feel like I've hit a wall."

"Okay . . ."

"Let me ask you something, Martha. Has Stephen Leahy ever struck you as crazy, paranoid, delusional?"

"Quite the opposite: very smart. Analytical. Very grounded."

"That's what I thought too."

"So how the hell did he end up in there?" Meyerstein asked. "It makes no sense."

Reznick sipped his coffee. "I think it does make sense with what I know now."

"I've worked with Stephen in the past. He's a good guy. Intense, but a good guy."

"That was the sense I got as well."

Meyerstein shook her head. "I'm not an expert in psychology, but it seems a stretch to think he would go from composed and smart to psychotic in a matter of days, especially when I only spoke to him about a week ago. But then again, what do I know?"

Reznick got to his feet. "Let's walk and talk. Stretch our legs. It's a troubling business."

He finished his coffee and dropped it in a trash can as they strolled down the path shaded by thick foliage. A mother pushed her child in a stroller. A middle-aged bald guy stretched out in a yoga pose on the scorched grass.

"This whole thing seems off, Martha. Stephen told me they said they found drugs in his desk."

"That's bullshit."

"That's what I figured. Stephen also told me that two CIA psychiatrists got him committed as he had paranoid delusions. Do you know his lawyer isn't even able to get independent experts in to examine him? It's been refused. In the interests of national security."

"That's interesting."

"Lawrence also said he's not allowed to access the medical records of Stephen or his father. He's their lawyer. The father used to work at the Agency as well."

"I knew him too. Michael Leahy. Old school."

"Here's the kicker. He drowned in a boating accident a short while after speaking to his attorney about Stephen's case."

Meyerstein turned and peered over her sunglasses. "Now that's stretching credibility."

"Precisely what I thought. Michael's widow down in Florida is scared. She told me to go away, as—get this—*they might be watching you.*"

"She said that?"

"Verbatim."

"Someone got to her?"

"And I'll tell you who. She got a visit from the CIA General Counsel and the Feds."

Meyerstein shook her head. "That's a heavy approach. I'm out of the loop on FBI machinations these days. But that in and of itself is revealing. It indicates that they're very concerned."

"Definitely."

"It's a lot to take in . . . What exactly was he so eager to speak to you about? I asked him at the time, but he wouldn't tell me. He just wanted someone to speak to, someone who I thought he would be able to trust implicitly. Someone who understands the world of intelligence and the military but is no longer part of it. You just mentioned military plans . . . Latin America. What the hell did he tell you?"

Reznick nodded. "I went there because I was curious. But, Martha, what he told me was so outlandish, it alarmed me greatly."

"You're not the sort of person who gets alarmed easily."

"Don't get me wrong. Initially I really did think he might be crazy. Florid psychosis; I've seen a few guys from Delta in hospital for shit like that. Hallucinations, delusions, loss of contact with reality from PTSD. But that was decidedly not the Stephen Leahy I met. He talked about an operation, highly classified."

"He should not have shared that with you."

"Correct. Do you want to hear the details?"

Meyerstein nodded.

"It's an operation on foreign soil."

"I assume you know, Jon, that you must not share classified intel?"

Reznick went quiet for a few strides, unsure what he could say. "I know."

"However, it's just you and me, shooting the breeze, right?"

Reznick felt uncomfortable sharing the information he had gleaned from Leahy. He knew Lawrence Morgan had been privy to some of it, as had Michael Leahy.

Meyerstein sensed his discomfort. "What's stopping you sharing what you know?"

"Primarily, I don't want to get you into trouble. I don't want you having the CIA or the Feds crawling all over your life."

"Don't worry about me, I can take care of myself. You're not passing documents to me. We're just having a chat. So, what's this all about?"

"Stephen methodically outlined a CIA/Pentagon false flag operation in Guyana. Signed off by those at the very top."

"Jon, I don't have to tell you that that is exactly what the Agency does."

"I'm well aware of that. What freaked out Stephen was that this particular operation, using narco-cartels and foreign mercenaries as the backdrop, would include mass shootings of civilians and the bombing of American oil facilities in the country."

"So we're going to invade Guyana?"

"No. It's simply the pretext. The violence will be blamed on Venezuela. Conservatively, hundreds of American citizens in Guyana and Venezuela could be killed. The carnage that would ensue could potentially kill hundreds of thousands."

Meyerstein took off her sunglasses. "And he objected to that?"

"Precisely. His was the sole voice in opposition. And within a week or so, he was removed and locked away in a psych ward."

"I guess the first thing Stephen should have done, if he had concerns about the operation and its legality, was reach out to the Inspector General. If we're talking about following protocol, procedure."

"Stephen told me he initially approached the Inspector General—"

"I know him—Eugene Buckley. What did Eugene say to him?"

"Nothing."

"What do you mean?"

"Stephen tried to speak to him. He sent secure messages. But he never heard back."

They walked on in companiable silence for a few minutes before Meyerstein spoke again. "Let's back up. I think a healthy dose of skepticism might be in order."

"I get it."

"We don't know that the plans are real. Do they exist? Or only in Stephen's head? Verbal or written discussions or leaks of highly classified data like that—if indeed it was verified—would be violating the Espionage Act. Remember, I work for the National Defense University, funded by the Pentagon. I've got to be very careful."

Reznick shook his head. "I know that. Stephen knows that. Help me out here, Martha. I'm stuck. I'm tempted to just say fuck it and head home, I really am. But there's part of me that's demanding I stay with this."

"For what purpose?"

"I don't know. Doing the right thing?"

Meyerstein checked her watch and put her sunglasses back on. "Listen, I need to give this a bit more thought. A *lot* more thought. Besides, I've got a lecture to give in an hour. How about we meet up for a drink tonight? We can talk more then."

Eight

Edward Black sat at his huge, polished, mahogany desk in a secure suite of offices in downtown Arlington, staring at surveillance footage on his computer screen. Light flooded through the floor-to-ceiling windows. It had been filmed by two highly trained operatives, taking both still photographs and video from inside a white AT&T van parked on Jackson Place, on the western border of Lafayette Square.

The images showed a meeting between two people in the heart of DC. One of them was the main target of the covert investigation, Jon Reznick.

Black's heart raced when he recognized the face of the woman behind the sunglasses.

This open-air meeting between Jon Reznick and former Assistant Director of the FBI Martha Meyerstein was alarming on multiple levels. Was Reznick divulging classified intel? If so, what was she going to do about it? Black shouldn't have been surprised. Reznick and Meyerstein had worked together for years while she was at the FBI.

He assumed the meeting was linked to Reznick's surprise visit to Stephen Leahy at the psychiatric hospital down in Maryland. He had been astonished that Reznick had gotten access to Leahy, especially as the senior CIA officer was being held under a false name to shield both him and the Agency.

Black sensed a major problem brewing if Reznick was on the scene. He had spoken to various people who either knew him or had worked with him. It was always the same—this guy was the toughest, meanest, coldest black-ops operator in America. But more than anything, he was smart and had a moral code. A dangerous combination at the best of times.

Reznick wasn't the sort of guy to look for glory. He usually operated under the radar, often working abroad at the behest of, of all people, the CIA. But something had changed to bring Reznick out into the open. Which was why seeing him appear on the footage was so disconcerting.

What did he want? Why was he getting involved? This wasn't his area of operation. It all seemed out of character. What the hell was going on?

Reznick reaching out to Meyerstein was troubling in the extreme. Black wondered whether Reznick was getting that relationship going again for professional reasons, drawing on Meyerstein's intelligence expertise and contacts.

Black was transfixed by the footage. Reznick was calmly drinking a cup of coffee as Meyerstein, wearing large tortoiseshell sunglasses, sat and chatted with him on a bench. It was like they were on a lunch break from the office.

A few minutes later, the pair got up and strolled through the park, deep in conversation, only one hundred yards from the White House. Meyerstein had left the FBI, but she was still involved in intelligence matters. She split her time between lecturing at Georgetown and the National Defense University. She was still connected to that world, and she groomed future American intelligence leaders. This was problematic.

"What the fuck are you two up to?" he muttered to himself.

He finished watching the video.

Black took a few minutes to absorb the ramifications of the meeting. He sent a secure copy of the footage—all eight minutes and forty-two seconds of it—to Don Schneider, a colleague in New York who specialized in forensic lipreading.

Black sat back in his seat. His mind was filled with scenarios he didn't want to contemplate. This was the last thing he needed. His global risk and security company had been formed to ensure that problems never materialized. When they inevitably did, he crushed them before they developed into full-blown crises.

He was the point man. His two major clients were the Pentagon and the CIA. No one knew this—the invoices detailed *Special Projects Consulting Services*, making his firm seem like they were in management consulting, like McKinsey. That was fine, so long as no one ever asked for a breakdown of their work. They were actually part of a black-ops special projects budget. Hidden from sight.

The nature of their work required multiple layers of vetting for him and his staff by Homeland Security and the Department of Defense. He had the very highest level of clearance. Top Secret. And this included special access programs—highly sensitive information and classified operations, both current and future projects.

Black had previously worked at Quantico, for the Defense and Counterintelligence and Security Agency. He had been the top executive responsible for vetting both individuals and companies working with, or being used by, the Pentagon. There, Black had overseen exhaustive background investigations. The organization had oversight of more than ten thousand vetted companies.

Five years ago, he had set up his private security firm, working secretly for the Pentagon on ultra-secretive, off-the-books projects. CIA involvement, invariably. The operatives he employed were mostly ex-military surveillance experts, ex-FBI computer experts, private security operators who had worked in Iraq and Afghanistan, some former Navy SEALs, all with top-secret clearance.

The highly lucrative work had made him a millionaire many times over. He maintained an enviable lifestyle. He owned a stunning ten-million-dollar home in a gated community in Falls Church, a second home in Aspen, a penthouse apartment on Fifth Avenue overlooking Central Park, and he enjoyed three vacations every year with his wife and kids: Tuscany, Dubai, and Seville in the last twelve months. What was not to like?

A ping from his computer indicated a secure email.

Black opened it. His eyes scanned a full transcript of the conversation analyzed by Don Schneider in New York. He read slowly, carefully. "Motherfucker!" It was clear that his deepest fears had been realized.

Reznick and Meyerstein were discussing classified plans Reznick had learned about after meeting up with Stephen Leahy at the psychiatric hospital.

Even more worrying, the discussion showed a detailed understanding of a high-concept, geopolitically important black-ops operation in Guyana that would precede a full invasion. A false flag event.

His company's task was simple: head off problems before they escalated. It meant shutting down any threat to the viability of a secret operation. Those threats, in this context, were real. And growing like a cancer.

At the center of it all was Reznick, black-ops specialist, ex-Delta Force. A man who had assassinated American enemies abroad: jihadists, financiers of terror groups, enemies by the score. Black took a deep breath. Coupled with Meyerstein's connections within the FBI and across the intelligence community, he knew he needed to bring this to the attention of his paymaster before it spiraled further out of control.

Black picked up his desk phone and dialed a familiar number; a private secure line he rarely used.

It rang for nearly a minute. "Come on. Pick up, pick up!" he said, impatient.

Eventually, the gruff voice of Brigadier General Michael Johnson. "Yeah, what is it?"

"We got a problem. One that's not going away."

"So deal with it."

"I would . . . ordinarily. But this is no ordinary issue that can simply be brushed away. Far from it."

"What kind of problem are we dealing with? Don't sugarcoat it."

Black got up from his seat, phone pressed tight to his ear, pacing the thick office carpet. "The kind of problem named Jon Reznick."

"I see."

"I just saw footage of him talking about Guyana with—and you're going to love this . . ."

"Who?"

"Ex-Assistant Director of the FBI, Martha fucking Meyerstein."

Silence.

"How far do you want me to go? I want a steer on this. We can deal with it any way you like. But I need to know and then we'll fix it."

"Jon Reznick is here? In DC? Are we talking *the* Jon Reznick?"

"Yeah, him. You know him?"

"Yeah . . . so he's involved in this?"

"He is."

"Reznick is a major problem. Cold as they come. What do you suggest?"

"Let's not panic. I suggest we stay on him. And find out where he's going with this. What's his motivation? What exactly does he know?"

"Don't let him out of your sight. We need to shut this down. We need to figure this shit out, fast."

Black focused his gaze out the window at the blinding summer sun bathing downtown Arlington in a golden haze.

"He mentioned Guyana specifically?" Johnson asked.

"I have the transcript. Reznick and Meyerstein, in Lafayette Square."

"I don't like this. Any of this. Get surveillance on Reznick around the clock."

"I already have."

"We need him to drop this."

"Carrot or stick?"

"Just get him the hell out of the picture."

Nine

Night had fallen.

Reznick caught a cab from outside the Sofitel across the city to Martin's Tavern in Georgetown. A classic bustling, noisy corner bar. The smell of steamed shrimp greeted him from a table near the door.

Reznick spotted Martha Meyerstein, sitting alone in a wooden booth, nursing what looked like a Bloody Mary. He walked over and sat down opposite her. He soaked her in for a moment. "You look nice."

Meyerstein curled some hair behind her ear. "Thank you. Good to see you again."

"Likewise. Glad you could spare the time. How was the lecture?"

"I don't know if it's me or my deadpan delivery, but my lectures on asymmetric threats always seem to dampen the mood in class."

Reznick chortled. "Sounds pretty riveting to me."

"I thought so too. Maybe that says more about me than my students. Tell me, what are you having?"

"Beer and Laphroaig."

Meyerstein burst out a laugh. "You really don't change, do you?"

"I try not to." Reznick grinned as he signaled a waitress and ordered his drinks and another Bloody Mary for Meyerstein.

"You want to eat? The burger and fries here are to die for."

Reznick picked up the menu and quickly scanned the dishes. "Sounds good. Make that two burgers and fries."

"Coming up, sir." The waitress picked up the menus, winked at him, and turned on her heel.

"She seemed to like you," Meyerstein said.

Reznick shrugged. "I don't think so. Just being friendly, I guess."

Meyerstein rolled her eyes. "Yeah, right."

Reznick read the metal plaque on the side of the booth where they sat. "The Richard Nixon Booth? You got to be kidding me."

Meyerstein grimaced. "Yeah, he used to drink and eat his meatloaf here. This exact spot—booth two. This was his seat, apparently."

"Nixon, huh? You old romantic, Martha."

Meyerstein laughed before she took a long sip of her Bloody Mary. "It's been a long time, Jon. I thought you would have gotten back in touch before now."

"I feel bad about that. But you know how it is. Never seem to find the time."

"I thought maybe I'd said something wrong. I still wanted to keep in touch."

Reznick looked away. "Last I remember, I think we agreed it might be best if we didn't stay romantically attached . . . or something like that."

"True. But I had expected a call. Maybe an occasional email, FaceTime. Maybe a lunch."

"What can I tell you? Here I am!"

The waitress approached. "Here you go, guys," she said, setting their drinks on the table.

Reznick picked up his bottle of beer and clinked it against Martha's cocktail glass. "To old times and old friends."

"Less of the old, if you don't mind."

Reznick took a sip of beer and looked around the bustling, buzzing bar. "I like it here. Don't think I've been in here before."

"Yeah, it's one of those great places. Just never changes."

"Just like me."

"Just like you."

Reznick studied her soft, peachy complexion, the beautiful blue eyes, manicured nails. "You look real nice."

Meyerstein flushed pink. "Yeah?"

"Oh yeah. I've missed you."

"Have you? Strange way of showing it."

"I miss working with you. I miss being with you. I miss being around you."

Meyerstein put down her glass and showed her hands. "Easy there."

"I'm serious. We spent the better part of a decade working together. And all the rest."

"And now here we are. Never a dull moment!"

After they'd been talking a while, the waitress arrived with steaming plates of food, carefully placing them on the table. "The plates are super-hot, guys. Be careful. Enjoy."

Reznick looked at the food. "I'm starving."

"Me too."

The pair ate in companionable silence. Reznick stopped occasionally to sip some beer as Martha drank mineral water alongside her Bloody Mary. He finished his burger and fries first.

"I thought I was a fast eater, Jon," she said. Meyerstein dabbed the corner of her mouth with a napkin. "That was really nice."

"Excellent. Quite a find, this place."

Meyerstein finished her drink and ordered another round.

"You not working tomorrow?" he asked.

"First lecture starts at eleven, so a few drinks the night before is perfectly allowable."

"I'll drink to that," Reznick said, sipping his single malt.

After the meal, Meyerstein made some small talk about the crazy hot weather DC had been experiencing, and about a twenty-something girl her ex-husband was dating. "Apparently an au pair from Ukraine, half his age."

"That must be tough."

"On me or the girl?"

"Fair point."

"Anyone special in your life, Jon?"

Reznick shook his head. "Not at the moment. Let's change the subject. Let's talk about why we're here. Stephen Leahy." He took a sip of his Scotch, feeling it warm his belly.

"What do you want to know?" Meyerstein asked.

"Stephen said that he was—maybe still is— Deputy Director of the CIA for Operations. Is that the capacity in which you knew him?"

"One hundred percent. He's the real deal. Very urbane, highly intellectual, sometimes rubs people the wrong way—quoting Voltaire, talking about Thomas Paine, whatever is running through his head. Some think he's arrogant: a throwback WASP, Ivy League, and all that."

"And is he?"

"Pretty much. I knew him from when he came back to DC after a long posting in Beirut, I believe. He actually lived a block from me in Bethesda. Loved opera. Visits the Met in New York at least four times a year."

"Interesting guy. What about his capabilities in the job? It's demanding to say the least."

"I remember—it must have been about a decade ago—Stephen's team was leading a major investigation. I think it was a joint CIA–FBI task force, cross-border Medellin Cartel operation. Stephen headed up what was a very complex operation—legally, logistically, militarily. He had these Agency paramilitary guys down in Colombia doing stakeouts, surveillance, and the FBI were involved in connection with the cartel operating in South Florida, Texas, Los Angeles. But he always struck me as a man of principle. What's right is right, what's wrong is wrong, that kind of thing."

Reznick leaned in closed, voice low. "We had a connection too."

"In what way?"

"He said his godfather was William Crenshaw. I was sent to the Middle East to, shall we say, deal with him."

"Crenshaw? I don't know that name."

"He was old-school CIA. I was dispatched to neutralize him."

Meyerstein closed her eyes. "You don't have to tell me that."

"I know I don't. But Stephen knew about it and said he was glad Crenshaw had been deleted. He was a traitor. Selling secrets to Moscow."

"You get around, Jon. That's for sure."

Reznick sipped his drink. "So, any more thoughts on what I told you this afternoon? Now that you've had a few more hours to mull it over."

"I've got a lot of questions. You mentioned that Stephen contacted the Inspector General?"

"Correct."

"That should definitely have been his first port of call."

"It was."

"The Inspector General investigates a wide spectrum of issues; fraud, waste, and abuse are some of the main areas. But he also, crucially, investigates potential illegal activities across the CIA."

"And I'm guessing that's why Stephen raised it with your pal Eugene Buckley, right?"

"Correct."

"Leahy's lawyer, Lawrence Morgan, was quite clear on the legal position of the plans, if indeed they even exist. That they are illegal under 18 USC 1119—the statute specifically referencing the foreign murder of US nationals."

Meyerstein nodded. "I concur."

"Clearly illegal. It's not like killing an American working for a terrorist group abroad, right? The name Adam Yahiye Gadahn mean anything to you?"

"Name seems familiar."

"He was an American convert to Islam. Ended up being a propaganda mouthpiece for Al-Qaeda. Taken out by a CIA Predator drone. And that's entirely legal, right?"

"Absolutely."

"But the plans down in Latin America? This is as cynical as it gets. These are innocent Americans—oil workers and their families, which means children. So, beyond the moral rationale Stephen Leahy has against this, it's also against the goddamn law. CIA planners, Pentagon planners, directors, everyone involved, they would all be liable to prosecution."

Meyerstein grinned.

"What?"

"I don't know . . . It's interesting to see you get worked up about a guy you only just met."

"What gets me far more worked up is the fact that we're potentially talking about the lives of hundreds of Americans as if it's a fucking game. That enrages me. And that's before we get to the real shitshow across the border in Caracas."

"Jon, let's not get ahead of ourselves." Meyerstein sipped her third Bloody Mary. "So Stephen really never heard back from Eugene Buckley or his office?"

Reznick shook his head. "Leahy told me he made repeated attempts to reach out—encrypted email, messages, and phone calls. But he didn't hear back. Not a thing."

"Office of the Inspector General would be crazy busy."

"I get it. But I would have imagined that him being such a senior CIA figure—Deputy Director of the CIA for Operation, no less—would mean that Buckley would address any complaint or issue raised as a matter of urgency. A matter of priority."

"I agree entirely." Meyerstein sipped her cocktail. "Mmm . . . that is good."

"You want another?"

"Absolutely not. I have a cross-fit class at nine o'clock tomorrow morning."

"Good for you."

"I know Eugene well. How about I arrange for you to meet up with him. Maybe he can tell you if the issue was really raised by Stephen Leahy or not. Maybe his team are working on it as we speak. But, going forward, I can't help you any further, Jon. I hope you understand my position."

"Of course."

"You need to figure it out."

"If I can speak to Eugene, hear his side of things, it'll hopefully clarify the whole thing. As it stands, Leahy seems to have been abandoned."

"I'll be in touch."

Ten

Early the following morning Reznick got up and changed into his running gear, left the hotel, and entered into Washington's steam-bath summer heat. He stretched for a few minutes, then headed off on a run.

He ran along the National Mall, past the Washington Monument. A blood-red sun peeked over the rooftops in the distance. He headed past the mighty Lincoln Memorial, the sun bathing the stone in a crimson glow.

His T-shirt sticking to his sweaty skin, endorphins racing through his body, he headed past the Reflecting Pool.

Reznick jogged over to the Vietnam Veterans Memorial. He looked at the names of the fallen soldiers carved into the black granite. Row after row. He bowed his head; his father had served in Vietnam, multiple tours of duty. As a boy his father had taken him to this same memorial.

He remembered standing to attention as his father had wept openly, touching the names inscribed in stone. Men he had known, served with, and who had died nearly ten thousand miles from home. His father, when he returned, had seemed like a different person to Reznick: quieter, angrier, drinking monumental amounts of bourbon and Scotch to black out the memories of what he'd witnessed. His father had spent his remaining years, after building his home from scratch in Rockland with his own hands and hard work—the house in which Reznick still lived—working at a canning factory in Rockland, hating his job, hating his life. But his father had always turned up for work at the job he loathed. He had endured the pain. When Reznick's mother died, his father did his best. Even as a boy, Reznick could see the terrible sadness in his father's eyes. He was never the same again.

Reznick stood for a few minutes in the shadow of the monument. He said a silent prayer to all the soldiers who had fought and died in a war in that far-off country. Vietnam had lost millions of people. America had lost nearly 60,000 men. But it was clear that America had lost its moral compass as well as its collective mind. The war that destroyed one generation radicalized a younger one.

Reznick headed back to his hotel, the ghosts of Vietnam still lingering in his mind. He thought of the black-and-white photos of his father taken in the backstreets of Saigon: photos in bars, alleys, standing on street corners, local Vietnamese kids looking haunted in the background.

Reznick got back to his room, sweat covering him from head to toe. He checked his cell phone. A text from Martha at 0702 hours, telling him that Eugene Buckley would see Reznick in his third-floor office over at George Washington University at 9:30 a.m.

Reznick showered and changed into a fresh T-shirt and jeans, sneakers, and a Red Sox baseball cap. He headed out again, stopping off at a nearby diner. The air-conditioning blasted ice-cold air in all directions. He had a light breakfast of toast, scrambled eggs, freshly squeezed orange juice, and two mugs of strong, black coffee.

A short while later, he headed to the Elliot School of International Affairs on East Street NW, part of George Washington University. Reznick walked up a flight of stairs and headed down a long corridor until he saw a sign for Buckley's office. He knocked a couple of times.

"Yes, come in," a voice boomed from inside.

Reznick opened the door.

A small man wearing a white shirt, navy bow tie, and matching suspenders stood up from behind his desk and shook his hand. "Eugene Buckley, I believe you know Martha Meyerstein."

"That's correct."

Buckley indicated for Reznick to take a seat opposite him. "Please, have a seat."

Reznick pulled out the chair and sat down. "Appreciate you meeting me at such short notice. I'm sure you're a busy man. I won't take up too much of your time."

Buckley sat down. "So you worked with Martha for many years."

Reznick nodded.

"Very unconventional for an ex-Delta operator to be fraternizing with the Feds. You guys not more at home killing people abroad?"

Reznick ignored the barbed comments, not wanting to get drawn unnecessarily into a discussion about his role. He sensed that Buckley was less than happy about being interviewed but was doing this as a favor for Martha.

"If you don't mind me asking, Mr. Reznick, what were you doing working alongside the FBI for all those years?" he asked sourly. "I've spoken to a few people within the Hoover Building who were less than enthusiastic about this unconventional arrangement."

Reznick ignored once more the dig at his expense. "Doing work related to classified and sensitive investigations, among other things."

"*Work related to classified and sensitive investigations,*" Buckley parroted. "Interesting. And you used to be in the feared Delta Force and worked for the Agency at one time?" he asked. "Do you mind me asking what you did at the CIA?"

"Classified work."

"Classified? Assassinations?"

Reznick stared across the desk at Buckley. He could see the type of guy Buckley was: a pompous ass. He decided to just roll with it. He had met many men like Buckley over the years—men who tried to unsettle him, toy with him, as if Reznick were a student, but also insinuating that they knew a lot about him.

"It doesn't matter to me, Jon. I know the Agency better than anyone. I know how it works. I know how it doesn't work. That's why they appointed me."

"What's your specific role?"

Buckley took in Reznick as if unused to answering direct questions. "I'm in the business of overseeing highly classified work as Inspector General of the CIA. I'm sure you know that."

"Interesting."

Buckley checked his watch. "So, Jon, I've got a class in less than fifteen minutes. I'm teaching an Oversight of an Intelligence Agency workshop. The students are, by and large, quite brilliant, very impressive. But I'm on a tight schedule today, so how can I help?"

"What do you know about a special access program called Yellow Rain?"

"Right to the point, eh, Jon? As you know, I can't discuss classified matters. I'm sure you understand."

"Does the name mean anything to you?"

Buckley shrugged, looking slightly bored. "This is very obtuse, Mr. Reznick. Is there a point to all this?"

Reznick mulled over why Buckley seemed so annoyed by his mere presence. Why do the favor for Meyerstein if this was how he'd planned to act? Reznick sensed he was getting underneath Buckley's skin. "Do you know Stephen Leahy of the CIA?"

"Let me think. Stephen . . . how do you spell his last name?"

"L-e-a-h-y."

"I know that name. Actually, it would be more accurate to say that I know *of* him; that's not a state secret."

"You know of him . . . Did you also know that Mr. Leahy, one of the Agency's most senior directors, is being held at a psychiatric unit in Maryland?"

The color seemed to drain from Buckley's face. "I see. Tell me, what exactly is your point, Jon?"

"My point is, Stephen Leahy, Deputy Director of the CIA for Operations, brought aspects of a highly classified program which concerned him to *your* attention. Your office's attention. Repeatedly he contacted you and your office. Stephen did not receive a reply. I'm just asking you to confirm if that is correct."

Buckley's expression changed. He seemed to take in Reznick on a different level now. "I can neither confirm nor deny that."

"Not hearing back from you, Stephen then showed an extract of this special access program which so concerned him to his father."

Buckley's face flushed. "Jon, I would caution you that talking about CIA officers sharing classified intel is, in itself, problematic."

"I'm well aware of that. Stephen's father, Michael Leahy, used to work at the Agency several decades ago, and he was also knowledgeable as to the workings of the CIA and the Pentagon's special access programs. I've learned that Michael tragically died in a boating accident shortly after reaching out to his personal lawyer in DC."

Buckley shifted awkwardly in his seat. "I'm very sorry to hear that."

"Michael was concerned about Stephen and where he'd been taken. I've spoken to the lawyer. And that's where it gets really interesting."

"You've been busy."

"The lawyer said that both he and Michael Leahy were refused access to the medical reports that got Stephen Leahy committed."

Buckley gave a patronizing smile, as if dealing with a student who hadn't understood a discussion point. "That's a fascinating story, Mr. Reznick."

Reznick said nothing.

"So, Jon, Martha has already told you, I'm sure, that there are very strict protocols in the CIA and Pentagon for dealing with highly classified and secret documents. You should know that better than anyone. National security, yes?"

"Agreed."

"Stephen Leahy, obviously with acute mental health problems, should have reached out to my office instead of reaching out to his father. I have no recollection of him trying to speak to me. In my opinion, for Stephen to pursue such a case, to share intelligence, shows a terrible lapse of judgment and a breach of trust. It's also illegal."

"Well, here's the thing, Eugene. Can I call you Eugene?"

Buckley glowered. "Sure."

"As I said earlier, Eugene, Stephen told me that he did contact your office, including sending several encrypted follow-up emails. You should pay attention."

Buckley flushed scarlet. "I heard what you said. I'm saying I have no recollection of that. If I did, my office would have dealt with the matter accordingly."

"You told him you would investigate. But he didn't hear back from you after that. Stephen's words."

Buckley eyed Reznick, face flushed again.

"Is it normal for you to ignore such a high-ranking member of the CIA if they reach out to you in confidence?"

Buckley gathered up the files on his desk and slid them into a case. "I'm not sure I like your tone, Jon."

"I don't really care if you like my tone. I'm asking you if it's true or not. Stephen was very clear."

"If what you say is true, then this is a delicate matter. I will of course look into any emails supposedly sent to my office. For now, I have to take your word for it."

"Stephen's word for it."

"My office has an incredibly heavy backlog of cases; I'm sure you understand."

"I'll have to take your word for it."

"I have to say, I have no recollection of having had such a conversation with Stephen Leahy."

"None at all?"

"If what you say is true then I would have remembered it. But I will of course investigate this matter and check through my call logs. I'm speculating that maybe Stephen, who you say is in a psychiatric unit, is paranoid. Has it occurred to you that maybe he's just making this shit up?"

Reznick nodded.

"Maybe he imagined that he called me. Maybe he imagined that he reached out to me."

Reznick saw through the tactic. Buckley was gaslighting him. "I've considered that possibility."

"Which was maybe the reason he was taken away for treatment in the first place."

"Don't patronize me, Buckley. I'm asking straightforward questions. I'm speculating that you brushed Stephen aside, ignored him, hoped he'd go away."

"That's not what happened."

"So, what did?"

Buckley sighed, seething, flushed. "Are you finished?"

"Not quite. When Stephen didn't hear back from you, he reached out to his father. And within a day or so, Stephen had been committed to a mental hospital and now his father is dead. Coincidence?"

Buckley's face drained of color. He turned a ghostly white.

"It's all very odd, very bizarre, don't you think, Eugene? Is this how you normally deal with complaints? Hush it up, don't deal with it, and hope it goes away?"

"When faced with allegations of illegality within the CIA, I can reach out to senior leadership. The Director, for example. But also the Department of Justice and the FBI, among others. I have a wide scope to ask questions. I have powers to hold people to account, Mr. Reznick."

"What about the Pentagon? Does your reach stretch that far?"

"I focus on the CIA, Mr. Reznick. Can I ask you something? Were you told by Stephen Leahy what he believed the special access program entailed?"

Reznick said nothing.

"Can you tell me what it's about?"

"How do I know I can trust you, Eugene? Besides, sharing intel like that would be in violation of the Espionage Act, right? Would that not incriminate Stephen if he did pass on details of that nature?"

Buckley nodded as he checked his watch. "You're an interesting man, Mr. Reznick."

Reznick sat and stared.

"I'll tell you what I'll do, Jon. I'm genuinely concerned about what you've said. Call me at my office tomorrow morning, after eleven a.m. I'll be able to clarify the situation then. It'll give me time to check my department's emails and phone logs to make sure we didn't miss anything. I can assure you I'll get to the bottom of this. I've had three office managers in the last twelve months, and to be fair, it's a bit of a shitshow. But call me and I'll clarify where we stand. I'll have answers to your questions then. I promise."

Eleven

Brigadier General Michael Johnson strode through a side entrance of the limestone and brick facade of the Metropolitan Club in downtown DC, two blocks from the White House. He was a member of the club and still marveled at the view of the Obelisk from the rooftop terrace.

The Metropolitan was widely known as the most exclusive private members' club in Washington, renowned as a bastion of the highest echelons of the political classes—partners at the top law firms, East Coast blue bloods, a sprinkling of State Department and Pentagon big shots, a few authors, not to mention assorted foreign diplomats, a couple of TV anchors, and a bunch of hedge fund guys.

It was a place where the rich and powerful could be themselves. Everyone from Henry Kissinger to JFK to Allen Dulles could drink themselves crazy without it being in the next day's papers.

Johnson was from a blue-collar family in Grand Rapids, Michigan. He didn't breathe the same rarefied air as the other members; he wasn't of this world. He felt like a fish out of water, not in his usual environment working deep within the Pentagon. He showed his membership ID and barcode to a doorman and strode up a flight of stairs, through a set of double doors, and into one of the club's famed bars, taking in the oriental rugs, leather seats, walnut wood paneling, and crystal chandeliers. The place reeked of power. Influence.

He was dressed business-casual in a button-down pale blue shirt, club necktie, tan chinos, navy blazer, and shiny black Oxfords. He always kept his hair short.

Johnson felt on edge. The operation was his brainchild. He had drawn up the blueprint. His title was Director of the Department of Defense Special Access Program Central Office. But he was also Director of Special Programs. A massive responsibility rested on his shoulders.

He felt apprehensive, which was unusual for him. But he had good reason to be.

Johnson walked over to the gray-haired, bull-necked man squeezed into a faded dark brown leather chair, nursing a large , reading *The Post*. The man in the chair, General Charles Schultz, was the head of the US Army. The club was Schultz's favorite place to be when he wasn't at the Pentagon barking orders to minions in conference rooms and corridors. Underneath those crystal chandeliers existed a place for him to be among friends, not underlings; a place to stay overnight when he didn't want to return to his home in the suburbs; a place where the staff knew him as Chuck. But Johnson never called him that. He wouldn't dare.

Schultz was not an easy man to please; even the toughest men were wary around him. He had won military honors for his bravery in the Gulf War and the invasion of Panama.

Johnson was always straight-talking with Schultz, and that seemed to be appreciated. Cold truths were better than warm words in their world.

Schultz looked up from his paper, eyes cold. "Johnson? What the hell is this? Can't a man have some privacy these days?"

Johnson leaned down. "Sir, I have some news I'd like to share with you."

"Here?"

"I believe time is of the essence."

"Can't it wait? I mean, this is my club."

"I know it is, sir. Mine too. But this can't wait."

Schultz indicated for Johnson to sit down in the adjacent chair. "What are you drinking?"

"Whatever you're having, sir."

The general signaled a waiter. "Two single malts, straight up."

"Very good, sir."

Johnson made small talk for a few minutes as the attentive young waiter fetched their drinks. Schultz spoke grimly about the heatwave knocking out power grids, the latest hurricane headed straight for Florida, with a few asides about the Nationals' current dismal run.

The waiter returned and delivered the drinks on a silver tray, carefully setting them down on circular leather mats in front of them. "Thank you, gentlemen."

Schultz picked up the drinks and handed one to Johnson. "That'll be all, Andrew," he said, barely giving him a sideways glance.

Johnson sat patiently as the waiter disappeared out of sight behind some curtains.

Schultz sipped his Scotch. "Damn fine."

Johnson did likewise. "Indeed, sir."

"I don't usually receive visitors here, Michael. It's a place of refuge for busy men. A place to forget about the world. So what the hell is going on?"

"Apologies once again, sir. But this couldn't be helped."

Schultz put down his drink, sitting back in his seat. "What's on your mind?"

Johnson leaned in close and lowered his voice to barely a whisper. "I thought you'd want to hear the news from me, face-to-face."

"Spit it out."

"Sir, I've been told that Jon Reznick has met up with three separate individuals in the last few days. Individuals who we assumed were not going to be a problem. This relates to the . . . the program."

Schultz's gaze wandered around the empty room as he took in this information. He turned and fixed his eyes on Johnson. "What individuals are we talking about, just so we're clear?"

"He met up with Stephen Leahy at the hospital."

Schultz picked up his glass and took a large gulp, draining it. He set it back down hard on the table. "In the name of God."

"Indeed, sir."

"Just so I'm clear. Jon Reznick visited Stephen Leahy in the hospital where we thought he would be out of sight, out of mind?"

"That is regrettable but unfortunately correct."

"We're at a critical juncture. The program has a green light. This is not the time for such distractions. Let's put an end to this."

"I'm well aware of that, sir. The second person he met with I found concerning as well: former Deputy Director of the FBI Martha Meyerstein. Professor at the National Defense University here in DC."

Schultz shook his head. "I can't believe what I'm hearing."

"The third person he saw in town was, tellingly, Eugene Buckley, the Agency's Inspector General."

Schultz fixed his glare on Johnson. "Are we sure?"

"Positive—face recognition, photographed, live footage analyzed."

"How did this happen? What brought a man like Jon Reznick into this? This is not his usual purview."

"My thoughts exactly, sir." Johnson took a few moments to scan his surroundings, making sure no one was within earshot. "It began, sir, when Stephen Leahy reached out to his father in Florida. And then his father, Michael Leahy—who is sadly no longer with us—upon hearing that his son had been committed, contacted the office of his private attorney, Lawrence Morgan."

"Morgan is a member here at this club. Did you know that?"

"I did not know that. Well, it was Morgan, the lawyer, who contacted Reznick."

"How did he get Reznick's number?"

"I've been asking a few questions about this. It transpires that Stephen Leahy has known Meyerstein for years. Back from when she was at the FBI. She gave Leahy the number in confidence, we're assuming. And he's obviously passed that on to his lawyer, Lawrence Morgan. And that is what sent Jon Reznick to that hospital."

Schultz's face darkened. "He's being kept under a false name, is he not?"

Johnson nodded.

Schultz closed his eyes for a moment. "How did Reznick find Leahy if he was being held under a false name?"

"Reznick is smart. Very smart. He's also working with, I gather, an ex-NSA wunderkind named Trevelle Williams. He helps Reznick whenever he needs it. Cybersecurity, military-grade hacking, you name it. So you can see now that this is a pressing matter."

"I'm glad you brought this to my attention. I see why you wanted to come here right away. I'm sorry I was rude."

"Not a problem, sir. My question to you, sir, is where would you like to go from here? Reznick is a driven, resourceful, man, a patriot to the core, but he's also highly volatile. He sails too close to the wind. I don't like it."

"It's not good."

"Though he's asking questions—reaching out to Meyerstein and Buckley—we don't know how he will move forward with this. He might just shrug his shoulders and say, pardon my French, sir, *fuck it, I'm out of here.*"

Schultz shook his head. "Then again, he might not. Let's keep our eyes on him—who he meets up with, locations. I want to know everything. But we have to tread carefully: Reznick is a lethal and complex man. We need to keep him on a tight leash. Bottom line? We want Reznick to back off and get the hell out of DC."

"What if he doesn't go for it?"

"Make sure he does."

Twelve

The following morning, Reznick was still in DC. A dusty pink sunrise was already bathing the monuments in a coral pink shimmer. He once again headed out of the Sofitel for a morning run.

He ran for five stifling miles in the high humidity, across the cinder paths around the monuments. He felt his endorphins kick in and his mood lift, his brain feeling sharper.

Reznick ran past the Reflecting Pool as the other early morning runners arrived, burning up the miles, pounding the trails. He went back over his meetings with both Martha Meyerstein and Eugene Buckley. Reznick was glad to have met up again with Meyerstein the previous evening. She seemed calmer than he remembered her being in her FBI days. He had lost count of the times Meyerstein had driven herself to the edge. She had been tough on herself, working long brutal hours, for months at a time, on complex, classified investigations. But she had also driven her team hard. And they were fiercely loyal to her.

Meyerstein knew that there were those on the seventh floor of the Hoover Building—where the most senior FBI agents were based, including the Director—who resented a man like Reznick, with his black-ops links to the CIA and Delta. They had no desire for him to get involved with the Bureau in any shape or form.

Reznick had never been bothered about that; he simply blocked out the white noise. Besides, he had Meyerstein in his corner. He had always trusted her. Trusted her judgment. She listened to those who had other opinions on the way forward. He liked that about her.

Reznick finished his run, drenched in sweat. He walked slowly back to the hotel, the city streets just coming to life. He showered, and pulled on a T-shirt, jeans, and sneakers. Famished, he headed out to Pete's Diner on nearby Capitol Hill for breakfast.

The diner was a firm favorite of Reznick's from years ago, when he had first visited the city on vacation. It was an easygoing, down-to-earth eatery. Occasionally, the blue-collar clientele would see a senator or congressman walk in for breakfast. But Reznick was relieved that, on that morning, there was no sign of any politicians, just a couple of construction guys wearing faded baseball hats eating breakfasts of eggs and sausages.

Reznick sat down on a hard wooden booth.

The waitress approached. "Morning. What're you having, honey?"

Reznick ordered a bowl of fresh oatmeal, pancakes and maple syrup, a squeezed orange juice, and a black coffee.

"You got it." The waitress shouted the order through to the short order cook.

Reznick checked his cell phone. He had a text message from Martha Meyerstein saying it had been nice to see him again and asking to meet up for lunch or dinner sometime. He was pleasantly surprised to hear from her so soon. He texted back, *Sounds good. I'll be back in touch. Got stuff to do. Nice seeing you again.*

The waitress returned with his breakfast. "Enjoy."

Reznick drank his juice and then started on his oatmeal. He didn't take long to finish that and then wolf down the delicious maple-syrup-drenched pancakes, energy levels rising. He took a gulp of his first coffee of the day, glad to get some caffeine in his system.

The gravelly voice of Leahy still echoed in his head. The raspy, smoker's voice had belied the composure, the quiet delivery. Leahy hadn't shown any signs of the disordered thinking that was often a sign of mental illness. Quite the contrary, Leahy's thinking had been logical, clear, and organized.

Reznick wondered what would happen if the plans, assuming they were real, played out. His head filled with apocalyptically crazy pictures of slaughtered civilians—Americans blown to pieces on oil installations in Guyana. He couldn't shake them off. The more he thought about what he had been told, the more a sense of foreboding washed over him. He believed Leahy was telling the truth. But what the hell was Reznick going to do about it? Was he going to be a lone voice in the wilderness?

Reznick assumed that most Americans would never have even heard of Guyana, let alone be able to point to it on a map. It was more Caribbean than Latin American, some said. It was only a four-hour flight south from Miami. He didn't think the average American cared what happened down there. But surely they'd care if they knew American lives were at risk?

Something was gnawing away at Reznick. Was it a moral code? Maybe a semblance of duty from his time in the military? Whatever it was, Reznick felt that, in all good conscience, he couldn't walk away until he had done everything he could to find out the truth. Maybe he needed to reach out to other people beyond Meyerstein and Buckley. But who?

Reznick finished his mug of coffee and got a quick refill. He finished that and paid the bill, leaving a decent tip.

The waitress smiled. "Thank you."

Reznick walked out onto 2nd Street and turned onto Independence Avenue. He stopped and gawked at the magnificent, glistening white stone of the White House, drenched in a golden glow in the blazing morning sun.

He asked himself whether the President had signed off on the plans Leahy had opposed. He had to assume he had, or ultimately the operation couldn't go ahead.

Reznick felt conflicted. He couldn't have this mission on his conscience—knowing about it and doing nothing. No matter the geopolitical and economic rationale for overthrowing the Venezuelan regime; the reach of the powerful narco cartels operating across the Southern Caribbean in fast boats, transporting tons of illicit drugs over the southern border, bringing addiction, misery, and gang violence to America.

But the major drug cartel route was not from Guyana or Venezuela, but rather Mexico and Colombia. Besides, in Reznick's eyes, nothing justified killing innocent Americans.

The news segment he had seen of the US naval buildup in the Caribbean and cartel boats being blowing out of the water was a portent of things to come. The media was already being used to shape the narrative. Softening up American public opinion for the war that was to come.

Reznick had read up on the situation down in Latin America. Whether the countries in the region liked it or not, America could operate with impunity there, especially if the interests of basket-case countries like Venezuela clashed with US economic or political interests.

That's why American intelligence agencies had applied the term "narco-terrorists" to the Venezuelan regime—deliberately conflating international cartel drug-smuggling with the government that enabled it.

The language used was important in shaping people's perceptions in the media: psyops—certain words were used deliberately to give credence to the narrative that US military and intelligence powers were being deployed to fight an external, government-level threat. The geopolitical reasons were simply that America wanted to control the region: oil, gas, minerals—the world's largest crude oil reserves. Besides, the US viewed Latin America as within its sphere of influence. America was the colonial master.

Reznick checked his watch. It was nearly ten in the morning. He suddenly remembered his call to Eugene Buckley's office at eleven.

He killed time for the next hour; he walked around Capitol Hill, enjoying the baking hot sun on his skin. He spotted a man standing on the other side of the Reflecting Pool, with a long-lens camera aimed in his direction. The man turned and walked away, disappearing from sight.

Reznick knew they wanted him to know that he was being watched: it was a warning. He walked on for a couple hundred yards more.

Out of the corner of his eye, he saw a tall, athletic man approaching, wearing expensive sunglasses and a red St. Louis Cardinals baseball hat. The guy walked slowly toward Reznick, then looked around as if making sure there was no one within earshot before he looked him in the eyes.

"You Jon?"

Reznick sensed this was to be his first interaction with those who did not want his inquiries to proceed. "Who are you?"

"Tom Steele."

"Do I know you?"

The man shook his head. "Not as far as I know, Jon."

"Who do you work for?"

"I work on behalf of a government agency."

"What do you want, Tom?"

"Can we have a little chat? I have a proposition for you."

"Sorry, got a few things going on at the moment."

"It won't take long. Couple minutes of your time."

Reznick shrugged and turned to walk away but Steele fell into step beside him. "What do you want?"

"I've been instructed to let you know that the people who hired me have requested that you back off. Whatever it is you think you're getting involved with, Jon, it stops now."

Reznick tilted his chin. "Why?"

"It doesn't matter why. What matters is that you need to realize that your actions will not be tolerated. What you are embarking on is rash, and I've been instructed to convey the message that if you don't stand down, people will get hurt."

"What kind of people?"

"You, in particular. I can't make it any clearer. The people I represent are reasonable. But they can't allow this to go on. What you are doing is almost certainly illegal, hampering the vital security work of the American government on sensitive intelligence matters."

Reznick stopped and faced Steele, who was three or four inches taller. "I don't take kindly to threats, veiled or otherwise. And I don't take orders from some bag carrier. Where you from? The Agency? State Department?"

Steele sighed, averting his gaze. "I was hoping we could come to an agreement. You walk away, and we're good."

"What if I don't want to walk away?"

"I can't tell. I do know it's not in either of our best interests."

"What does that mean?"

"Let's not go there. What I've been authorized to say, Jon, is that we are prepared to offer you a one-off *ex gratia* payment. This can be made to an account of your choosing, anywhere in the world: Switzerland, New York, Grand Cayman, your choice. You want it in Bitcoin? That can be arranged. One million American dollars, tax free, untraceable."

"Are you kidding me?"

Steele shook his head. "All you have to do is sign a contract acknowledging that you will not divulge anything you have heard or learned in the past week. It's a great deal. My advice? Take it."

Reznick's senses switched on. He wondered if this was a bit of FBI entrapment. "You wearing a wire?"

"I am not wearing a wire. You want to frisk me? Go right ahead."

Reznick's attention wandered around the area, mindful that he might very well be under surveillance at that very moment.

"I am not law enforcement. I'm not even carrying my cell phone. This is confidential. My work is strictly professional in nature."

"Who authorized you to approach me?"

"A government agency."

"CIA?"

"I'd rather not say, Jon. They have allocated the million dollars from the budget already, and we're good to go. I'm on a retainer, if you must know."

"You working for the Feds?"

Steele shook his head and took out his card, handing it to Reznick. "Absolutely not. I would be disbarred or prosecuted, maybe both."

Reznick studied the neat black font on a white card. It showed that Steele was a managing partner of Feinstein, Steele, Murray and Slaven, a New York law firm based on Lexington Avenue. "You're a lawyer?"

"I am an attorney, based in Manhattan, as you can see from my card. Our clients include American government agencies, intelligence agencies, and the Pentagon. We are contracted by the legal departments of two particular government agencies to make problems disappear. We specialize in national security laws, advising our clients on risk, geopolitical strategy, and cybersecurity. We also deal with security clearance, insider threats, what is and isn't legal."

"Quite a résumé there. Interesting. If this conversation is to continue, I need to know who hired you."

Steele took a few moments to think it over.

"You either tell me or I walk away," said Reznick. "Right here and now."

"The Defense Intelligence Agency, if you must know. And alongside senior legal counsel acting for the Joint Chiefs of Staff, if that helps in any way."

Reznick saw another piece of the jigsaw slotting into place. He could see now that the plans must be real if the Joint Chiefs had sent a powerful attorney all the way from New York, authorizing a million dollars for his silence. He was surprised that Steele had given up the names of the agencies involved so easily. And he was even more intrigued. He knew the DIA well. A support agency of the Department of Defense, it informed the Pentagon and policy-makers on the capabilities and intentions of foreign governments. But what was doubly interesting was that Steele was working for the Joint Chiefs of Staff. The people who Leahy believed had signed off on Operation Yellow Rain.

"Take the offer, Jon. It's on the table. It's genuine. The money and your signature, and we're all good. Just take it. I would."

Reznick walked on, with Steele following alongside. "Are you really a Cardinals fan?"

"Hell no. Mets and Knicks."

Reznick shook his head, breaking into a smile. "You're killing me."

"Jon, please take this offer. I want to help you. You see . . . I don't know where this will end if you don't accept the offer. It's a one-time deal."

Reznick checked his watch, saw it was nearly eleven a.m. "Listen, it's been nice talking to you."

"What's your answer?"

"It's a no, son. Don't take it personally. I just don't want to cut a deal. It's not what I'm about."

Steele put his arms out to his sides. "You really should just take it."

"Have a safe trip back to Manhattan." Reznick turned and walked away toward Seward Square, then down a side street. He crossed and doubled back, checking that he hadn't picked up a tail. He headed across 6th Street SE, cut back through the grass and sat down on a bench, under the shade of a huge oak.

He checked his watch; it was just after eleven now. He took out his cell phone and called the number of Eugene Buckley's office.

A woman's crisp voice answered. "Good morning, the Office of the Inspector General, how can I help you?"

Reznick looked around at the moms pushing strollers and the handful of joggers passing by. "Morning, looking to speak to Mr. Buckley. He asked me to give him a call around now. He's expecting to hear from me. Name's Jon Reznick."

"Let me see . . . I'm just checking his diary, sir. Mr. Reznick you say?"

"That's right, ma'am."

"I'm sorry . . . It appears he's not in his office today. Actually, I'm checking his diary. He won't be in for a little while."

Reznick sensed he was getting the cold shoulder from Buckley. "Must be some sort of mistake. He didn't tell me that he would be out of the office."

"I'll check again, sir . . . I can see from his diary that he will be overseas for at least the next two weeks. Private business."

Reznick felt a flash of anger. He knew he was being toyed with. "Overseas? That's weird. He specifically told me to contact him at his office today at eleven. I was with him yesterday at his office in the Elliot School of International Affairs at George Washington University. Less than twenty-four hours ago."

"I'm looking at his schedule. I believe he flew out last night."

"Last night?"

"I'm so sorry but there must have been a mix-up in scheduling. Mr. Buckley is definitely out of the office until the end of the month. This was updated at 5:24 p.m. yesterday. So it's all up to date."

"Are you absolutely sure?"

"Positive. He's out of the country, on private business. I'm sorry. Would you like to leave a message?"

Reznick felt frustrated. "No. I'll catch up with him when he returns." He ended the call. Then he called Trevelle. "I need a favor."

"How's old DC treating you?"

"It's interesting, that's for sure. I met up with Martha yesterday. That was nice."

"Cool."

"And I got a face-to-face encounter this morning with an attorney from New York, offering me a million bucks to forget about it all."

"Are you kidding me, Jon?"

"Nope. Partner at a powerful New York firm that works for the Pentagon, Joint Chiefs, etc., etc."

"Heavy hitter?"

"You better believe it. What does that make you think?"

"It would make me reconsider exactly why I was still hanging around there. They want you out of the way. And they're offering a million bucks? Take it."

"I turned it down."

"You did what?"

"Listen, I think I'm getting messed with by the Inspector General. The guy I met with yesterday: Eugene Buckley."

Trevelle whistled. "You're making waves, Jon. It won't go unnoticed."

"I know."

"What exactly do you need, man?"

"I need a cell phone number for Buckley."

"Why?"

"He didn't tell me he would be out of the country today. I called his office, like he told me to, and they said he was overseas."

"Interesting. Give me a few minutes, Jon. I'm going to try and figure this out. I'll be back in five."

Reznick ended the call. He was irked that Buckley was playing games with him. Had the powers that be gotten to him? Maybe Buckley had something of his own to hide.

But why would Buckley tell him to call if he was going to be out of the country? Why not just say *I've changed my mind, Reznick, don't bother me again?* The more he thought about it, the more it irritated him.

He stood up and walked on until his phone buzzed in his hand.

Reznick checked the message which had just come in from Trevelle. It was Eugene Buckley's cell phone number. He replied to Trevelle: *Good work. J*

He headed along Constitution Avenue and past the Smithsonian before he called Buckley.

"Eugene Buckley speaking, who is this?"

"Eugene, sorry to bother you, it's Jon Reznick here. We met yesterday?"

"Oh, hi Jon," Buckley said, his voice languid, bored almost. "How are you today?"

"I called your office as you said I should, just after eleven this morning. But I was told by a very helpful lady who checked your diary that you're abroad. For the next two weeks."

"Apologies, Jon, I feel like such an idiot. I must've gotten mixed up with my work and lecturing diaries, assuming I was back in the office today. It's an overlap thing—not backed up to the cloud or something."

Reznick sighed, knowing it was bullshit.

"I realized late in the afternoon I had to fly off to a conference in Lisbon. My wife had to frantically find my passport. Everything got a little crazy. Listen, I haven't forgotten about you, I want to reassure you about that. Let's catch up when I get back. How does that sound?"

"I'll be back in touch."

Reznick ended the call. He sensed, not for the first time, that something was off. He was getting the brushoff. He felt increasingly as if he was going around in circles. And now, not getting any confirmation from Buckley of call logs or emails from Leahy? It was all a bit much. Then again, maybe Eugene Buckley wasn't at liberty to disclose those details because of data privacy laws, and he was just being diplomatic. Reznick couldn't discount that possibility.

He called Trevelle again.

"How did it go?"

"Got a problem, man."

"Again?" He laughed. "That's all you seem to deal with. You should have taken the money!"

"Tell me about it. Listen, can you do me one more favor?"

"You got it."

"Can you tell me which country Eugene Buckley is actually in? I'm just curious to see if he's giving me the brushoff. He said he was in Lisbon, but I want to know if that's actually where he is."

"So that would make it just after four in the afternoon in Portugal . . ." The sound of tapping on a keyboard. "Well, well, well . . ."

"What?"

"It shows that his iPhone and iMac are together in the same place. Why do you think that is? I'm assuming he hasn't taken his desktop iMac onto a transatlantic flight."

"Definitely not. Is he where I think he is?"

"He's sure as hell not abroad."

Jon groaned in irritation. "So where the hell is he?"

"Eugene Buckley is fucking with you. According to his electronic digital footprint, at this precise moment, he is at his home in McLean. Just across the Potomac. Half an hour away."

"Son of a bitch."

"The guy giving you the runaround?"

"Pretty much. One more thing, Trevelle. Text me his address."

"You're going to pay him a visit? At his home?"

"Seems rude not to."

"He might take that as intimidation."

"He can take it however he wants to."

Reznick ended the call as the text from Trevelle pinged with Buckley's home address. He felt the sweat running down his back. The sun blazed down through the broadleaf trees on the sidewalk. He knew what he was going to do: a surprise visit to Buckley's front door might unnerve the man. That was good. It might persuade Buckley to give some straight answers for once. It also might open Reznick up to threats and intimidation, perhaps playing right into the hands of those who were so keen to get rid of him. He had to assume he was on their radar now, and they would be able to track him down to Buckley's door.

He pushed those thoughts and concerns aside as he headed over to Metro Center station.

Reznick caught a Silver Line train out to McLean. It was a relatively quick twenty-seven minutes to the affluent town, not far from the sprawling Langley complex. Outside the station, he caught a cab to Buckley's house in the leafy Franklin Park neighborhood.

The taxi pulled up outside a grand, Tudor-style property on North Kensington Street, sprinklers soaking a lush, expansive, emerald green lawn. It was cut to perfection. Manicured to within an inch of its life.

Reznick paid the twenty-five-dollar fare and gave a ten-dollar tip. "Thanks, pal," he told the driver.

"You want me to hang around?"

"I'm fine, thanks."

Reznick slammed the taxi door shut and walked up the paved path adjacent to the driveway. He watched the cab turn around and head back into McLean. He buzzed the doorbell a couple of times.

A few moments later a sixty-something woman opened the door, smiling. "Yes, how can I help?"

"Good afternoon, ma'am. I'm looking to speak to Eugene Buckley."

"Eugene? I believe he's working upstairs in his office. Are you from work?"

"No, but there's something I need to speak to him about. Classified stuff. It won't take long. Just tell him Jon Reznick is here. He'll know what it's about. I met with him yesterday."

"Oh, he didn't tell me. Lovely to meet you." The woman turned and called upstairs. "Eugene, a Mr. Reznick is here for you!"

The sound of footsteps coming down the creaking wooden stairs.

Buckley turned to his wife. "I'll deal with this, honey. Private matter."

His wife nodded graciously. "Of course. Nice meeting you, Mr. Reznick."

"Nice meeting you too, Mrs. Buckley."

Buckley's wife headed back down the hallway. "I'll be out in the garden if you need me, darling."

"Thanks, honey," Buckley replied. He stood and glared at Reznick, eyes hooded. "What's the meaning of this?"

"I was about to ask you the same thing, Eugene."

"Why are you here?"

"Thought I'd just pop by, hoping you don't mind. Imagine my surprise when I found out you're not enjoying the delights of Lisbon."

Buckley waited until his wife was out of earshot before he leaned in close, voice low. "What the hell are you doing? Are you crazy?"

"I'm starting to question that myself. So, do you want to argue on the doorstep, Eugene, or would you rather invite me in and have a civilized discussion?"

Buckley shook his head. "Unbelievable." He waved Reznick in, and locked the front door behind them.

Reznick followed Buckley upstairs to a handsome second-floor office. Books and papers were stacked on wooden shelves that ran floor to ceiling. An iMac sat on a writing desk—as Trevelle had guessed—with papers strewn across it. In the corner of the study, a sofa and a leather chair were turned toward one another, as if they were in a psychiatrist's office.

"Apologies for intruding."

Buckley slumped in the leather chair and pointed to the sofa.

Reznick sat down and put on his most pleasant face. "I think there must be some misunderstanding," he lied.

"What the hell is this? Turning up at my home? Are you out of your fucking mind?"

"Not yet. I'm just a bit confused as to why you said to call you, and then when I did, your secretary said you were in Lisbon. What was that all about?"

"I can't answer that."

"But here you are, in lovely McLean. I've got to say, this is very salubrious. Beautiful town. And so close to Langley. What's not to like?"

"Are you spying on me?"

Reznick shook his head. "Me? That's a no, Eugene. I'm just a regular guy looking for straight answers."

"I don't think you know what you're dealing with."

"I think I've got a pretty good idea."

"So what do you want to know?"

"Just a few more questions, Eugene. That's all I ask."

"I've got a good mind to report this. This is intimidation."

Reznick rolled his eyes. "I'm not intimidating you, Eugene. Don't be so dramatic, it doesn't suit you. Tell me, why did your secretary lie to me? What's that all about? If you didn't want to talk to me, why didn't you just say so?"

Buckley looked sheepish, eyes down. "That was my fault. I asked her to lie."

"Okay . . ."

"Jon, you've put me in an awkward situation."

"Seems to me like you put yourself in an awkward situation."

Buckley closed his eyes for a moment.

Reznick leaned forward, hands clasped. "Let's clear the air. And let's get some honest answers. The scenario, the plans, concerns over the operation's illegality . . . was any of this brought to your attention at any time by Stephen Leahy?"

Buckley nodded.

"You told me that you were going to check the emails and phone logs. But I'm betting you knew about this all along. What are you trying to hide? What changed?"

Buckley turned around and picked up a legal pad and pen before scribbling down a note. It read: *I believe my home might be bugged. I don't know for sure.*

Reznick's senses switched on. He nodded to show he understood. He saw that Buckley was scared. "Stephen Leahy is fucking crazy. That's the official version. That's what they're saying, right?"

Buckley scribbled down more, showing the writing to Reznick. *I have no proof of that. I got a visit after Leahy reached out to me. Four guys visited me here at my home. Two of them were from the CIA's Office of Security, the other two from the FBI. They said Leahy had gone crazy and I needed to forget what he had told me. They said they had bleached the emails sent by Leahy as the contents broke the Espionage Act.*

Reznick had not anticipated the meeting with Buckley proceeding in such a strange manner. He understood now why Buckley had been afraid or reticent to talk to him. Reznick knew the gravity of the situation. The CIA operatives would be deemed to be assisting the FBI, allowing them legal cover for operating on US soil. The Office of Security was a little-known part of the CIA. Part of their duties in protecting intelligence programs meant protecting classified operations and covert activities. Anything that could even inadvertently endanger those plans would have to be treated as a problem to be shut down. Sharpish.

Buckley had been approached first by Stephen Leahy, then the Office of Security, and then Reznick himself. No wonder he was scared.

Reznick took the pen and pad from Buckley's hands and wrote: *Where does the guy—the independent overseer of the CIA—go when faced with this predicament?*

Buckley took the pen back and wrote: *I have the authority to contact an independent attorney who can review what I've been told. I could share what I know with my Deputy Inspector General, Dawn Gates. I'M FRIGHTENED. PLEASE GO.*

Reznick's gaze lingered on the words on the page. Buckley's cocky confidence of twenty-four hours earlier was gone. In its place was a man literally terrified of the consequences of his actions.

Reznick sensed the palpable fear in Buckley. It couldn't be clearer. He had to assume Buckley was being genuine and not pulling an elaborate stunt to get rid of Reznick. Buckley's eyes were filled with tears. He was that scared. Maybe for good reason.

"I would appreciate it if you would leave. I'm a busy man and I don't like interruptions to my private life."

Reznick didn't want to cause Buckley any more undue stress and alarm. "Very well."

Buckley took a lighter out of his pocket and began to burn the pad of paper he and Reznick had written on. He placed it in an empty metal trash can beside his desk. It burned for a few minutes until it was reduced to ash. "Please don't try and contact me again."

Reznick nodded and shook Buckley's trembling hand. He headed downstairs, letting himself out. He called an Uber and walked to the end of the street, shaking his head at what in God's name he had gotten himself mixed up in.

Thirteen

Edward Black seethed. He hung up the phone having just been told about Reznick's latest trip. He felt a mounting sense of fury as he paced back and forth. He kicked over a chair, seething at the latest developments. He stared out of the windows of his thirty-third-floor office on North Moore Street in downtown Arlington, gazing at the dark waters of the Potomac. His problems were deepening. Reznick appeared not to be going anywhere.

A few moments later, his cell phone rang.

"Eddie, it's Jimmy in vehicle three." The voice of one of his most trusted surveillance operatives.

"Reznick is hanging around McLean? What's going on?"

"Not good, I know. I'm about to send you our covert footage. Taken eight minutes ago out in McLean. You can see for yourself."

"You sure it's our friend from Maine?"

"Face recognition has confirmed it. The fucker is visiting the Inspector General's *home* this time, not even his office."

"Shit. Shit. Shit. This is what I was worried about. That he wouldn't stop trying to figure it out, that he'd continue speaking to people. Fuck!"

"You okay, boss?"

"No, I'm not fucking okay. Do I sound like I'm fucking okay?"

"I'm just telling you what we know."

"I know you are. Listen, send it over."

Black ended the call and sat down behind his desk. He turned on the huge monitor in front of him. A few moments later an encrypted message pinged from Jimmy and he clicked on the link.

Black peered at the high definition long-range video, presumably shot through a side window of the surveillance vehicle. A cab pulled up on a suburban street. An imposing man emerged. He recognized the profile immediately: Jon Reznick. The man himself. The same, impassive expression, mean as they come.

Black felt his stomach tighten. He watched as Reznick walked up to the door of the house and rang the bell. A woman answered. A few moments later, a small, bespectacled man came into view. The man ushered Reznick inside.

The footage cut to thirteen minutes later. Reznick emerged onto the street from the house of Eugene Buckley, Inspector General of the CIA, making a call on his cell phone.

Black decided to double-check the man's identity. He ran the facial features through the most advanced military facial recognition software in America. It pulled up a one hundred percent positive match. "What are you up to, you fucker?" He took in Reznick's implacable face. The eyes always cold. Blue.

He called Jimmy and got the lowdown on what exactly had transpired.

Black listened, took notes. He ended the call and contacted his source at the Pentagon. The one man he was allowed to speak to. The phone rang and rang. Eventually, it was picked up.

Black's heart was pounding, waiting for a voice at the other end.

"Brigadier General Michael Johnson."

"Our friend from Maine seems to be reaching out to important people in the city again. He rejected the offer from the lawyer out of hand. And now he's made a surprise visit to McLean."

"Why am I not surprised? Give me some details."

"Reznick just turned up at Eugene Buckley's house out in McLean—unannounced, apparently."

A long silence stretched between them as if the news had shocked Johnson into silence.

"Mikey, are you still there?"

"I'm still here. Reznick? He just turned up? Without any warning?"

"First he shows up at Buckley's office at the university. Then the following day at his home. I swear to God, I've just seen the footage."

"Are you kidding me?"

"Negative. Facial recognition is all green. It's him alright. The motherfucker is not going away. We tried blandishments—soft touch, light touch, call it whatever you want. He gave us a polite thanks but no thanks to a million bucks!"

"Are you one hundred percent sure it's Jon Reznick? *The* Jon Reznick."

"Completely sure. It's him. A long way from Rockland. He's worrying me."

"And so he should. What I can't wrap my head around is why he even gives a shit. I mean, what the hell is it to him?"

"What do you want me to do? Where do we go from here?"

Johnson sighed. "We need to move things up a gear. Ultimately, we need to neutralize this threat. Whatever it takes. Draw up plans. A more robust face-to-face might be in order."

"That can be arranged."

"Good. Deal with it. This has gone too far. I want Reznick out of the picture for good."

Fourteen

By the time Reznick walked up the steps of Metro Center station in downtown DC, he realized, definitively, that Stephen Leahy was not delusional. He was as sure as he could be that Leahy was indeed telling the truth. But that revelation left Reznick with even more questions than answers.

The bottom line: What could he do about it? What next?

Reznick was interested in the genuine fear that Eugene Buckley had seemed to exhibit. It was no act: Buckley was frightened. Terrified. And writing down their conversation before burning it? That was off-the-scale paranoid. But Buckley had been quite clear that he was being spied on. And they were almost certainly tailing Reznick through the city.

The unprecedented intervention by the CIA into the internal workings of the Office of the Inspector General seemed to Reznick to compromise the purportedly independent position of Buckley and his office. Buckley's job was to hold the Agency accountable under the law. But he was running scared. The CIA guys must have put the heavy hitters on the diminutive Buckley.

Reznick had found it notable that Buckley had said that the CIA/Feds "bleached" the encrypted emails Leahy had sent to Buckley's office, citing the electronic communications as being in violation of the Espionage Act.

The more Reznick thought about it, the more certain he became that a state-level cover-up was underway to conceal the truth at the highest levels of government. Reznick was headed back to his hotel when he took out his phone and called Trevelle. He relayed what Eugene Buckley had told him and how he had communicated with pen and paper, terrified his home might be bugged.

"That is seriously messed up," Trevelle said. "It's not good."

Reznick asked Trevelle to make a digital record of Reznick meeting Buckley.

"I got it, Jon," he said. "This is getting crazier by the minute. A whole lot crazier. As it stands, I assume you believe the plans do actually exist?"

"Yes."

Trevelle went quiet for a few moments. "Buckley lying about being out of the country, that's telling. He's running scared."

"He is absolutely running scared. It's just another part of the jigsaw. Leahy approached Meyerstein just before he was taken to the hospital. Maybe he sensed his days were numbered. And Michael Leahy? Both father and son—the only people believed to have seen some or all of the plans and, crucially, be opposed to them—have been neutralized. The father dead, the son locked up in a psychiatric hospital. Out of sight. And a lawyer representing the Joint Chiefs of Staff telling me to back off and offering me a million bucks to clear out? I mean, none of that is a coincidence."

"Jon, I'm kinda moving in your direction of thought. But I've got to be honest, I'm worried."

"What are you worried about?"

"I'm worried for your safety. What's going to happen to you? I think you're at risk. You're making connections they don't want you to make."

Reznick walked on through downtown DC.

"I've got a bad feeling about this, Jon. If the plans are in place, like you say, it might put you in the crosshairs of someone who wants to take you out, to silence you. You already know way too much."

Reznick ducked out of the blazing sun and into a nearby bar. He sat in a corner booth with line of sight to the entrance. "Here's the problem. I believe the plans are real. Now I need to talk to someone that knows about national security, someone who would have extensive contacts."

"Meyerstein?"

"I was thinking about someone outside of traditional intelligence circles, as much. as I admire and respect Martha. I want someone who knows about the world of national security and intelligence, but from the other side of the fence."

"What about Caroline Sullivan?"

Reznick signaled a waiter. He put down his cellphone for a few moments and ordered a beer and some fries. He picked up his phone and thought about the journalist as he contemplated reaching out to her. "That might work . . . *New York Times*, right?"

"You're breaking up. You still there?"

"I'm still here."

"So what do you think? Caroline Sullivan? She's got national security connections on speed dial. Bestselling author. She knows that world, Jon."

Reznick thought about that. Caroline had made her name as a *New York Times* investigative journalist. She had helped out Reznick and Trevelle when they were protecting a young student dissident from Hong Kong from Chinese operatives sent to kill him. Caroline had also written several geopolitical bestsellers focusing on American national security.

"Interesting. She might fit the bill."

"You need a sounding board. A person you can trust with this kind of intel. She checks those boxes. She knows her shit."

Reznick was handed his cold beer. He took a sip. "I know. She's tough too."

"Yeah, and she knows about the ongoing threats from China and Russia in Latin America. And Europe and beyond. She would be a good fit for what you're looking for."

"I get it. But this is different. This is a complex, external US intelligence operation on foreign soil. Something she might not know too much about: false flags."

"Maybe. But I trust her."

"So do I," said Reznick. "If what Leahy said is correct, and I don't doubt the veracity of his claims anymore, this is a threat to our citizens abroad."

"I read an article Caroline wrote a few years back about French intelligence agents trying to re-enter Algeria on false passports, which Algeria viewed as unwanted interference from a foreign power, trying to destabilize the government. She has a good handle on this world."

Reznick knew all about the shadowy world in North Africa and the Middle East—former colonial powers fighting for influence as China and Russia expanded their geopolitical ambitions, not to mention the Islamists' growing influence there, year by year.

"What do you say I reach out to her?" asked Trevelle.

"And say what?"

"That you'd like to meet up. That you've learned about something you feel is a national security issue. She might know some trusted intelligence or military sources who can help you verify your information. That's what you're missing. Verification."

Reznick could see the validity of that. "It's worth exploring. Certainly won't do any harm. Okay, reach out to her."

"Where do you want to meet?"

"DC works best for me."

"Consider it done."

Fifteen

When Reznick made the call to Trevelle, little did he know that the award-winning journalist in question was only three miles away, at her home in Georgetown. A few hours later, Reznick received a text in his hotel room from Trevelle: *You're in luck. Head to the Tune Inn Restaurant & Bar, three blocks from the Capitol.*

Reznick got dropped off outside the tiny diner/bar thirty minutes later. He tipped the driver and headed into the dimly lit dive. Baseball on the TV. The Washington Nationals playing the Mets. He sized up the unpretentious, down-to-earth place.

His gaze wandered around the drinkers and diners until he saw her.

Caroline Sullivan sat alone in a booth, drinking a bottle of beer and picking at a basket of fries. She looked even more stunning than Reznick remembered. Her sparkling eyes lit up when she saw him.

Reznick sat down opposite her. "Now what are the chances, huh?"

Caroline might even have blushed. "Long time no see, tough guy."

"Glad you could meet up at such short notice. You fly down from Connecticut?"

"Nope. I've had a place in town for years. A little pied-à-terre. I was visiting a contact on Capitol Hill earlier today, then did some work back at my townhouse in Georgetown. So, it's nice to have some company this evening."

Reznick opened his arms and grinned. "Don't expect much in the way of sparkling conversation."

Caroline laughed, eating a couple of fries at the same time. "Good one." She signaled the waitress. "Two large Vienna lagers."

Reznick nodded his approval.

Caroline waited until the waitress was out of earshot. Then she leaned in and narrowed her eyes in mock anger. "When I got a call from Trevelle, I thought, what the hell have I done to deserve this? You're not going to get me into trouble now, are you?"

"Perish the thought."

Caroline chuckled to herself as the waitress returned with the two huge glasses of beer.

Reznick picked up his and clinked it against Caroline's. "To old friends."

"Old friends."

Reznick took a couple of large gulps, sating his thirst. "Wow. That's good."

"Locally brewed," Caroline said.

"So, you know this place well?"

"It's an old dive hangout of mine from when I was at college. We'd come here for a few drinks before heading out to see a band at the Blues Alley Club. That was another hangout."

Reznick felt right at home. "I like it. A down-home feel."

"I occasionally drop in to catch up with old college friends who want to reminisce. Usually, we just end up blind drunk talking about Mötley Crüe or Nirvana."

"Sounds like a blast."

Caroline took a couple of gulps of beer. "What can I tell you? Now, what are you doing in DC? You're not thinking of becoming a senator, are you?"

Reznick laughed. "Kill me if I ever consider that, seriously."

Caroline looked at him with her dreamy eyes. "I wanted you to call me. I so wanted you to call me."

"A lot of stuff got in the way."

She rolled her eyes. "What kind of stuff? I haven't heard from you in a couple years, Jon. Maybe more."

"I had to fix a little problem in the Middle East. And there was also a tricky matter in LA."

"Jon, you are so fucking closed off it's crazy. Why is that?"

Reznick pursed his lips. "What can I say? I don't think I can change at my age."

"You're probably right," she said. "Though I could try."

"You could. I don't know if you'd get anywhere."

"Why am I here, Jon? I'm assuming this isn't a romantic liaison?"

"I'm looking for your help." He leaned closer, voice low. "Does the name Stephen Leahy mean anything to you?"

Caroline curled some loose strands of hair behind her ear. "Most certainly. One of the highest-ranking CIA bigshots at Langley."

"So you know him?"

"I do."

"How well?"

"I've met him before."

"Is he a contact or source of yours?"

"I couldn't possibly say, Jon. Journalistic code of ethics and all that."

Reznick considered this. "When was the last time you saw him, face-to-face?"

"Not long ago. Three months back, tops."

"Interesting."

"How so?"

"Are we talking off the record?"

"I hope so," she said. "You got any juicy gossip or secrets from the bowels of Capitol Hill you can reveal?"

"Probably something better than that."

Caroline narrowed her eyes. "Tell me what you've got."

"A brief disclaimer—it is highly confidential and illegal, okay?"

"I understand."

"What if I told you, in strictest confidence, that Stephen Leahy is being detained in a psychiatric hospital?"

"Bullshit."

Reznick shook his head.

"Are we talking about the same person?" she asked.

"Deputy Director at the CIA for Operations. That guy."

"How did you hear that?"

"I didn't hear it. I saw it with my own eyes. I saw *him* with my own eyes."

"What are you talking about? This doesn't make sense."

"I'll tell you what I'm talking about. I met him at a psychiatric hospital in Maryland."

Caroline leaned closer, a floral perfume hitting his senses. "Don't mess around with me. I'm a serious journalist, you know."

"I know you are."

"This is extraordinary. Is it really true? How did you first hear about this?"

"His lawyer called me. He told me Stephen wanted to meet me. And listen to this, he's being held under an assumed name: *Toby Breslin.*"

Caroline was wide-eyed at what he was saying. "Can I make a note of that name on my iPhone?"

"Sure."

Caroline took out her cell phone and entered the fake name in her Notes app. Then she put her phone back in her pocket.

Jon spread his hands across the table. "You got any questions?"

"Damn right I have. So, why you, Jon?"

"Why me what?"

"Why did he get his lawyer to reach out to you?"

"Leahy, by all accounts, is on friendly terms with former Assistant FBI Director Martha Meyerstein."

"The lady you used to work with?"

"Correct. And Leahy, apparently, asked her if there was someone in her orbit who she would trust more than anyone. To listen to the story he had to tell."

"And she named you?"

Reznick nodded. "I went to the hospital and spoke to him. But I checked beforehand. Or rather Trevelle checked the hospital's systems. That's how we found out he's being kept there as Toby Breslin."

"How did you figure that out?"

"We checked the dates of birth of all the patients. And we got a match."

"That's crazy. And you saw him inside?"

"Face-to-face."

"And they didn't stop you?"

"I went in under a fake name too. They didn't think anything of it. I'm assuming the staff, or most of the staff, have not been told the true identity of Breslin."

"And it was definitely Stephen Leahy?"

"It was him alright. He was no farther from me than you are right now, smoking up a storm. I mean, he was puffing like crazy on these terrible French cigarettes."

Caroline smirked a touch. "That's Stephen. And that is, by any standards, an astonishing story."

Reznick sipped some more beer. "That's not even what this is all about—interesting though it is."

"It's what he told you, right?"

"Correct. Here's the thing. I believe he has been committed to a psychiatric hospital to get him out of the way. He knows too much."

"Do you have proof of that?"

"No, I don't. What he told me is not only disturbing, it is illegal. According to Stephen, advanced plans are in place for a foreign covert operation. A war. But it will start with a manufactured pretext. A false flag."

"Did he go into details about these plans?"

Reznick nodded. "Oh yeah. A lot of detail. He has an incredible mind—went into intelligence matters, geopolitical strategies, covert operations for the military, Latin American politics, energy security. It was truly unbelievable to listen to him."

"I guess my next question is, why are you reaching out to me?"

"I need help."

Caroline grinned. "Tough guy Jon Reznick asks for help? What a time to be alive!"

Reznick shook his head and smiled. "Yeah, you got me."

"Talk me through this."

"I can't see a way forward. I can't do any more for Stephen, at least I don't think I can. I don't know what exactly I'm dealing with. The point is, I've been scratching away for a few days at this. There's stuff going on that you wouldn't believe."

Caroline was quiet for a few moments as she digested everything Jon had just told her. "What exactly did he tell you? Let's start there."

Reznick took a few minutes to explain, in its entirety, the complex false flag operation that was being planned in Guyana as a pretext for an invasion and war in Venezuela.

"This is so fucking fantastical it can't possibly be true. Seriously?"

"There's more. Layers of intrigue."

Caroline beamed.

"What?"

"Layers of intrigue . . . that perfectly defines Stephen. He's very mysterious in some respects. What was that quote from Churchill about Russia? *A riddle wrapped in a mystery inside an enigma.* That phrase could refer to Stephen Leahy."

"Caroline, here's where it gets super interesting. Within a couple of days of Stephen being committed, his father, Michael Leahy, who used to work for the CIA back in the day, met up in Washington with his lawyer—the same lawyer Stephen reached out to. You know what happened next?"

Caroline shook her head.

"Michael, an experienced sailor by all accounts, drowned in a boating accident down in Florida. I mean, what are the odds?"

"I guess accidents happen, right?"

"Absolutely. Boating accidents, car accidents; part of life. But if that wasn't crazy enough, I spoke to Eugene Buckley. Does that name mean anything to you?"

"I know him. Well, I've spoken to him over the years. Strange little man. Why did you speak to him?"

"Stephen told me that he had contacted Buckley with serious concerns about the plans. I wanted to try and establish whether or not that was true."

"You wanted to authenticate what Stephen said?"

"Correct. Martha Meyerstein suggested I reach out to Buckley since she knows him quite well."

"So you met up with Buckley?"

"Here in DC."

"You've been investigating all of this by yourself?"

"Pretty much. During my conversation with Stephen Leahy, he said, unequivocally, that he had reached out to Buckley and the Office of Inspector General multiple times. But he heard nothing back."

"That's weird."

"Isn't it? One of the most senior directors in the CIA ignored, in effect. So that seemed off to me. But I wanted to know if it was true."

Caroline sipped her beer. "I get it."

"Stephen was clear and lucid. He was appalled at the plans he had assessed and read. He reached out to Buckley through secure channels. But when he didn't hear back, he went down to Florida to talk to his father, Michael Leahy. And it all spiraled from there."

"Getting back to Buckley, what exactly did he say? I'm amazed that he even met with you."

"He was kind of evasive."

"How?"

"Nothing seemed to add up with him. Deliberately vague in his answers. I first went to meet him in his office at George Washington University where he lectures on intelligence matters."

"I didn't know he lectured there."

"When I spoke to him about Stephen, he said he didn't know anything about Leahy trying to contact him. But he said he would check if he had missed anything as his office was busy. And he told me to call back the following day. When I called, his secretary told me he'd left the country."

"Holy shit."

"To Europe."

Caroline nodded vigorously, as if she understood where this was going.

"He was giving me the cold shoulder. Fair enough. But Trevelle tracked him down."

"Where was he?"

"At his goddamn house in McLean."

"So you turned up at his door?"

"I did. Buckley was super nervous."

"I'm not surprised. You showed up at his door, Jon. A trained killer. That would make anyone uneasy."

Reznick considered that for a moment. "That wasn't it though. I went inside, up to his office. He said he had been visited by four guys a couple days earlier. That's what was scaring him. Two CIA and two FBI. They had warned Buckley that Stephen Leahy was crazy, and that the emails that Leahy had sent to Buckley had been bleached, and that he should forget the whole thing on the grounds of national security."

"That's one hell of a story, Jon."

"Buckley thinks his home might be bugged."

"This is getting weirder and weirder by the second."

"He answered most of my questions by scribbling answers down on a notepad. Then he burned it. The guy was freaking out. Does that sound like Stephen Leahy spun a tall tale to you?"

Caroline was quiet for a few moments, as if trying to get a handle on all the crazy stuff Reznick had just told her. "I mean . . . holy shit, Jon. I've got so many questions. I guess the thing that jumps out at me is that maybe Leahy has been, as you say, committed for objecting to the illegality of the plans. The nature of the plans."

Reznick nodded. "My thoughts exactly. I don't want you to record what I've said in any way. I'm telling you verbally, off the record. For your information. For background."

"Got it."

"What are your thoughts on what I've told you?"

"Playing devil's advocate . . . I don't think Leahy is crazy."

"Caroline, he was as sane as I am. Very composed. Analytical."

"So no red flags like . . . I don't know, being defensive, being wary of you, hostility?"

"None of that. He was chatty, composed, and very with it. No hypervigilance or anything like that, which I've seen with some of my Delta friends who've been put in psychiatric units. There's no comparison."

"But we have no proof that what he was saying is true? It might just be the utterings of someone who's brilliant but not very well. But Buckley's response is quite telling. And what he told you about the visit from some Feds and Agency men."

Reznick's voice was a whisper now. "I'm in a bind. I don't know where to take this. Which is why I'm talking to you. Stephen told me that he showed his dad an excerpt from the plans when he visited. If that's true, it could be the key."

"That's illegal, obviously."

"Completely. The problem is there's no way to verify that. Michael Leahy is dead. Within days of speaking to his lawyer about Stephen."

"I'm getting a really bad feeling about this."

"I forgot to mention, I also visited Leahy's parents' home down in Florida."

"Jon, you're like a dog with a bone."

"Stephen's mother, the widow of Michael Leahy . . . she was lovely, but she was wary too. Wanted me to leave."

"So you saw her?"

"Gated community in Boca Raton."

"I can't believe that you've been digging into all this."

"The only thing that makes sense is what Stephen said. Classified plans for a covert war. Stephen wanted someone to know what was about to happen. When he came back from seeing his father in Florida, he reached out to Martha Meyerstein."

"And that's how you got involved?"

Reznick nodded. "She gave him my name. I didn't ask for this. But now that I know what I know, I'm kind of stuck. I've got no way of proving that what Stephen Leahy is saying is true. I just believe it is. Buckley's visitors, Michael Leahy's death, Stephen Leahy's institutionalization . . . A picture has formed. But it's still only circumstantial evidence at best. I can't actually prove it."

Caroline stared at him. "I'm in shock. But it could just be a collection of strange coincidences, right?"

"It's a possibility. We can't discount that."

"But you don't buy that, do you?"

"I don't. It would be the easiest thing in the world for me to say this is all bullshit and head back home and forget all about Stephen and everything he told me. But I can't. I feel it in my bones. Something is very wrong. Something is keeping me here."

"Your conscience?"

"I don't know. The problem is, if I'm right and the plans do exist, how can I prove it? I would need an insider. And I guess that's why I'm speaking to you: your contacts across the intelligence community. People who speak to you in confidence."

Caroline sipped her beer, looking thoughtful. "That's a lot that you just threw at me."

"The coverup is only half of it."

"You talking about the plans themselves?"

Reznick swiped a couple of her fries. She pushed the basket over to him. "What I'm going to tell you is at the heart of the matter. It strikes right to the core of Leahy's fundamental objections. If this plan goes ahead and grants the pretext for war, it's possible that hundreds of American lives will be sacrificed."

Caroline said nothing.

"*Hundreds*. That's the figure Stephen told me he had seen mentioned in the special access program. But I've got no way of proving that. Killing Americans abroad—clearly illegal. United States Code—"

"Title 18?"

"Correct. Section 1119."

"Foreign murder of United Stations nationals, right?" Caroline said.

Reznick nodded.

"Nothing could justify that."

"What are your thoughts?"

"I'm torn . . . it's so outlandish it can't be entirely made up," Caroline said. "But it could be part of an elaborate disinformation campaign from within the CIA, using Stephen Leahy as the bait."

"Maybe it is," Reznick said. "It did cross my mind that I might be being played. But the question then becomes, what would be the purpose? And why involve me?"

"Who the hell knows?"

"If, hypothetically, Leahy is setting this whole thing up with the CIA, for this disinformation plan to be leaked . . . I don't know . . . that might be stretching a contrivance to new levels."

Caroline winced. "That does sound implausibly convoluted. But it's not an impossibility."

"I'm not a betting man, Caroline. But I would bet on the plans being bona fide. Stephen told me, quietly and firmly, that if these plans went ahead, hundreds of Americans could lose their goddamn lives in Guyana. Oil workers, their families, engineers. Not to mention Americans living and working in Venezuela. Guyana is the pretext. But the ultimate aim? Regime change in Venezuela. I don't think I'm being played, Caroline. I really don't."

"Neither do I."

"So can you help me?"

"Maybe I can," she said. "Tell you what I'll do. We need insiders, like you said. How about I reach out to a couple of former very senior military and intelligence experts who've worked at the highest echelons within the Pentagon. Highly placed until recently."

"Sounds like a plan."

Caroline's gaze wandered around the tiny dive bar. "This is a new one, Jon."

"In many ways it's not. It's what the CIA does. It plans coups—Guatemala, Honduras, Argentina, Brazil . . . we've been at it down there for nearly a hundred years. The CIA is adept at shaping public opinion in foreign countries and at home. It cultivates people with access to power in such countries: generals, wealthy businessmen, landowners."

Caroline stared at Reznick long and hard.

"You okay?" he asked.

"I don't know. I'm still processing. It's a lot to take in. It takes a lot to surprise me, but I've got to say, this sequence of events that you just relayed to me is shocking."

"So you'll help?"

"I need to head back to my house. I'll make a few calls. And hopefully we can meet tomorrow and see what it's produced."

After Caroline Sullivan left the Tune Inn, Reznick hung around by himself and had another beer. He thought about their conversation and ruminated on who she was going to reach out to.

Reznick was grateful for her time. It had also been nice to spend an hour with her. He wondered if through her myriad connections she might be able to find out something else about the false flag operation. He had to imagine that someone she knew might be able to shed some further light on the plans. Maybe they could get him the evidence he needed in order to verify once and for all that Stephen had told him the truth.

When he finished his beer, he caught a cab back to his hotel, showered, and lay back on his bed, staring at the ceiling. He felt himself begin to drift off to sleep far earlier than normal. Into a black lake. Billions of white pinprick stars glistening. He was floating downstream. There was the sound of screams from the shore. He turned his head and the corpse of a headless man floated by.

Reznick woke bolt upright in a cold sweat, surrounded by darkness. He took a few moments to get his bearings. He was lying in his hotel bed. His cell phone was buzzing on his bedside table.

He groggily reached over and picked up.

"Yeah, who's this?"

"Jon, it's Caroline Sullivan."

"Caroline . . . you okay?"

"I'm fine."

"What are you calling for? It's four in the morning."

"Do me a favor. Turn on your TV."

"Now?"

"Yeah, now."

Reznick reached for the remote and switched on the huge TV on the wall. The light bathed the room in an icy blue glow.

"Turn it to NBC 4."

Reznick navigated through the channels. He watched the screen. A young female reporter was speaking to the camera. Blue flashing lights and police tape in the background.

The reporter said, "Everyone is asking the same thing: how did a prominent Washington lawyer who represented politicians across the political divide come to be in a high-crime area of the city late at night? Police sources say Lawrence Morgan had no need to be in this part of town, had no clients in the area. His body was found outside a liquor store by witnesses who'd been walking their dog. He had been stabbed repeatedly through the chest and neck."

A photo of Lawrence Morgan wearing an expensive suit, shirt, and tie appeared on the screen.

The reporter wrapped up her report. "Mr. Morgan was one of the city's most celebrated attorneys. Anyone with information regarding his death is encouraged to call into the Crime Line at . . ."

Reznick muted the TV as he gaped at the screen in shock. "What the hell?"

"This is not normal, Jon. None of this is normal."

"Well, I guess one thing is clear?"

"What's that?"

"I'd bet my house on this being directly connected to what we were talking about."

"They've neutralized Stephen Leahy in a psychiatric hospital, his father in a boating accident and now his attorney outside a liquor store."

"So, what now?"

"We need to work fast."

"I want answers."

"I'm on it, Jon. I'll be in touch. Stay safe. If they can get to Morgan, they'll come after you next."

Sixteen

The men, and it was only men, who sat around the Pentagon conference table in windowless, secure room 2E924, were waiting impatiently for the emergency meeting to start.

Brigadier General Michael Johnson sat quietly, perusing his notes, waiting to give a briefing to the Joint Chiefs of Staff (JCS). His eyes flicked around the faces of America's most senior military personnel. Focused, serious faces stared back at him, awaiting his latest update on the covert operation which was about to be unleashed in Latin America.

He loved this conference room. Affectionately nicknamed "The Tank", it had been built to be a vault where the JCS could gather to discuss the most classified and sensitive intelligence and military matters—and this time, the subject was the covert operation he had been planning for the last eighteen months. His notes laid out the preparations, equipment, safe houses, movements of operatives on the ground, and preliminary sabotage of communication facilities such as satellite communications, but also provided instructions on how to sow seeds of confusion and spread fear by planting disinformation through social media channels, newspapers, and TV. Nothing would be left to chance.

Johnson's problem was that even his best-laid plans had begun to fray around the edges. Stephen Leahy, currently locked up in a psychiatric hospital, had gone from the lone dissenter to actively pushing back. He had revealed classified secrets. And so he would have to pay an even bigger price than he had already paid. But at this moment, Leahy wasn't the real and present danger to this operation: it was the presence of Jon Reznick in Washington, DC, reaching out to influential and powerful people in the know. That's where the real problem lay.

Johnson could see his reflection in the highly polished table. He saw the dark shadows under his eyes, from getting barely two hours' sleep every night. He knew the importance of the plans. He felt the squeeze of pressure from above. His plan was critical to the country's future economic prosperity, aligned with energy security that would last for centuries to come.

Sitting to his right, his boss—the head of the army, General Charles Schultz—crunched loudly on a couple of lemon drops. Schultz seemed to be on his best behavior for a change, which was a relief. Johnson had lost count of the number of times Schultz had exploded in a rage at any members of the JCS who hadn't been briefed and informed to within an inch of their lives. Schultz loathed tardiness, reaming out anyone who breezed in late to a meeting. Even small slights, real or imagined, could incur his wrath.

The chairman, General Max Silver, cleared his throat rather theatrically before formally starting the meeting, pointing across the table at Johnson. "Brigadier General, you're briefing today?"

"Yes, sir."

"Well, what're you waiting for?"

Johnson glanced again at the double-spaced, typewritten notes he had quickly updated a couple of hours earlier. The briefing he already knew by heart. He was the point man for the special access program Operation Yellow Rain. He had drawn up the plans from scratch. He had known they would be controversial to some. That had been proven by Stephen Leahy, who had voiced his clear, unfiltered objections. But Leahy's had been, rather crucially, the only objection among the most powerful military decisionmakers. The nexus of the Pentagon, CIA, and the Directorate of Intelligence had all agreed to this plan, save for Stephen Leahy.

Johnson's finalized plans had been shown to his military superiors around the table nearly two weeks ago. They had all signed off on them, again minus Leahy. But what he was about to tell them would be a sharp shock for the members around the table.

His gaze wandered across the faces of the men, who were all listening intently. "Gentleman, I have an update of grave concern with regard to our forthcoming special access program: Operation Yellow Rain. The President signed off on the latest draft of our plans only ninety minutes ago. I'm pleased to say that this has now been formally green-lit."

Silver beamed widely. "About time."

Johnson stayed quiet. He dreaded what their mood be like when he gave them the critical update.

Silver said, "Go on, Brigadier General. You have another matter relevant to this operation to discuss?"

"Sadly, there is one thorny issue which has recently emerged. I have been monitoring this situation closely. I believe it is of paramount importance to bring this matter before you all today. It is an issue I alluded to in a meeting two days ago in this same room. Today I can categorically confirm that we have what can only be described as an emerging problem, giving me real cause for concern."

Silver looked across at Johnson, face lined, eyes black. "Go on, Johnson."

"The problem threatening the secret nature of the plans is a man—none other than Jon Reznick, a Medal of Honor recipient."

A few hushed whispers echoed around the table.

"Some of you may have heard of him. Reznick appears to have become involved over the past week, and unfortunately this has seen him drawn into our orbit here in Washington. We have evidence which indicates that Reznick has been made aware of the nature of our covert plans."

Silver held up his hand to silence Johnson. "We are quite sure of this?"

"Definitely sure."

"Go on." The chairman gestured for Johnson to proceed with the briefing. "This is alarming."

"It indicates that a major leak of information has occurred. What is even more alarming, from my point of view, is that Reznick has already gained first-hand access to Stephen Leahy." Johnson looked across at James Raban, Leahy's replacement.

Raban looked down at his notepad. "I can add that Stephen Leahy's mental decline blindsided us, it was so rapid. That situation has been resolved."

"I welcome that, James," said Johnson. "I know how hard you have worked to make such significant contributions to our future in Latin America. Sadly, James's former colleague, Stephen Leahy, as he has indicated, has been diagnosed with paranoid schizophrenia after dabbling in psychedelics, and is seeking treatment in a psychiatric hospital where he is getting the best possible care. He had a psychotic breakdown—as was mentioned at our last meeting."

The faces around the table were stern, eyes hooded. Silver turned to Johnson. "Getting back to Reznick. His involvement. How did this come about? I mean, how was Jon Reznick alerted to these highly classified plans in the first place? I'm shocked to the core that this has taken on a life of its own."

"We are in the process of sorting this situation out," Johnson replied. "We believe this all started when Stephen reached out to his lawyer shortly before he was committed, to give him Jon Reznick's number. Then his father, Michael Leahy, now sadly deceased, on learning his son was in a psychiatric hospital, reached out to the same attorney, Lawrence Morgan, who seems to have been the victim of a violent attack in DC last night. It's all a very sad, unfortunate, strange state of affairs. But the problem for us now is that Reznick, who got this crucial call from Lawrence Morgan, headed to the hospital in Maryland where Stephen is a patient. There he entered the hospital under what we believe was a false name, and met up with Stephen who, as you know, was committed under a false name for his own privacy, protection, and also to ensure foreign adversaries did not try to exploit his vulnerable situation."

Raban nodded, finger in the air. "Brigadier General, sorry to interrupt. I can confirm exactly what you're saying. Reznick gave the identity of James Levy. The Agency has launched an internal investigation into Stephen Leahy, with initial conclusions that he has been badly compromised. There are indications of unauthorized meetings in Geneva with military attachés from Cuba, an ally of Venezuela. I will of course keep you all informed."

Johnson nodded. "Many thanks for that, James. So, after the visit to the hospital—a brief visit—Reznick appears to have then hooked up with former FBI Deputy Director Martha Meyerstein, who has worked with Stephen Leahy in the past. Reznick also visited Lawrence Morgan in DC, before he flew down to Florida and spoke to Michael Leahy's widow."

The chairman shook his head. "This is outrageous! Reznick has crossed a line. We need to arrest him. Now!"

Johnson took a few moments to compose himself, making sure his voice did not betray the anger bristling under the surface. "Subsequently, I have learned from a surveillance specialist that Reznick then spoke to Eugene Buckley, the Inspector General, on his cell phone. He also visited his office at the university and his home out in McLean. Leahy has caused absolute chaos in the leadup to the operation. What also concerns me, and I'm sure others around the table, is where this all ends?"

Schultz slammed his hand down on the table. "What the hell is he up to? Who the hell does Jon Reznick think he is? Is he a one-man crusade? Beyond all of that, how has he retained the highest level of clearance through the years? What the hell is that all about?"

Johnson cleared his throat, annoyed at the interruption from his irascible boss. "Sadly, sir, it does not end there. Only last night, I've been told by the surveillance firm who are currently monitoring his movements, Jon Reznick met up with Pulitzer-winning national security journalist and author Caroline Sullivan at a bar near Capitol Hill. A bar frequented by politicians and intelligence committee members from both sides. Sullivan, I've discovered, actively helped Reznick on a previous assignment he was working on regarding Chinese spies in New York. She is a specialist in the area. But what concerns me most are the widespread connections she has within the Pentagon itself and the CIA."

General Schultz turned to him. "I don't give a shit if Leahy is mentally ill or fucking crazy or whatever they say he is. We need to send him away to Guantanamo or some black site in Poland or Ukraine and fucking leave him there to rot."

Johnson nodded, although he could see that Schultz wasn't helping the mood of the men around the table. "I'm getting to that, sir. General, and Joint Chiefs of Staff here today, there are two separate issues. Operation Yellow Rain must proceed, as it has been formally approved by the President and the Secretary of Defense, the Director of the CIA, and every senior military and intelligence officer around this table. All those who agree raise their hands."

The chairman raised his hand first, followed by a unanimous show of hands around the table.

"Secondly, there is the issue of Jon Reznick. My analysis indicates quite clearly that he is a real and growing threat to this program: to its secrecy—the element of surprise. We should not underestimate this man. Reznick is highly dangerous. The information he has gathered, presumably from his conversation with Stephen Leahy, is the stuff of nightmares. He's a one-man asymmetric threat, punching above his weight, pushing boundaries, probing to find weakness. It's like he's testing us. Stephen Leahy, for exposing classified information and putting American lives at risk, must either be prosecuted at a later date with the full force of the law, or stay incarcerated, out of sight, until the end of his life. But that's a matter for another day. My final thoughts? We need to stay focused. But Reznick, in my opinion, needs close surveillance."

"So when do we arrest him?" the chairman bellowed.

Johnson looked around at the stern faces in the room. "We could arrest him, in theory. It's a viable option we shouldn't take off the table. But my concern would be, bearing in mind he has already reached out to Caroline Sullivan, that it would be a red flag for her if Reznick were to be taken off the streets and into secure custody. That said, he needs to be managed. I propose that we reach out to him via a third party. We've already tried a softly-softly approach via a partner at a New York law firm: polite, man to man, a sizable payoff just to get him to head back home to Maine. This pathway, Reznick rejected."

"So what do you propose now?" said the chairman. "What about further leaks? This needs to be contained. It's like Reznick is on a one-man mission. Like Leahy, he's gone rogue. He needs to stand down!"

"Agreed," Johnson said. "There are options—less palatable ones. But first and foremost, we need to make contact again. He needs to know that it is not in his interest to pursue this. We will turn the screw. There will be less carrot, more stick. He'll get the message this time, trust me."

Seventeen

Reznick stepped out onto the terrace of Caroline Sullivan's Georgetown townhouse. Another sweltering Washington morning. Her place had killer views of the Potomac, complete with wraparound views of the water, the Key Bridge, and the Arlington skyline.

"All this from book royalties?" Reznick said. "I'm in the wrong line of work."

Caroline tutted. "Not quite. I bought a hundred Bitcoin when it was going for four hundred bucks each, way back in 2016. I cashed it in last year. Ten million bucks."

Back inside, Reznick gazed around at the modern art adorning the walls. "Not bad."

"You hungry?" Caroline said.

"Famished."

Caroline headed to the kitchen, where she made some scrambled eggs, toast, and coffee. They ate at a granite worktop breakfast bar while a small TV showed CNN. The talk was of the Middle East, Ukraine, and American debt. A studio discussion started on the ratcheting tensions in the Southern Caribbean. Gunship diplomacy. Illegitimate elections.

When they'd finished eating, she showed Reznick to a huge living room. Light flooded in through floor-to-ceiling windows.

Caroline quickly assembled a whiteboard. "Okay I'm trying to figure out a way forward, how we proceed with this investigation, if indeed it is an investigation."

Reznick slumped down on a huge sofa. "Any ideas?"

Caroline picked up a marker. "I've been thinking about this overnight. A lot. And I've been making calls." She scribbled down a timeline of the chain of events. She started with Stephen Leahy being incarcerated in the psychiatric hospital in Maryland. Michael Leahy's drowning in a boating accident. Reznick's visit to see Stephen. Then the lawyer, Lawrence Morgan, stabbed to death in a sketchy part of town. A separate list included Michael Leahy's widow being warned off by Pentagon and CIA operatives.

Caroline sat down next to Jon as they ran through the names on the whiteboard. "There is a thread through all of this. Stephen Leahy. What do we know? Like what actual, provable facts do we have? It's been bugging me. What we do know is that Stephen said he brought that information to his father's attention, and the father brought it to the lawyer's attention, and now two out of the three of them are dead."

"It's no coincidence."

"It would be a stretch, wouldn't it? They must have thought with Stephen Leahy in the hospital, he'd be out of the equation; he's too high profile to eliminate, so stash him in a psych ward and silence him that way. But his voice was still heard. And now all this happens in the past couple of weeks. I want to try and run with this scenario before I give some suggestions for where we go from here. You want to jump in?"

Reznick leaned forward, hands clasped. "We need to see for ourselves if the plans exist, right?"

"We need hard proof."

"Stephen Leahy said that he copied part of the plans onto a micro-SD card and showed it to his father."

"That could be crucial."

"Agreed. That to me is an important aspect we can't and shouldn't overlook. That file may—I stress may—still exist. I don't know. Trevelle has trawled through all the relevant cloud accounts. Any and all MacBooks, phones—anything connected and linked to either Michael or Catherine Leahy in Boca Raton, anything of Stephen's—but so far he's drawn a blank. So we're at an impasse. I've been down there already and tried to reach out to Catherine: nothing." Reznick shook his head. "Let me ask you something, Caroline. You have contacts. Military contacts I'd imagine. Experts in the field who help you with national security. Contacts at all the intelligence agencies."

"I've been drawing up a list of people I think could help. I haven't wanted to rush into this by being rash and reaching out to any and all long-time contacts, in case they report it. And then we really would have problems, as we'd be sharing intel on classified operations. The problem I have, as a journalist, is that special access programs are especially tightly controlled. Any leaks and the leaker would lose their job and be prosecuted, right?"

"Right."

Caroline looked at the scribbles on the whiteboard and faced Reznick. "What about . . . and this is just me thinking out loud . . ."

Reznick shrugged. "Shoot."

"I was thinking, what about a person that *had* the highest level of access at one time when they were still in the Pentagon, but who's left military services? And that person still has clearance at the top-secret level."

"Retired?"

"Precisely," she said. "I wanted to speak to you before I do anything about it. Here's what I'm thinking. There's an expert I know, a military contact with the highest level of clearance. He's very, very well connected. It might be a long shot; he might not be willing to help. But in my estimation, having known him for the better part of ten years, it's worth a try, and I believe I should try. But first I wanted to hear your thoughts."

"Who is it?"

"It's a long-standing contact of mine. I don't reveal sources, ordinarily. But this is no ordinary case. I'm assuming what I tell you is in strictest confidence."

"Caroline, that goes without saying. Who is it?"

"Former Vice Chairman of the Joint Chiefs of Staff, General Andrew Stone. That name ring a bell?"

Reznick nodded.

"When he retired three years ago, I kept in touch. I assiduously cultivated him and his deep knowledge of the military, Pentagon and intelligence future thinking. We meet up a couple times a year. Lunches with contacts are the name of the game in my line of work. And I know for a fact that Andrew has maintained his top-secret clearance since he retired from the Department of Defense. The clearance enables him to engage in highly lucrative consulting work and private employment, including sitting on a special committee of the board of directors of a multibillion-dollar defense contractor, Phoenix Systems. The company he advises is involved with myriad classified US government contracts."

"How lucrative?"

"Think offshore accounts in the Cayman Islands. Eight-figure income. I would imagine he's doing very well. I know he's doing well. But I think our entry point is stronger with him because of this continuity from Pentagon top dog to the rarefied atmosphere of private defense contractors and their lavish expense accounts."

Reznick shook his head.

"What? You don't want me to reach out to him?"

"No, quite the opposite."

"So why the shaking of the head?"

"Simply a matter of principle. I don't agree with allowing classified Pentagon access to people who are out the door. The revolving door between government and private contractors is obviously problematic. No?"

Caroline shrugged. "It's a long-established collaboration between private companies and the government. The military-industrial complex, if you will."

"I understand the rationale. I just don't agree with it."

"Let's leave any reservations on that score aside, at least for now. Andrew is a man in demand. He also advises several corporate entities involved in global management, technology services and program solutions, predictive and big data analytics, and advanced systems engineering integration."

"I'm surprised he's got time to sleep."

Caroline smiled.

"Problem is he must have signed a classified information non-disclosure agreement—all that top-secret clearance comes at a price," said Reznick. "In which case he can't discuss it."

"Probably. But I'm hoping because of what we know, and the serious ethical concerns around these plans, that he might at least be able to steer us in the right direction. He has the access. And that could be very valuable."

"I think it's a long shot. He might not want to risk this new world he's inhabiting."

"We won't know unless I ask."

"You really think this will work? A guy like that would have too much to lose to risk leaking any intel on this."

"I think I'm a pretty good judge of character. He's a really good man. I went to college with his daughter. And he is a patriot to his bones. I've known him for twenty years. I can talk to him about delicate geopolitical matters knowing our conversation will stay between us."

"And to me?"

Caroline grinned. "And you."

"Do you trust him?"

"Implicitly."

Reznick leaned back on the sofa. "I guess we have nothing to lose."

Eighteen

After leaving Caroline's townhouse, Reznick caught a cab back to his hotel and headed up to his room. He changed into his running gear, laced up his sneakers, picked up a small bottle of water from the minibar, and headed back out. He walked over to the National Mall. The stifling humidity was like a steam bath in the ninety-five-degree heat.

Reznick liked to keep in shape. Maybe not the Delta Force elite-fighting shape from twenty years ago, but good enough. He ran every day, walked miles every day, and he also hit the gym, lifting weights in his basement five times a week. When he stayed in hotels with swimming pools, he always swam fifty lengths at a minimum.

He set off down the cinder paths between the Capitol and the Lincoln Memorial. His legs found their pace as he jogged, on either side of him the beautiful structures of the Smithsonian. Then on to the World War II Memorial, and finally the Lincoln.

He felt his thoughts clarifying as he ran alongside the stunning Reflecting Pool. His mind was sharper. More focused.

As he jogged all the way back to where he'd started, he felt good. Sweat was dripping off his brow. He did some calf stretches for a few minutes, making sure his muscles didn't tighten up later. Then he strolled back to the Sofitel to shower and change.

Reznick was starving. He headed out for a late lunch at a bar he had spotted three blocks away. He sat down in a corner booth, ordered an IPA and a turkey club sandwich.

He was thinking of Caroline Sullivan's ex-Pentagon contact when his cell phone rang.

"Hey Jon." The familiar voice of Trevelle. "You're getting around, man."

"Unfortunately, not making much progress. Feel like I'm going around in circles."

"You thinking of calling it quits?"

"Not quite. I'm still scratching around, trying to figure out exactly what's going on. I met up with Caroline Sullivan last night and this morning, and she might be able to help. It could be a way forward. Maybe pass on the baton to her. Investigations are her thing."

"Tell me more. What's she thinking?"

"She came up with an idea. Wants to reach out to a contact of hers, an ex-Pentagon chief who still has full security clearance."

"That's a big ask, Jon. He might alert his friends still at the Pentagon."

"That did cross my mind. But she seems to trust him. Let's see how it goes."

"I see problems ahead, I'm telling you."

"I think you're right. I'll give it another twenty-four hours. See what's what. After that, if the whole thing is seeming like speculation and dead ends, I'm out of here."

"That sounds like a plan. Besides, if there is an operation in motion, plans will be locked in, the timescale set. Nothing will stop it."

"True."

"You need anything, just holler."

Reznick ended the call and slid his cell phone back into his pocket. The bar's glass doors opened. He looked over. Three men in suits walked in: one tall; two thickset like wrestlers. He sensed they weren't there to get his autograph. The tall guy sat at an adjacent table. The two chunky guys sat down on either side of Reznick, boxing him in.

He figured they were either Feds or worked for the government in some capacity. He sipped his beer. "Well, this is cozy, guys. To what do I owe the pleasure?"

The guy on Reznick's left looked around the restaurant before glaring at Reznick, inches from his face. "We'd like to talk to you, Jon. I'm sorry this is a bit sudden."

The guy's bad breath hit him hard.

"You need a mint, my friend. Listen, I don't need life insurance, thanks all the same. I can always tell from what a person is wearing whether they're trying to sell me something."

"Don't be a wise-ass, Jon."

Reznick took a bite of his sandwich. "You should try this, guys, it's phenomenal."

"You got a minute?"

"Depends? Who are you?"

"We represent a client. The client is the American government. My client wants to relay a message—they believe you're getting involved in something you know nothing about. And they are urging caution. We think you're snooping around as if you know what this is all about. But you need to know that you don't. With all due respect."

Reznick took another large bite of the club sandwich. "With all due respect, you should try this."

"No thanks. We're here to talk."

"So talk."

"We respect you, Jon. No question. But this is not the time to grow a conscience. It's important that you understand the gravity of the situation. You may think you have a handle on a story. But you're being misled. You're miles off base."

"Interesting."

"So my client is asking, respectfully, that you stay in your lane. Respect the authority of the government, and back off. And we can all get back to our day jobs."

Reznick finished his food before sipping his beer. "You guys are really missing out on these sandwiches. Epic."

The guy to his right cleared his throat. "I've read a summary of your file. Very impressive. I'm former military myself."

"You get thrown out?"

The guy flushed dark red. "Don't push us. It's time for you to realize the foolishness of wasting time on this. You don't know what you're dealing with."

"No idea what you're talking about."

The guy to his right leaned in as if to intimidate. "Don't let anyone pull the wool over your eyes. Stephen Leahy is an enemy of the United States. And he is weaving a fantastical tale for anyone to soak up. Don't head down that road, Jon. That's gonna be a dead end for you."

"Is there a point to this rather bizarre conversation."

"You need to leave town, and soon. Next flight home. That's the best advice my client can give you. Pack your bags, get back to Maine or whatever shithole you live in. Do we have a deal?"

"You know, it's funny you should say that, but I'm starting to like DC. Real nice place. People too—you excluded, obviously. That and the fucking politicians, right? Who doesn't hate them?"

The man shook his head. "We've been authorized by our client to share that if you have any concerns about intelligence matters, we are aware of what this is all about, and it's all in hand. We can reassure you that this country only takes decisive actions when we are threatened. You should know that better than anyone. You know what I mean?"

"No, I don't know what you mean."

The guy's eyes got more menacing. "You've been talking to people. Word gets around. But you need to know that the route you're going down is not a smart one. Not for a guy like you. It doesn't lead anywhere. And it might get you in serious trouble."

Reznick took a large gulp of beer and dabbed at the corners of his mouth with his napkin. "What a fascinating story. I wish I had more time to spend with you guys. Riveting company." He got slowly to his feet. "Now, if you'll excuse me, I need to use the bathroom. I'm assuming that's okay with you?"

The guy to his left got up from his seat to let Reznick past.

Reznick headed into the bathroom. He figured the heavies were security contractors working for the Agency. Maybe out-of-shape ex-military wannabes. Maybe ex-cops. He splashed water on his face, drying himself off. He looked in the mirror. The door opened and the two grinning heavies in suits blocked the door. "Well, this is nice. You guys like hanging out in bathrooms, huh? I'm not judging. Whatever floats your boat, right? I'm as open-minded as the next man."

That wiped the smiles off their faces.

The slightly bigger guy moved first.

Reznick stepped aside and kicked his legs out from under him, stomping on the guy's face, cracking his jaw. It happened in the blink of an eye.

The man groaned, blood pouring from his mouth.

The second guy pulled a hunting knife, moving it expertly from one hand to the other. "You going to try that shit with me?"

Reznick feigned a move, and the guy lunged forward. He stepped aside, grabbed the man's wrist, twisting it hard until the knife fell from his grip. He headbutted him, blood exploding from his nose. Then he grabbed him by the throat, squeezing tight on the carotid artery. The man temporarily blacked out.

Reznick bent down and grabbed the man's right wrist—the hand that had been holding the knife. He twisted the thick wrist and exerted more pressure, pushing it back as far as he could. Then he heard it crack.

The guy screamed, his wrist broken, hanging at a weird angle.

Reznick stood up and kicked the man in the head, knocking the guy out cold.

He stepped over both men, walked out of the bathroom, and headed back toward his booth. It had all happened in less than a minute.

Reznick approached the tall man, who was still seated and suddenly looked nervous. Jon dropped a fifty-dollar bill on the table beside the check. "You might want to call an ambulance. Your two pals seem to have had a nasty fall."

Nineteen

Edward Black was driving to a meeting in Chevy Chase when his cell phone rang. It was one of the three operatives he had sent to the diner. He sensed disappointment before he even answered.

"Boss, that didn't go as planned." It was Brad Falk, one of Black's most experienced and trusted employees.

Black's mood dropped like a stone. "What happened?"

"We sat down for a powwow with Reznick. He was just being a wise-ass. He's a piece of work."

"What are you saying?"

"Reznick didn't get the message. So, when he headed to the restroom, I sent Ron and Pedro to be a little more forceful, to make sure our message was received loud and clear."

"Excellent. So, what the hell happened?"

"What happened was Reznick fucked them up bad."

"Both of them? Are you kidding me?"

"Compound fracture of the wrist for Pedro, burst nose and mouth. Ron's got a broken jaw and fractured eye socket, blind in one eye."

Black spiraled into a rage. "Are you fucking for real? Are you shitting me? Why didn't you put a gun to his head? He'll get the message then, loud and clear. Why not just smash him over the head with a fire extinguisher? Knock the fucker out."

"We thought the two-on-one scenario in an enclosed space like a restroom would limit his options."

"Didn't you listen to what I told you fuckers? What don't you understand? Reznick is no ordinary GI Joe."

"With two on one and a knife, and him being unarmed, we thought he'd get the message."

"But he didn't. The guy is a serious piece of work. He's a machine."

"I'll remember that the next time."

"There won't be a next time, Brad. Take a hike. It was a simple exercise."

"Boss, come on. This guy is crazy to have dealt with Ron and Pedro so easily. Reznick walked out of the restroom cool as a cucumber, dropped a fifty-dollar bill on the table, and strolled out as if it was nothing."

"Hand in your cell phone and all your communication equipment to head office. We're done."

"Boss, gimme a second chance."

"Don't ever call me again, you piece of shit."

Black ended the call, fuming. Raging. Seething. "Dumb motherfucker!" he screamed as he drove. He headed past Washington National Cathedral and on through North Cleveland Park. They should have just blown Reznick's fingers off. He'd have bled out and then he'd get the message. But no, that seemed to be too easy for those jacked-up, steroid-chewing bodybuilders.

He headed into an underground parking garage underneath a nondescript office building. He got out, locked his car, and walked over to a set of security doors, with fingerprint entry into the building.

He took the elevator to the sixth floor.

Black stepped out and headed down a corridor until he arrived at a thick metal outer office door. He stood in front of the biometric face scanner. A few moments later, the door clicked open.

He headed inside, careful to shut the door behind him. His heart sank.

The client was already sitting in a chair, staring out of the window. Black felt sick.

Brigadier General Michael Johnson turned around and faced Black, eyes cold. "Take a seat, Eddie."

Black slumped in the black leather chair behind his desk. "I can explain."

"Your guy just texted me how it went."

Black closed his eyes, humiliated.

"The government doesn't pay such exorbitant fees to receive *explanations*. We pay to achieve *results*. The objective was clear: Jon Reznick needs to leave town, even if you have to fuck him up bad to make that clear. So, who the hell did you send to deal with him?"

"My guys are former military."

Johnson laughed. "You sure? From what I hear, your boys got a serious beating: broken bones, one eye blinded. Is it possible they underestimated Mr. Reznick?"

Black sat in silence, avoiding Johnson's piercing gaze.

"One job to do, and your guys couldn't even achieve that. Have they never heard of the element of surprise? Getting one's retaliation in first? You've got to play dirty. And you need to be able to kill if need be."

"Michael, they were complacent. They shouldn't have been. But I will rectify this."

"How?"

"I'm going to gather my team. And we're going to figure this out. This won't happen again, trust me."

"I want him out of the way. Whatever it takes. This has gone on too long."

"Permanently?"

"*Whatever it takes.* Do you understand what that means?"

"You want him dead?"

"Neutralize the fucker. He's ruffling feathers. We can't have that. He's crossed a line."

"Of course. Michael, I swear, we will fix this and make it right."

"So, here's what's going to happen. I want you to continue to keep running surveillance on him. I want to know who he meets. When and where. And, when the time is right, and only when the time is right, you will take him down."

"I hear you, Michael."

"What your guys need to know is that they will be on welfare if this happens again. Your contract will be torn to shreds."

Black felt sick to the pit of his stomach.

"I gave you leeway. I fought to get your contract renewed. And this is how you repay me?"

Black sat sullenly.

"The government has plans. Plans that are going to reshape Latin America for the next hundred years. The US empire is not going to go down without a fight. And that's why any impediments or threats to its classified missions will be crushed. If your firm can't handle that, I know several others who can."

Black nodded meekly.

"We watch him. We figure out who he's speaking to. And then, we move. But when we do, I want him gone for good. Reznick is a dead man walking."

Twenty

It was early evening when a text pinged Reznick's phone. He was still processing the altercation at the bar earlier that day. He had come out on top, but he knew that next time he might not be so lucky. The message was clear: *they* were on to him. And they wanted him out of the way.

It had been the second approach. The first was the New York lawyer. He had offered a soft touch in the form of a bribe. The second incident had added a bit more muscle. But Reznick had brushed it off. At least so far.

Reznick knew he couldn't get complacent. He picked up his phone and read the text. It was from Caroline Sullivan. *See you at my house at 8pm. Someone I'd like you to meet.*

He figured it was one of her ex-Pentagon contacts. He headed downstairs and caught a cab from the Sofitel over to her home in Georgetown.

Reznick pressed the button on the security video phone next to her front door.

"Hey Jon, come up."

The door buzzed and Reznick checked that it had closed fully before he walked into the townhouse. He hugged Caroline and they climbed the stairs to the top floor of the house and stepped out onto the rooftop terrace. Sitting on a sofa was a well-dressed gentleman, clean-shaven, mid-sixties.

The man stood up and shook Reznick's hand. "General Andrew Stone, retired. Pleasure to meet you, Jon."

"Likewise," Reznick replied.

Night fell slowly in the summer in DC. The rooftops of Georgetown were bathed in a burnt orange glow. Off in the distance, the silhouettes of the Washington Monument and the dark waters of the Potomac. Handshakes out of the way, both men turned to Caroline.

"So, Jon, I wanted you to meet Andrew. Please, let's all sit."

Reznick sat down on a wicker chair opposite Stone.

"We can talk through what we know, and where we go from here," Caroline began.

"Sounds like a plan," Reznick said.

Stone sat back down on the sofa as Caroline headed inside to the kitchen. "I've heard a lot about you."

"None of it good, I imagine."

Stone smiled. "You have a phenomenal résumé, Jon. Caroline has painted a fascinating picture of you. It's a privilege to meet you."

"Likewise."

Caroline returned from the kitchen with three Scotches on the rocks and handed out the glasses. "Cheers, gentlemen."

Reznick clinked his glass against the others'.

"Jon, would you like to start things off? After all, you know more about this than anyone."

"Sure thing . . . Down to business. I'm assuming Caroline has briefed you on what we know so far, Andrew?"

Stone took a small sip of the Scotch, putting his glass down carefully on the table. "It's very troubling. When Caroline spoke to me, I was very, very concerned. Not only that an alleged, highly classified special access program had been leaked, but that, in legal terms, the operation itself was deeply problematic."

Reznick was somewhat surprised that Stone was sitting before him. He imagined the former general was putting his neck on the line by meeting up and discussing hypothetical classified intel belonging to the United States government. His natural instinct was to be wary of those he didn't know, whereas, as a journalist, Caroline obviously felt free to discuss anything with the ex-Pentagon chief. He debated whether Stone could be trusted. But he would have to defer to Caroline's judgment on that.

"You mind me asking a quick question before we get into it?"

"No, of course not. Fire away."

"I'm assuming, Andrew, that if your former colleagues still at the Pentagon realized you were meeting up with us, that could jeopardize the position of trust granted to you—your continued high-level clearance and access to the inner sanctum of the Department of Defense. Would you agree?"

"It probably would."

Reznick sipped his Scotch. "And that doesn't concern you?"

"Not as much as knowing the details of what Caroline has described."

"I appreciate your candor."

"I'm here simply because what I've been told has concerned me enough to make me want to meet with you and Caroline. Maybe help in some way. But what is said between us is obviously in confidence. I'm assuming that's a given."

Reznick nodded. "Absolutely."

Stone cleared his throat, glass in hand, leaning forward. "What can I tell you? Over the last twenty-four hours, after speaking to Caroline, I've reached out to contacts within the wider intelligence community—long-standing friends from my military days, at the

Pentagon, CIA. They include retired colleagues as well as those currently serving."

"I'm guessing you want to try and verify what Jon was told?" Caroline took out her cell phone and placed it on the table in front of them. "You okay if I get this verbatim? I'll take contemporaneous notes as well."

Stone nodded. "Strictly for your ears only. Refer to me as a source close to the Pentagon. Absolutely no names. Your microphone on the cell phone working okay?"

"We're good."

"I'll give you some background, which might be useful for Jon, too. Since retiring, I've worked for the Pentagon, on behalf of companies across a broad spectrum that specialize in products and services essential to our advanced economy. I represent clients including oil companies, data analytics firms, mining companies, mineral exploration. I understand better than most people the rationale for wanting to secure resources for the United States for the next hundred years and beyond. Resources so we can function as a complex advanced society in the twenty-first century, moving into the twenty-second century, especially when there are competing interests from countries like China and Russia."

Reznick listened carefully. Stone glanced at the cell phone on the table, recording light on. He continued, "Jon has been told verbally about an alleged classified operation. But we need to know, first and foremost, if his information is correct and if there is a bigger picture. One hypothesis is that the CIA and the Department of Defense want to secure the resources of a mineral-rich country on our doorstep—Venezuela. Latin America is within our sphere of influence. And we absolutely don't want Communist China getting their foot in the door, accessing the vital oil, gas, and rare minerals."

"Aren't we getting off the beaten track with this analysis?"

Stone waved away Reznick's interruption. "I'm only outlining the rationale for the operation. I'll get to the crux of the matter soon. What's important to know, geopolitically speaking, is that China has opened up serious investment in South America. Beijing, for example, has lined up sixty billion dollars' worth of direct investment in Venezuela on economic development and industrial investment. Think about that."

Caroline nodded. "I have sources saying it might be nearer one hundred billion."

"There you go. Why would they be doing that? What are they getting out of modernizing the country? I'll tell you what: a multitude of factors. Number one: influence. Deepening bilateral relations between China and not only Venezuela, but across Central and South America, including the Caribbean. We believe this is a real and present danger to America's future national security."

Reznick said, "I believe Russia has paramilitary forces in Venezuela to help prop up the government."

Stone hummed in approval. "Russia is a major creditor of Venezuela. No question. So you can see the problems emerging. The American companies I represent have long-term concerns that China is building a bridgehead into Latin America, getting its tentacles into Venezuela, all of this aligned with Russia. But let's not lose sight of what this is all about: Venezuela has more than a thousand years of oil and gas reserves—the world's largest proven oil and gas supplies. So that's the big picture."

Reznick put down his drink. "I understand the rationale. But maybe not the means of going about it."

"Good minds can agree to differ on that," Stone said. "But the rationale for going in is only one part of the equation. Now to answer the question about verification of these special access program documents Leahy was talking about. I have some news."

Caroline seemed deep in thought as she listened to Stone.

"This morning," Stone said, "I was given highly privileged access to the classified documents as per my highest level of clearance and my position as retired Vice Chairman of the Joint Chiefs of Staff. I was taken to a secure viewing room and was briefly allowed to read the summary in full. No notes were allowed to be taken."

Caroline shifted in her seat, impatient. "And? You're killing me with the suspense!"

Stone sipped his Scotch, eyes slightly heavy. "What Stephen Leahy laid out to you, Jon, I can confirm, categorically—it is true. The plans are very stark. Very sobering."

"Andrew, what details of the operation can you share with us?" Caroline asked. "And also, where does this leave us?"

"Jon, like you, I have grave concerns about the plans. You already know the basics. I can confirm that they call for coordinated explosions starting in the oilfields of Guyana. A lot of it offshore, out of sight. The plan estimates that there might indeed be up to two hundred American contractors, engineers, oil experts wiped out in Guyana. But that would just be the start. There would be simultaneous shootings and stormings of gated communities used exclusively by American oil executives and their families. This would spread to killings of Americans living and working in Venezuela. I have a figure of twenty-five thousand Americans—teachers, doctors, engineers—living and working in and around Caracas with their families."

Reznick felt as if his insides had been ripped out. How could anyone justify using the killing of Americans as a pretext?

"It's very sobering. The American embassy in Guyana will be attacked by rocket fire from CIA-backed mercenaries from Colombia, some special forces, some former prisoners, but also a lot of cartel narco-traffickers and their gangs. They will leave fake

Venezuelan military IDs at the scene. A classic false flag. And that's what Stephen Leahy tried to warn you about."

Willliams scribbled down shorthand notes of everything Stone was saying. "You are one hundred percent sure about this, Andrew?"

"No question about it. I couldn't photocopy the plans, obviously, and my cell phone was confiscated during the visit. It's all in my head. But this is going to happen. You can bet your bottom dollar on that. And it's just the start. This is about giving us cover to go to war with Venezuela, topple its communist, virulently anti-American government, and install our own hand-picked regime of Venezuelan generals, all of whom have been trained in American military schools. The report estimates it will cost tens of thousands—maybe hundreds of thousands—of Venezuelan lives, not to mention thousands of American military casualties. But the rationale is that this is a small price that's worth paying."

Caroline wrote furiously, flipping over her legal pad. "Is this for real? This isn't just a draft plan, playing fucking war games?"

"Categorically not. These are actual war plans. False flag as a pretext for a full invasion and war against Venezuela. It's a regime change."

Reznick spun the empty glass of Scotch on the tabletop. "This is insanity. We're killing Americans? This is criminal."

"Before I came over here, I spoke to my attorney," said Stone. "He advised me in no uncertain terms against speaking to you both, even if it was off the record. He said it would leave me wide open under the Espionage Act."

"You're willing to face the full consequences?"

"Jon, the US Code says it all. And everyone who signed off on those plans would be prosecuted further down the line."

"Apart from the President?"

Stone nodded. "I believe that to be the case, yes."

"Andrew, can you reiterate what you just said, once again, for the record, so there is no ambiguity?" asked Caroline.

"The invasion plans are real. Operation Yellow Rain is a green light. This is not a drill. Not a war game. And it's been signed off on by the CIA, Pentagon planners, and, within the last couple of days, the President. The ramifications of the false flag being revealed would leave America as an international pariah. Make no mistake, this is an ultra-high-risk operation. It actually reminds me of Operation Northwoods in the early sixties. That one had to be scrapped."

Caroline nodded. "The time of the Cuban missile crisis?"

"Exactly. A proposed false flag was drawn up to kill American civilians and military targets in the Miami area, and sink American ships. It would have served as a pretext to invade Cuba. But it never got off the ground, despite the Joint Chiefs agreeing to the plans."

"Getting back to Operation Yellow Rain, you're satisfied the document you saw was genuine?" Jon asked.

"It's not a fake. I know it's genuine. I checked the markings carefully. But I also spoke to a serving member of the Joint Chiefs, a very close personal friend. I mentioned at lunch what I had learned."

"What did he say?" Caroline said.

"He just smiled. I told him I thought it was unconscionable. And he told me, *this is all about the big picture, Andrew.* Gas, oil, significant deposits of iron ore, gold, diamonds, a strategic mineral called coltan which is used in the manufacture of cell phones and computers, vanadium, and critical minerals used for advanced batteries. That's the big picture."

Caroline was shaking her head. "Andrew, this is about America getting its hands on the most valuable resources on the planet, right? One thousand years of gas, oil, minerals. We would have it all. But at what cost?"

Reznick turned to look at Caroline, her face impassive, steely blue eyes exuding a quiet determination.

Twenty-One

Brigadier General Michael Johnson was sitting in his windowless office, deep within the bowels of the Pentagon, using military-grade messaging to communicate with operatives and contractors on the ground in Guyana. The groundwork was being laid. He was also receiving twice-daily updates on the preparations. He was satisfied, as were his operatives on the ground, that the men and equipment were in place, just waiting for the green light from him.

The remote explosives had been carefully placed on oil platforms just over one hundred miles from the coast by expert teams three weeks earlier. The oil fields were located east of the Essequibo River. The two geographical areas Johnson had focused on were strictly within Guyana's Exclusive Economic Zone in the waters offshore—the Stabroek Block and the Orinduik Block. Hundreds of other mercenaries and dozens of CIA operatives had been smuggled into the Guyanese capital of Georgetown over the previous six weeks, stowed on cargo ships and light aircraft, awaiting final instructions.

He was satisfied the operational logistics were in place.

Johnson checked his watch and logged off. He left his office, careful to lock his door, and headed out onto the concourse to get a coffee from Starbucks. The Pentagon in many ways was like a small city. On a daily basis he passed by a post office, shopping mall, coffee shops, restaurants, cafés, and a police force.

He picked up his coffee, and returned to his office. He answered a few emails from Schultz about drawing up new budgets for Operation Yellow Rain before the phone on his desk rang. He picked up right away. "Brigadier General Johnson."

"Mike, it's Eddie. Eddie Black."

Johnson's stomach tightened, sensing more bad news. "What's the latest?"

"You're not going to like this."

"What've you got?"

"I'm going to send you a secure video file. It's drone footage shot earlier this evening in DC. And it's self-explanatory."

Johnson's computer pinged as the message arrived. He opened it up. The footage was shot from two mosquito-sized military drones, invisible to the naked eye, hundreds of yards away from the target.

"You got it?"

Johnson downloaded the file. "Affirmative."

"Watch it."

On his computer screen he had a drone's-eye view of the rooftops of Georgetown in DC, as the drone edged through the darkening night sky. The technical details in the right-hand corner showed that the tiny drone was hovering just over half a mile away from the target. Then the ultra-high-resolution 8K camera began to zoom in with pin-sharp accuracy, with a perfect line of sight to the target.

Three people sat on a penthouse roof terrace.

Johnson gawked, incredulous. He immediately recognized *New York Times* journalist and author Caroline Sullivan. He had read a flattering profile of her a couple of years back in *The Atlantic, part of an article* on security and intelligence threats to the US in the twenty-first century. The camera panned slowly across the terrace.

And there it was: the familiar, impassive face of Jon Reznick, nursing a Scotch, by the looks of it—no doubt a single malt. His name popped up on the display, identified by the drone's facial recognition software. But it was the third person Johnson was most shocked to see.

He recognized the short gray hair and tanned, handsome features immediately: retired Vice Chairman of the Joint Chiefs of Staff General Andrew Stone. A man beloved by those in his command. People were fiercely loyal to him. Johnson knew there was talk that Stone might one day enter politics, starting a glittering new career. But he could not understand what had compelled a decorated general like Stone to meet with Reznick and Sullivan. The dangers were obvious.

Stone was a retired military man of the highest caliber. Were Reznick and Sullivan passing on details of what they knew about the classified operation from Stephen Leahy? He didn't dare even think it.

Johnson toggled the night-vision footage, zooming in closer. The trio seemed immersed in their discussion. General Stone appeared the most animated, doing most of the talking. And Johnson knew that this was the most worrying and potentially dangerous development since Reznick had first appeared on the scene.

Johnson assumed it had to be Caroline Sullivan, with her extensive network of military, intelligence, and State Department contacts, who had reached out to Stone. He knew that Stone's interest would be piqued if Reznick was relaying what Stephen Leahy had told the ex-Delta Force black-ops specialist in the psychiatric hospital. But maybe he was reading it wrong. Maybe Stone was there to listen and relay to the Department of Defense via a backchannel what he had been told. The problem was that this was one more person who theoretically now knew about the so-called secret operation. Johnson began to kick around the idea of bringing the plans forward by a week. Or, as a last resort, scrapping them on security grounds.

Black said, "Michael, I'm sorry to bring this to you."

"You did the right thing. This is valuable."

"I know you're a busy man. But while the optics are not good, not good at all, I would suggest that this might be useful for future prosecutions."

"They could argue it's a social gathering."

Johnson felt as if he was living a nightmare. These plans had been meticulously drawn up, black-ops budgets agreed on, precise timescales laid out and structured. He imagined the meeting between the three could lead to even more people being informed of the operation. Politicians. Members of intelligence committees. He knew Andrew Stone was good friends with the chair of the Senate Select Committee on Intelligence. *Shit.*

"We have a problem. The problem seems to be gaining traction, at least to my eyes. And we need to fix it."

"Mike, I'm on this. I got this. Whatever it takes, this will end. Tell me if there's anything else I can do."

"I want you to trawl the emails, messages, notes in the cloud . . . anything Andrew Stone uses. Does he use Dropbox? I don't know if he's gone rogue. I don't know if he knows what he's getting himself into. Is he hoping to share this information with one of the companies he's associated with? He could profit personally off this, right? We need to know that. But also, maybe we need to keep track of his buying and selling of shares to see if there's any insider trading. We could get the fucker on that. Anything else I need to know?"

"General Stone met his lawyer, Fred Eagleham, earlier today."

"That's interesting," Johnson said.

"I'd imagine his lawyer was giving it to him straight as to the legal quagmire he might be getting himself involved in.

Disseminating or sharing classified Pentagon files with journalists—I mean, come on."

"Let's get into Stone's life. I want to know more about him. I thought he was a straightshooter. But I guess not. Who else is he communicating with? He's also a non-executive director of numerous military and technology companies. He's very well connected. I don't like this. He has powerful friends on Capitol Hill, bipartisan support. And I believe he may even golf with the President."

"This could be disastrous."

"So, let's do something about it. Let's fix this. Let's lock it down."

Twenty-Two

The morning after their meeting with Andrew Stone, Reznick sat in a Georgetown diner across from Caroline, enjoying a nice brunch. They discussed the need to get more than one-source verification, although they both agreed General Stone was highly credible. But they would need more.

Caroline wiped her mouth and set down her napkin. "I'm happy that he confirmed what you were told. Andrew Stone is not the sort of person to make shit up."

"The problem is, what now?" Reznick said. "I can't see what else I can do."

"I get it. But for me, this is only just beginning. I'll be reaching out to numerous other contacts in the coming days. Does anyone else know about this? More importantly, can anyone else verify it? I'm build up a bigger picture."

"Then what?"

"Fly to New York, speak to the *Times* investigations editor and executive editor, and see what they say. I'm hoping they'll think we have enough to go on."

"Do *you* think you have enough?"

"I have more than enough to start an investigation. Maybe I could start with the fact that Stephen Leahy is in a psychiatric hospital, being held under a false name. Then maybe build on it when we learn more about this apparent false flag military operation in Latin America. But we'll see. I'll need another source willing to go on the record. It needs to be watertight."

Reznick took a gulp of his hot black coffee. "As it stands, I don't see much point in me hanging around here. I've done everything I can. But hopefully you can use your clout to get the story out. No doubt in my mind the plans are real. But I think time is of the essence."

"I really appreciate you reaching out to me on this. And the time you've spent on it."

"Gives you your next big story. Hopefully you can do something with it."

"I'm kind of an old-school journalist in the sense that one of the basic tenets of investigative journalism, at least that I was taught, is to hold the powerful accountable. And how much more powerful can you get than the American government? I can assure you I won't stop. You have my word. I'll get to the bottom of this, no matter the consequences."

"I admire that. So, I can hand it over? I can stand down?"

"It's in safe hands. I won't let you or Stephen Leahy down."

Reznick had done his bit. He had taken this as far as he could. He was starting to think ahead, about putting his feet up at his home in Rockland—enjoy some peace and quiet for a while. But it was an all-too-brief, fleeting moment.

His cell phone started vibrating on the table. "Are you kidding me?" He picked it up. A text message from a number he didn't recognize.

Tonight get the 8:07 pm American flight from DCA to Miami International Airport arriving 10:55pm and await instructions. I have what you're looking for.

Reznick showed Caroline the cryptic message.

"Might be a trap," she ventured. "Especially after your encounter with the goons at the diner."

He thought that was a real possibility. But he also wondered if maybe the person was someone close to Stephen Leahy, finally reaching out to him.

Caroline looked skeptical. "You're not actually thinking about going down there, are you? That would be a risky move. Besides, didn't you just tell me you were finished with this."

"I don't know. I'm not sure I can ignore this."

"Jon, you can't be serious. You don't even know who this is. I would not follow that up. Besides, I believe I can develop this story and get it out to the public, hopefully sooner rather than later. Let me handle it."

Reznick tapped his finger against his mug. He had imagined arriving back in Maine, heading to the Rock Harbor pub for a few drinks. Shooting the breeze with a few local friends. Maybe heading over to the Myrtle Street Tavern to play pool with some old-timers, have a few drinks over there.

"I think you've done your bit," Caroline said.

"Maybe I have."

"Think of the risks. Enough is enough!"

"What if it's Catherine Leahy reaching out to me? I did pass on my details, and she is in Florida. What if she changed her mind and this is her way of communicating with me?"

"What if these are the people who were involved in the death of Michael Leahy? Or Lawrence Morgan? You don't know what you're getting yourself involved in. It could be a setup."

Reznick nodded, conceding that possibility.

"If I were trying to lure you into a trap, I'd make you believe it was coming from Catherine Leahy. Maybe that's their thinking."

Reznick shrugged. "I get it. I just think it might—and I stress *might*—be worth the risk. I've come this far. What harm could it do?"

"What harm could it do? You could be walking right into a trap." Caroline put her head in her hands. "Jon, please, you don't have to do this. I'll find an independent second source who can verify the plans."

"What if you don't?"

"Jon, I will find a second source. And a third if I have to."

Reznick was quiet for a few moments as he considered what might lie ahead. He had a hard choice to make.

"Jon, please, I don't want to lose you."

Reznick averted his gaze.

"You're going to go, aren't you? Despite the risks?"

"Life is full of risks."

"You don't have to jump headfirst into one."

"I feel like I have to."

"Why? I told you, I've got this."

"I don't want to walk away just yet. I need to do this. This person has my number and might be connected to Stephen Leahy. They might have the proof we need to blow this wide open. It might give us a breakthrough."

"What if it doesn't?"

"Nothing ventured, nothing gained."

When Reznick arrived back in his room at the Sofitel, he called Trevelle.

"Hey Jon, you still mooching around DC?"

Reznick explained the text that had come in asking him to head down to Miami. "I need to know who it was from. I'm looking for a name and anything else you can find."

Trevelle trawled the databases at his disposal. "And we're in! I believe I have what you're looking for."

"Who is the owner of the phone?"

"Don't think it's the owner. It was sent from an old-style Nokia cell phone bought by a woman called Jewel Johnson of Pompano Beach, Florida."

"And who is she?"

There was a pause. "She works for Baptist Health hospitals across South Florida. She's a nurse."

"So, she's a legitimate person?"

"I'm checking her social security records . . . and she's a tax-paying person, excellent credit score."

"Question is, how did she get my number? Is this someone pretending to be her, registering the phone in her name? What does she know about this?"

"Theoretically, the number might have been spoofed. You know what I mean? Saying the call is coming from Florida, but it could be anywhere."

Reznick considered this possibility. He knew taking that flight was a risky proposition, especially knowing the dubious circumstances under which both Michael Leahy and Lawrence Morgan had lost their lives.

"You could be walking into a trap," said Trevelle, knowing what he was thinking.

"I know that. Caroline said exactly the same thing."

"She's right, Jon. I think it might be time to seriously reconsider your actions. I don't think this is going anywhere. Besides, now Caroline has her teeth into the investigative side of things, she'll get the story out there when she can."

"I think it's worth the risk. A calculated risk."

"Why won't you let this go?"

"I don't know."

"What if this is what they want you to do? You might be walking into real trouble. Have you considered that?"

"I have."

"And?"

"Well, I guess we'll find out soon enough how it plays out."

The lights of Miami twinkled in the darkness below.

Reznick's plane touched down on time. A few minutes later, he was headed through the cramped, crowded hallways with passengers milling around the terminal. His cell phone pinged. It was a message from Trevelle: *Go to Communitel Baggage Storage, second floor of Central Terminal, Concourse E. Backpack waiting.*

Reznick headed there, showed his ID, and picked up the backpack. He knew inside there would be a 9mm Beretta with ammo. At least now he had some firepower at his disposal. He slung the bag over his shoulder and headed for the exit.

A few moments later, Reznick's cell phone buzzed again. It was from a new number he didn't recognize. The message read: *Get the Metrorail to Earlington Heights.*

Reznick didn't know for sure if it was from the same person who had told him to come to Miami. And he could so easily be getting played by agents of the state. But for some reason—maybe the thought of Stephen Leahy being kept in that psychiatric hospital, or because he was haunted by the insane covert operation plans for Guyana and Venezuela, or maybe because of the possibility that Michael Leahy's widow might finally be reaching out to get in touch—he felt driven to find out more.

It was a crazy risk. But life was a risk. For Reznick, this was at least a calculated one.

Reznick knew the area of Earlington Heights, which wasn't far from the international airport. It was near Liberty City, a rundown enclave in downtown Miami. Trevelle used to have a compound based in that part of town. He remembered the first time he had driven through the sketchy area in the dead of night to meet up with the ex-NSA cybersecurity expert. It had been worth the hassle, and he had managed to hook up with one of the finest computer security experts in the world. Trevelle had been invaluable to his clandestine operations ever since.

In the metro, he headed to Level 3 and boarded a northbound Orange Line train to Earlington Heights. He sat at the back of the carriage, with a line of sight to every passenger. Backpack in his lap, cell phone in hand.

Reznick was jolted on his seat as the train pulled away. His gaze wandered surreptitiously around the carriage. A Black guy was whispering into his cell phone, glancing around occasionally. Two Hispanic kids nearby were watching a music video on their phone. His senses were switched to the max.

A couple of old Hispanic women sat up front, side by side, laughing. A white guy with a backpack slung over his shoulder was standing chewing gum, surly, dead-eyed, staring down the carriage, gaze locked onto Reznick.

Reznick stared back, and the guy quickly looked away. He wondered if he was on drugs, maybe paranoid—possibly the guy thought Reznick was a plainclothes cop. But then again, maybe he was watching Reznick, following him to the next stop.

A couple of minutes later, the train pulled up. The station overlooked the busy airport expressway, a trail of headlights as far as the eye could see.

Reznick stayed seated. A text pinged on his phone.

Walk to the Metrorail Parking Garage nearby and go to Level 4 and wait.

Reznick got up and slung his backpack over his shoulder, Beretta tucked into his waistband. He saw what was happening. The sender, whoever they may be, was moving him around, maybe checking that he wasn't being followed. He stepped off the train and waited.

He walked toward a sign for the parking garage and bounded up the concrete stairs to Level 4. He stood and waited. He sensed he was being watched.

His mind flashed back to the concerns of both Caroline and Trevelle. He knew that under the circumstances, and especially after the violent encounter in the bathroom of the diner—coupled with the meeting with Andrew Stone—this could be viewed as ultra-high-risk. It might even be foolish. But despite wanting to walk away, here he was, unable and unwilling to do so.

He was being inexorably drawn deeper into the story.

A guy walked by, cell phone in hand, before getting into a Mercedes. The sound of the engine revving up echoed off the concrete walls. The lights of the vehicle bathed the parking garage in pale white light as the guy pulled away.

He glanced out of the window as he passed Reznick, as if he suspected the dude hanging around in a Miami parking garage late at night was up to no good.

Reznick watched the Mercedes head down the ramp and out of sight. He waited and waited. Still no sign of anything.

He looked around again to see if he could see any sign that he was being watched at that moment. Maybe by an observer from afar. Maybe someone crouched down in the garage.

Reznick remained at the location. He stood and waited. He knew he was a target. The minutes dragged on. He checked his watch. He had been waiting for nine long minutes.

He glanced at his cell phone. No message.

In the distance, the sound of screeching tires.

Reznick observed a navy Suburban approaching fast, before it skidded to a halt in front of him. The passenger door flung open.

The driver, a Black guy he didn't recognize, leaned over and shouted, "Get in, Jon!"

Twenty-Three

The car sped away, heading fast down the winding exit ramp and out onto the dark Miami streets. The guy floored it and raced through the city's Design District, past upscale art galleries and stores.

"Who are you?" Reznick asked. "And why the attention-grabbing speed?"

The driver glanced in his mirror anxiously. "Shit."

"What is it?"

"I think we're being followed."

They turned down NW 40th Street, past Ralph Lauren and then Dior.

"I need to lose this fucker."

Reznick glanced in the side-view mirror. A BMW was closing in as they turned onto North Miami Avenue, past a huge graffitied mural on the corner. The driver accelerated and doubled back, trying to lose the tail. They headed down NW 41st Street as they rushed through Little Haiti.

"Who are you?"

"Someone who wants to help."

Reznick glanced again in the side-view mirror. He saw a sign for Biscayne Boulevard. "Get on there!"

The driver sped along the boulevard, whizzing along, the head-lights of other cars flashing by. He accelerated through a red light.

"Who are you?" Reznick asked again. "How do you know me?"

The driver was preoccupied with his tail.

"I asked you a question."

"I was sent to help you. I'm Michael Leahy's son-in-law. I'm married to his daughter. Her brother is Stephen Leahy."

Reznick glanced over at the speedometer. "Take it easy, man, you're going to get us killed."

"You know what this is about?"

"I've got a pretty good idea. Stephen told me about it in the hospital."

The guy reached into his jacket pocket and handed Reznick a 1 TB micro-SD card. "It's all on that. I'm risking my life for this shit."

"Why?"

"It was either I do it, or my wife, Kathleen, said she would. I said absolutely not. And here I am." The guy shook his head. "What was I thinking? I must've lost my fucking mind."

Reznick examined the wafer-thin memory card. "What's on this?"

"Plans. Stephen gave that to his father."

Reznick placed the SD card in his jacket pocket, zipping it up.

"It's all on that. That's what I've been told."

"Who else has seen the contents of this?"

The driver doubled back and headed down a dark side street. "I can't see the car following us. But I think we've got a problem."

"Keep driving. Let me ask you something: how long have those guys been on your tail?"

"I think I caught sight of them just before I hit the highway in North Miami Beach."

"That would indicate they were following from the start. Tracking you."

"How?"

"I don't know. Maybe a GPS device in this vehicle. Is it yours?"

"Yes."

Reznick's mind was racing. He pointed to a sign for Edgewater. "Go there."

The driver was breathing hard. He accelerated. They were going faster and faster. Speeding past the skyscrapers and lights as they approached downtown Miami.

Reznick checked the side-mirror again and saw that the car chasing them was still close behind. "You see them?"

"Shit."

"Don't worry about them. Keep your eyes on the road."

"What do you mean don't worry about them? Who the hell are they? Why are they following us?"

"Why do you think?"

"How did they know where I was?"

"Like I said. Maybe they're tracking your car, cell phone, I don't know."

"Shit. Shit. Shit. I can't believe I'm doing this. What a fucking idiot."

Reznick's voice was calm, trying to reassure him, keep him focused on not crashing. "Just drive, you'll be fine."

"How do you know I'll be fine?"

Reznick needed to engage with the guy to distract his attention from the car following them. "What's your name?"

"Bob."

"Bob what?"

"Bob White."

"Okay, Bob White, and you're Michael's son-in-law?"

"Was. He's dead."

"Who gave you the memory stick?"

"Catherine Leahy, my mother-in-law, Michael's widow, spoke to me. She said she was visited by you. And she decided she wanted you to have this. She instructed me to give it to you. She's scared. But she didn't want her husband's death to be in vain."

Reznick nodded.

"She doesn't believe her husband drowned at sea. He was a careful sailor. A careful person. Always wore a lifejacket. I can vouch for that. Michael Leahy was a good man. And she told me to let you know that her son, Stephen Leahy, is not crazy."

"I know he's not. Mrs. Leahy is very brave. So are you."

"I don't feel very brave. So you've met Steve?"

"I met him in the psych hospital in Maryland. I know he's not crazy. Far from it."

Bob glanced in his mirror. "They're still there."

"We'll figure this out."

"They want Steve out of the way, don't they? That's what Catherine said."

"I believe they do. He knows too much."

Bob glanced in the rearview as he hung a right. "No sign of the BMW. Must've lost them."

Reznick pointed straight ahead. "Drive on." He wanted to learn more about Stephen Leahy. But he was also keen to distract Bob White from worrying about the tail. "Tell me how well you know Stephen."

"I've known him for ten years. Man, he's a super-smart guy. Loves to travel. Reads everything. I mean, he's Mensa-level, man. Fascinated by the Romans and empires, their rise and fall. History."

"You don't think he had a breakdown? Maybe he had previous mental health issues you didn't know about?"

"No chance. Stevie had a full medical six months ago. He was proud of it. He aced it, he said. Only his lung capacity and smoking got flagged. I'm sure you saw, he's a super-heavy smoker. He's tried everything to quit: nicotine gum, patches, vaping. But apart from that, his mind and general fitness are excellent. His mind is so sharp. He can talk about anything: politics, history, religion, philosophy, the money markets. Taylor Swift."

"Taylor Swift? Stephen Leahy of the CIA likes Taylor Swift?"

"Thinks she's great. He's a big fan, he's gone to a few of her gigs in Europe. But he's interested in everything. Loves the news. Fascinated by the world."

Reznick took out his Beretta and pulled back the slide.

"Woah . . . what the fuck, man."

"Just as a precaution. You got a problem with guns?"

"Complete opposite. I have guns. I know guns."

"Assume the guy tailing you also has guns."

"Just as well I came prepared."

Reznick tried to figure out what Bob was talking about. "I'm sorry?"

Bob pointed to the passenger door and Reznick shone his cell phone light on it, illuminating a steel-reinforced compartment with a tiny numerical keypad. "What've you got in there?"

"Check it out. Eight-digit code: 56149926."

Reznick reached down and tapped in the number. The compartment clicked open.

"Just for emergencies. It's Florida, right?"

Reznick reached inside and carefully pulled out a foldable AR-15 rifle. "This could do some damage."

"Damn right."

"Who do you work for, Bob? Military? Police?"

"I'm a tax attorney and analyst."

"What?" Reznick checked the weapon. "You've got nice taste in guns for a tax attorney."

"Rifle club member. A buddy of mine at the club suggested it. He's an army vet. I just have it in here for absolute emergencies. Carjackings, crazies." He glanced in the rearview mirror. "Shit, the BMW's back. I thought I lost them. Shit."

Reznick snapped the barrel into place and disengaged the safety, muzzle pointed down.

Bob was frantic. "What do I do?"

Reznick was about to respond when the rear window exploded and shattered in a hail of gunfire. "Floor it!"

Bob hit the gas as he gunned down Biscayne Boulevard, racing through red lights. "What now?"

Reznick glanced in the side-mirror. He saw two guys in the back seat, windows down. They were doing the shooting. "Get on the bridge!"

Bob accelerated fast toward the MacArthur Causeway Bridge, which would lead them to South Beach. Lights flashed by, warm winds buffeting the inside from the blown-out rear window.

"I'm scared, man. I'm really scared. I fire shots, I don't engage in firefights."

"First time for everything, Bob." Reznick clambered into the back seat, gripping the rifle, as Bob weaved in and out of lanes.

"What the fuck are you doing, Jon?" Bob shouted.

"Drive! Don't stop! Faster!"

Reznick peeked his head over the rear seat. The car tailing them had switched lanes and dropped back around fifty yards. He waited for a few moments until it started to catch up. Closer and closer. Foot by foot. Inch by inch.

He positioned himself. He poked the rifle over the back seat and peered through the sights. The occupants of the chasing vehicle were in his crosshairs. "Motherfuckers!" He squeezed off two shots in quick succession, spiderwebbing the BMW's windshield. The driver looked terrified, trying to crouch down while driving.

The tailing car veered off violently to the right, then the left, as the frightened driver struggled to control the vehicle.

Reznick watched as the car swung wildly. He took careful aim a second time. He had the driver's head in the rifle's crosshairs. He waited. And waited. Slowly, he squeezed the trigger. A single shot. It tore off one side of his face, blood spattering, spraying the inside of what remained of the windshield.

The chasing car had a dead driver at the wheel, with one of the men in the back seat desperately trying to climb into the front to steer the car. But it was too late.

Reznick raked the chasing car with a hail of gunfire. The BMW veered wildly to the right, smashing through the concrete barrier, toppling over a metal rail, and plunging off the bridge, disappearing into the dark waters of Biscayne Bay.

Bob screamed. "What the fuck, man!"

Reznick flicked the switch on the left side of the rifle, activating the safety. He climbed back into the passenger seat. "You okay?"

Bob was breathing hard and fast. "Am I okay? No, I'm not okay. What the fuck? Are they dead?"

"Almost certainly."

"Sweet Jesus! This is fucked up. Oh shit! I didn't want this."

"It's fine."

"Don't keep saying that! It's not fine. This is crazy. I'm scared. The cops will be on us. We're fucked."

Reznick placed the AR-15 carefully back in the rifle compartment, locking it again.

Bob sped across the bridge, shaking, trembling. "I deal with tax returns, deductions. I deal with the fucking IRS. I deal with invoices. I deal with refunds. This is not what I do. This isn't me! I don't kill people."

Reznick could see Bob was in total shock. "Focus. Keep driving."

The car headed over the bridge. A few moments later they were in South Beach. Reznick knew the area well, having visited the Art Deco district with its pastel-colored hotels, bars, clubs, and restaurants on numerous occasions for vacations or trips to meet ex-Delta buddies. He pointed off to his left. "Head down Alton until 14th Street."

Bob was breathing faster and faster as he began to hyperventilate. "I don't know this area. I don't want to be here."

"You're doing great. Relax, you'll be fine. Slow your breathing. That's all."

"I don't know what I'm doing. What was I thinking?"

Reznick patted him on the shoulder. "You're doing fine. Trust me."

Bob drove on and turned down a dimly lit 14th Street. "I am fucked. If the cops don't arrest me, my wife will kill me."

"Why?"

"For getting the rear windshield shot out. This is way out of my comfort zone."

Reznick had to stifle a laugh. "That wasn't your fault. That was theirs. I'm proud of you."

"You killed them."

"That's on me. Not you."

"I'm freaking out."

"I can see that."

"I mean what the fuck just happened? Did you have to do that?"

"Drop me at the edge of Flamingo Park, up the street."

Bob drove on for another half-mile, skirting the park.

Reznick said, "This'll do."

Bob pulled up sharply. "Go!"

Reznick patted him on the back. "I owe you one, Bob. Tell Catherine thanks."

"Man, you're fucking crazy."

Reznick got out of the car and slammed the door shut. He watched Bob accelerate away, rear windshield blown to shit, tires screeching, speeding off down Michigan Avenue. He turned and headed into the semidarkness of Flamingo Park. A few moments later, he spotted a group of stoned kids smoking weed on a bench.

"You got any money, man?"

"Not tonight, son," he lied.

Reznick strode past them and out of the park. He walked along Meridian and then headed east back down 14th Street. He walked on until he got to the corner of Washington and 14th. Across the street sat a late-night store that sold electronics.

He stepped inside, looking around. He knew what he wanted.

The bearded guy behind the counter grinned. "Shutting up soon, bro, so you better be quick."

Reznick scanned the shelves of products. He bought a high-capacity SD card reader and a cable. He paid for the purchases in cash, leaving a fifty-dollar bill.

"Man, that's too much."

"Keep it."

Reznick ripped off the packaging and handed it back to the guy behind the counter. He connected his iPhone to the reader with the cable and inserted the memory card.

"Someone's in a hurry," the guy said.

The light was flashing as it read the data on the card, and then quickly began to download it.

"Everything working okay?"

"Perfect."

He put his phone—along with the reader with the card inside and the cable attached—into his jacket pocket, zipping it up tight. Then he walked in the direction of Ocean Drive, toward a neon-lit bar he knew well—Mac's Club Deuce, a favorite of his when he visited the beach.

He walked in, ordered a beer, handed the bartender a twenty-dollar bill, and sat down beside the pool table.

Reznick gulped down some beer to sate his thirst before he took the device and phone out of his pocket. The green light was still flashing away, downloading the contents. He called Trevelle, SD reader still attached to his phone.

"Quite a night you're having, Jon."

"Tell me about it. Trevelle, I'm downloading what I believe might be encrypted data from a reader onto my phone. I don't know for sure yet. But are you able to access this remotely via my cell?"

"Might take a few minutes. Bear with me . . ." Reznick waited as Trevelle worked. "Okay, I'm in."

"Are you getting this?"

"Hang on . . . it's not decrypting, but something's coming through . . ."

"That's something."

"Oh yeah . . . It's coming through fast now," Trevelle said. "I'm getting it."

"Do you have it on your screen?"

"Motherfucker! Jon . . . It's only just over one gigabyte of data. But this is it. Wait . . . I need to upload the decryption software. So we are . . . Yeah, that's it, you beauty!"

"What does it say? What are the markings?"

"Department of fucking Defense. Special operations. This is the real deal. Right from the top."

"The markings are authentic?"

"Running a recognition on the markings . . . one minute."

Reznick waited impatiently. "Come on, hurry up!"

"You got it, Jon. You did it. This is it."

"You sure?"

"Affirmative. Holy shit. It's all here. Guyana. Oil platforms. Casualties. It's marked *Copy for Stephen Leahy, CIA*."

"Lock it down. Now!"

Twenty-Four

It was midnight.

Edward Black hadn't gone home. He paced, wired, crazed, balling his fists, wearing down the carpet in his office in Arlington. He wanted to shoot someone. Anyone. He was enraged. He began to shout expletives at the huge TV screen on the wall. The live news report was further enraging him.

He felt his breathing pick up. "Fucking hell! What is this? You stupid fuckers!" Real-time footage from a Miami-Dade police chopper, lights scanning the dark waters below, the chyron giving him reason enough to kick over the trash can beside his desk. He vowed revenge.

Black knew this was the work of Reznick. But even knowing Reznick's skillset, he was shocked to the core.

His team had assured him that attacking the vehicle from the rear, blowing out the window and unleashing their firepower against the car would bring the required result. The end of Reznick. But it wasn't the end by a long shot. It was a clusterfuck of huge consequence for not only himself and the three dead operatives, but for his entire organization. It was all on the line, hanging by a thread.

Black could read the runes. He saw it for what it was. Reznick had sent his own message. *Don't fuck with me. I don't care who the fuck you are. I am calling the shots.* He assumed that Reznick had been passed secure documents via the driver, Bob White. What else could it be?

What a shitshow. And there was no end in sight.

It would be all out in the open soon, exposed to the public gaze. The level of publicity would inevitably lead back to his firm's door. He wouldn't be able to escape it. He was responsible. It would bring scrutiny like he had never experienced before. Maybe by the FBI. *Fuck.*

Black crossed his arms and watched the footage on the TV. A semi-submerged car, a vehicle used by his firm, was partially visible as police patrol boats circled. The helicopter lights illuminated the surreal scene.

His firm still had to tell the widows of the three men that their loved ones had been killed down in Miami. Maybe those loved ones were watching the same damned news channel. It was more than he could stomach.

He turned up the volume. So far, Fox News was the only network covering the developing story.

A young news reporter at the scene, microphone in hand, looked into the camera. "Gunfire erupted on the MacArthur Causeway Bridge leading to Miami Beach around midnight, local time," she said. "That's how we believe this began. Police sources say a chase seems to have developed. But sources have ruled out a terror attack. The FBI and Miami police have confirmed they believe this was gang-related."

Black saw the coverup was already underway. It was one small crumb of comfort. He picked up his phone and called a member of his support team down in South Florida.

"Chico, what the fuck is going on?"

"Boss, this is another-level crazy. I was watching it remotely from a drone following the vehicle. We thought we had him in our sights. Our guys hit the car Reznick was in."

"Then what?"

"All hell broke loose. The driver of the vehicle that picked up Reznick—guy called Robert White, he's the brother-in-law of Stephen Leahy—gunned it across the bridge to South Beach, with our guys in pursuit. But then the tables turned. Our car got raked by semiautomatic rifle fire. The drone footage showed Reznick shot twice to break the windscreen and the third shot killed Marty, the driver. More shots into the vehicle and it crashed through the barriers. Our other two guys drowned, that's all I know."

"Your brother Sam?"

"Yeah, my brother Sam."

"I'm so sorry."

"Me too. He was one of the two in the back. Now he's dead. What am I going to tell his wife? His kids? Huh?"

"I'll deal with that."

"No, I'll talk to them first."

"So after the gunfire, the car was obviously out of control."

"Yeah. The car went over the fucking edge, man."

Black closed his eyes for a moment, feeling sick to his bones. He had known Sam for the past three years—a tough former street cop and surveillance expert from Chicago. He felt overwhelmed with anger. He wanted to shoot Reznick through the head himself. "Shit, Chico, I'm sorry. I'm so sorry."

"Boss, I want to take this fucker down. I want to do this."

"You'll get your chance. I'm sorry about Sam. He was a good guy."

Chico sobbed down the line. "He was my brother."

"I know. How could this happen?"

Chico sniffed. "Boss, our intel showed that Reznick would only have a handgun, if that. But whoever was driving the car must have had a high-powered rifle onboard."

"And Reznick was the shooter?"

"Drone shows, quite clearly, the driver still in position. It's the passenger who maneuvers to the rear seat, takes out a long rifle, and fires like crazy. Pinpoint accuracy. Devastating. We've run the footage a few times. It's Reznick. The motherfucker. He's the one."

Black felt as if he had gone over the edge with his men. But his despair couldn't cloud his judgment. He needed to think. To focus. His men would sense vulnerabilities in not only him, their leader, but the company. They might not want to work for such a firm. And who could blame them? This could be the beginning of the end.

"I want the chance to avenge my brother."

"You'll get that, Chico."

Chico sobbed again. "I'm serious, boss. He always looked after me on the streets when we were kids. He was the one who looked out for me."

"Listen to me very carefully. I'm going to figure this out. I'm going to figure out how we can get Reznick for good. He needs to be neutralized permanently. I've had enough."

"I want to be part of that team."

"I think it might be best if you maybe take a few months off, Chico. You're not in any fit state."

"No boss, that's my brother. We served in the force at the same time. We were inseparable."

"Tell me more about this fucking Robert White character. Who the hell is he? The whole story."

"The driver of the vehicle? White is the son-in-law of Michael Leahy. Upper-middle-class background. Smart guy. Tax attorney and analyst." The sound of tapping on a keyboard. "I'm pulling up some background. Shit."

"What?"

"He might have a well-paid white-collar job, but this explains everything. He's also a member of a gun club in Deerfield Beach. Rifle City it's called."

"Motherfucker. Shit. Shit. Shit! I'm wondering if . . ."

"Robert White had the long gun? He handed over the plans? Is that possible?"

"Shit, shit, shit. Yes. Listen, I'm so sorry, man. You need to take some time off to grieve."

"Negative. I want to avenge my brother. I need to be part of anything that takes down Reznick. I'm not walking away from this."

Black got the message that Chico wasn't in the mood to be denied. He figured it might be better to get him busy immediately, working out how they could neutralize Reznick with a one hundred percent chance of success. Maybe Chico could channel his rage and use it to take down Reznick. Maybe that would be better for everyone. "Okay, fine. I'll get back to you. Stay safe. And once again, I'm so sorry. I'll be thinking of your family."

"I'll send you the drone footage," said Chico. "It's not an easy watch."

Black ended the call. He looked up at the TV footage. The helicopter lights were still trained on the car, which was floating on its side, semi-submerged in the water.

A pinging sound. A text message.

Black slumped back down in his desk chair, staring at the iMac, before he clicked to open the secure message: a three-minute, twenty-two-second video clip.

He watched in rapt horror and fascination at the footage of the high-speed pursuit through the streets of downtown Miami. He felt sick as the cars sped across the causeway that straddled the city and the beach. The footage was trained on Robert White's Suburban. Gunshots from the tailing car exploding the rear windshield of the vehicle. The drone zoomed in.

Reznick was ducked, spreadeagled across the rear seat, only the rifle peeking over. Black freeze-framed the image—grainy, but unmistakably Reznick. The Delta black-ops specialist. The man who was turning his firm inside out. A law unto himself.

Black took a screenshot and sent it in a secure message to Brigadier General Michael Johnson. A few moments later, his phone rang.

"Is this for real?"

"I just watched the drone footage from Miami. This has been verified as Jon Reznick. The guy is fucking with us. The footage clearly shows him in the vehicle. And he's hooked up with Michael Leahy's son-in-law. A tax-lawyer-slash-analyst, down in Miami. Michael, I've never seen anything like this. We couldn't have known it would turn out like this. It's catastrophic."

"You're telling me. This is going from bad to worse. I just saw the Miami police chopper footage. Those are your guys inside the car?"

"All three. The driver shot through the head."

"Through the head? How?"

"Reznick. Guy is a crack shot."

"Jesus."

"He then raked the vehicle with semiautomatic fire before it went over the edge."

"Holy Christ."

"And I just learned that Robert White is a member of a gun club. He must have come prepared. I don't know if he brought the rifle with him as protection. But clearly Reznick took control of the situation, and used it to obliterate my men."

"So where does this leave us? We're at a crossroads. What do we do? Which direction should we go in?"

"I'll fix this."

"You said that before. Reznick is running circles around us. Why can't he be stopped?"

Black paced the room, glancing out into the darkness of the Arlington night. "Three of my men are dead. Two more hospitalized after getting the living shit beaten out of them in a diner. And this is all caused by one guy. How is he able to do this? This is no ordinary soldier."

"I know that. You should have known that. But that's not my concern. My main concern, from where I'm sitting, is the leak from Stephen Leahy. That leak has not been plugged. We've tried to paper over the cracks, but nothing is working. This situation is threatening to get out of control. Forensic analysis by the CIA of Stephen Leahy's personal iPhone shows, get this, he not only communicated with his father, but he hoped to show him an extract of the special access program on a memory card."

"We know that for sure?"

"The CIA know what they're talking about. I can only assume that Stephen's brother-in-law reached out to Reznick in some way. I'm worried; we should all be worried. Do you understand the gravity of the situation? Do you really understand the fucking gravity of what I'm dealing with? It's escalating to a fucking crisis point. We're making the news in fucking Miami."

"Michael, you need to trust me, we can nail this fucker. We just have to be patient."

"I'm not a patient man, Edward. We need this runaway crazy to be stopped. Problem is, we're running out of time. The plans are already underway. We can't have any threat to the timetable now. It's set in stone. The question is, does Reznick have a copy of the plans or some version of it? I believe he might. We have no option but to neutralize him on sight, regardless of collateral damage."

Black sighed.

"Do you understand what I'm saying?"

"Absolutely."

"The government needs to be able to operate without the threat that our enemies will be alerted to our plans—plans that cannot be jeopardized. But I'm watching live TV showing a vehicle with your guys in it being fished out of the water down in Miami. What do you want me to say? This is a fuckup. Am I wrong?"

"I don't disagree, Mike. We tried the soft approach with the lawyer, which failed. We tried to up the ante, but he smashed up two of my guys in DC. And now we've taken the very direct approach in Miami. All have ended in failure. We clearly need to draw up a more complex final plan for Reznick. Something a bit more sophisticated. Cunning. We need to get him in the kill zone with no way out."

"This sounds more like the kind of plan I understand. Draw something up and get back to me. Remember, we have Andrew Stone and Caroline Sullivan hanging out with Reznick now too. Ideally, we take them all out. I don't need this shit!"

"Leave it to me."

"Figure it out. And fast. Reznick *must* be neutralized."

Twenty-Five

Reznick needed to be on the move. He pulled back the curtains of his hotel room and looked at the street below, chewing on some Dexedrine. He had checked himself into the small two-star hotel on Washington Avenue five hours earlier, using a false name and credit card to get a room and get off the streets. But wired on amphetamines, thinking of the crazy chain of events that had taken place after he had touched down in Miami, he hadn't slept a wink all night.

He had thought it might get crazy down here, but what had happened was ridiculous. All that said, he had, miraculously, retrieved the memory card containing the plans. It was a major step forward and should help Caroline Sullivan in her investigation. But it had come at a cost. The last thing he had wanted was to draw attention to himself and leave a trail of dead bodies floating in Biscayne Bay.

Reznick pushed those thoughts to one side. He believed he had found the final missing jigsaw piece. His mind had raced all night, running over the events in his head. Earlier he'd watched local news footage of the car being hauled out of the water, cops swarming the bridge, stopping sightseers. It was showing on a loop, or at least that's how it seemed.

His cell phone rang, snapping him out of his reverie.

"Jon, it's Trevelle."

"Hey man."

"Making quite a splash in Miami, I see."

Reznick chortled at Trevelle's dark sense of humor. "Yeah, good one."

"Listen, pack up your stuff, head out the back of the hotel, and meet me in Collins Court in two minutes."

Reznick was surprised. "You're outside?"

"I live in Florida, remember? I was thinking about the SD card. I want to secure the hard copy. The last thing we need is for this original evidence to be taken from you."

"You downloaded the contents?"

"All of it."

"And when you get the card, where are you going to take it?"

"A secure underground vault."

Reznick picked up his backpack, headed out of his room, down a flight of stairs and through the rear door of the hotel, cell phone pressed to his ear. "One minute."

"Copy that."

Reznick vaulted over a small perimeter wall and dropped down into an alley—Collins Court. He saw Trevelle pull up on a motorcycle. Reznick handed him the SD card.

Trevelle pushed the card deep into the pocket of his jeans and dismounted from the bike. "Get on!"

Reznick climbed on and checked the bike's mirror. Behind him, a handful of revelers were ending their night as day broke. "You not coming too?"

"I've got a place nearby I want to store this. The contents have been saved to multiple secure cloud servers in Europe as well as my own onsite servers on Captiva."

"Send it to Caroline Sullivan, strictly for her eyes. Tell her to check and reverify the validity with a second source. I want to be sure this is rock solid. I'm guessing she'll want to do exactly the same thing."

"Leave it to me. Now go. I'll be in touch."

Reznick pulled on his backpack and accelerated away, weaving through the narrow streets of South Beach. He figured that Miami International Airport would be crawling with cops, Feds, or contractors working for the Agency.

He wanted to get back to DC and meet up again with Caroline Sullivan as soon as possible. He didn't know if that was viable, or even wise. But it was the best plan he could think of at that moment.

Reznick's mind raced as he tried to think of a smaller airport where he could depart for DC. He vaguely remembered using Punta Gorda Airport on the Gulf Coast, north of Fort Myers, in the past. It was a long ride. He figured it must be nearly two hundred miles. But it was a little-known airport from which he had flown out to Europe in past missions on Gulfstreams operated by private companies. It might get the job done, and it was low-key.

He checked the tank. He was in luck, it was full.

Reznick sped on up toward Fort Lauderdale. Mile after mile. On and on. He tore up the miles riding west along Alligator Alley, the stretch of I-75 to Naples. Then up the Gulf Coast to Punta Gorda Airport. It took him two and a half hours.

He dropped off the motorcycle at a parking garage and headed down to the small terminal.

Reznick used a fake ID and credit card in the name of Bud Chertoff to book a ticket. He decided not to head directly to DC after all. Instead, he caught a flight to Asheville Regional Airport in North Carolina. He had a two-hour layover before the flight back to Dulles. It was a convoluted route, but after what had just happened, it might give him a better chance of evading detection.

Reznick's flight landed in DC after a tortuous journey. He caught an airport bus to the nearby Westin Hotel and checked in, again under the name Bud Chertoff. He went to his room and locked his door. He showered and lay down, the events of the last twenty-four hours still racing around his head. Then he felt the waves of tiredness wash over him. He closed his eyes and felt himself falling into a chasm of blackness.

Reznick floated in darkness. The river moved slowly downstream to an unknown destination. He peered up at the billions of stars in the inky black sky. He sensed he was not alone. He saw corpses floating by. Limbless corpses, the sound of dogs barking in the distance. Men on the banks of the river, firing. Gunshots echoing in his head. On and on, gunfire. Relentless. The sound of screaming in the distance. A woman's wail. Then corpses falling from the sky. In slow motion, they plunged into the water, disappearing farther downstream. He tried to turn his head. Dark whispers. You will never return home.

Reznick made out a silhouetted figure on the riverbank. It was his father, beckoning him over. Reznick looked at his face, tears streaming down his father's cheeks. His father was crying. Beseeching him to leave the water. More corpses floated past as his father turned and walked away, disappearing from sight.

Reznick awoke in darkness, drenched in sweat. His nightmares were back: flashbacks to what he had seen in Iraq. He took a few moments to realize his cell phone was vibrating on the table. He reached over and checked the caller ID. It was Caroline Sullivan.

Reznick sat upright in bed, turning on the lamp.

"Jon, are you okay?"

"Just getting a bit of sleep."

"I was worried about you. How did it go down in Miami?"

Reznick's mind replayed the crazy events of the previous night. "It was . . . interesting, that's for sure."

"That sounds terrifying."

"I think I made a bit of a splash."

"Jon, that's not funny."

"It happened alright, what can I tell you?"

Silence, then: "You killed people?"

"We were being followed. And they started shooting first. But I got you the documents, right? Did Trevelle send them across?"

"He did, thanks to you."

"It's the real deal?"

"I was shaking reading it. It's the highest classification. Stunning. But I'm still working through it. Tell me more about Miami."

"It was a close call."

"Who were they?"

"No idea, but if I were to hazard a guess, I'd say private security contractors from the same company who tried to strongarm me at a diner in DC a few days ago. Maybe working on behalf of the Agency."

"The CIA wants to kill you?"

"I think so. I know too much."

"Why would they use a private security firm? Plausible deniability?'

"Precisely. They don't work for the government directly."

"This is very unsettling . . . I don't know . . . I'm scared just hearing all this."

"I didn't mean to scare you, Caroline."

"I know you didn't. Are you back in DC?"

Reznick rubbed his eyes. "I'm on the outskirts."

"Why the outskirts?"

"Long story. How are things on your side of the fence? Any further developments?"

"There's a guy I reached out to. I'm hoping he can get us over the line, so to speak. He used to work at the Agency."

"Retired CIA. Interesting. And you can trust this guy like you trust Andrew Stone?"

"In my line of work, Jon, I operate on trust. There has to be a level of respect or I'd never get a story, never get a contact or source to speak to me. There has to be mutual trust. But there are rules."

"Are you meeting him today?"

"You want to tag along?"

Reznick was thinking he had done his bit. And then some. But somehow, it didn't come out like that. "I don't want to cramp your style."

"You won't be doing that."

"Will your source be okay with me tagging along?"

"Won't be a problem. Do you know Fairfax, Virginia?"

"I know where it is. Why?"

"My contact lives there. I think he can also give us a path forward."

"And regarding the—"

"Plans? I'm confident he'll be able to steer us in the right direction."

"Where in Fairfax?"

Caroline gave him an address.

Reznick felt conflicted. He really wanted to go home to Rockland, get back to his old life and put all this behind him. But the story seemed reluctant to give him up. He looked inward to determine if the real reason was that part of him felt uneasy that Caroline Sullivan might be left at the mercy of whoever it was that had Reznick in their crosshairs. "I'll catch a cab. See you in thirty minutes."

The cab pulled up outside a large suburban house, cloaked behind oaks and beech trees. Fairfax was picture-perfect: brick-facade homes in the Federal style. Reznick paid the driver and got out, headed up the pathway. He rang the bell.

The door was opened by a sixty-something woman with gray hair. She stepped aside and waved him in. "Hello. And you must be Mr. Reznick, right?"

"You got it."

"Your friend Ms. Sullivan is here already." The woman showed him upstairs to a second-floor office. She knocked and opened the door.

Waiting inside were Caroline Sullivan and an older, bespectacled man in chinos and a white button-down.

Reznick felt as if he was intruding as he walked into the room.

The man looked up. "You must be Jon. Ernest Steiner, nice to meet you."

"That's me." Reznick shook Steiner's hand. "Nice place you've got."

"Just paid off the mortgage two years ago. A lifetime of work and toil and for what? A home in the suburbs." He sounded bitter.

Reznick smiled at the self-deprecation. "You've made a lovely home for your family."

Steiner indicated for him to sit down on the sofa beside Caroline. "So here we are. Caroline was telling me all about you and your work. She mentioned your connections with special forces, FBI, and the CIA. Long spells overseas. And Delta Force?"

"I've been around."

Steiner chuckled. "I don't know about you, Jon, but I always missed home when I was abroad. I missed my family. I missed my children growing up. But someone has to do it, right? Sacrifices."

Reznick nodded, remembering the feeling of being away from his daughter as she was growing up.

"People don't know what it's like. Men like you do. Men who have served in wars. Overseas for years. You have a family, Jon?"

"I've got a daughter."

"You married?"

Reznick felt awkward. He shifted in his seat. "At one time, yeah." He wasn't going to get into talking about Elisabeth. He'd believed for years that she had died on 9/11. But a few years ago he had found out she had been hiding out in Switzerland all this time, working for the CIA, using an alias. It couldn't have been much more devastating. She had since relocated to Connecticut, but there had been no visits. It was all in the past now, he mused.

Steiner looked at him thoughtfully. "We don't think about it . . . but it takes its toll. The long absences. The separate lives. Not easy."

Reznick said nothing.

"Anyway, down to business," Steiner said. "Caroline reached out to me, as is her wont as a top journalist. I believe you guys are looking for verification of what you believe may be a highly classified special access program? It's a bit irregular to say the least."

Reznick nodded. "I believe it is bona fide."

Caroline intervened. "Jon, just so you know, Ernest has retained the highest level of security clearance, like yourself, since he retired. He has helped me on numerous national security stories, when I've needed to verify the facts and accuracy of a story. He previously headed up the Directorate of Intelligence at the CIA, specializing in Latin America."

"The department is now called Directorate of Analysis," said Steiner. "And Latin America is what this story is all about after all."

Caroline nodded. "Pretty much."

"I'm going to be talking candidly among friends. I trust that what we say stays within these four walls. Legally, as you know, I shouldn't be speaking to you with regard to this documentation. When Caroline told me how this had all transpired, it took my breath away. However, I had to think long and hard about this. I am loyal to the Agency. And to my country. But Caroline is very persuasive."

She batted her eyelashes. "What can I tell you?"

Steiner observed Reznick. "You look hungry. You want some food?"

Reznick shook his head. "I'm fine, thanks."

"Coffee?"

"No, I'm good."

Steiner laughed hoarsely. "I'm sorry, I'm an old man. I don't receive many visitors. My social graces are not what they were. And I ramble on . . . So this morning, after Caroline gave me a rudimentary idea of what had happened, I agreed for her to send over to me, securely, of course, what you found during your eventful little trip to Miami."

"Do you know what happened down there?"

"I heard. Car tailing you, shooting out the windows, and you fight back, right?"

"Precisely."

"What does that tell you?"

"Someone wants to silence me?"

Steiner grinned. "You better believe it. Anyway, enough of this preamble. I know all there is to know about you, Jon."

"All good?" Reznick joked.

"You're not too dissimilar to me. You see, I'm a patriot. I believe in this country. But I believe what's driving you with this case, if you want to call it that, is that you are not blindly following the flag. I believe, sometimes, you have to adhere to your principles, no matter the cost. Sometimes it means crossing a line. You've crossed the line. By speaking to you it means I've probably crossed the line as well. I could be jailed. All of us could be. But I'm guessing we all understand the risks we're taking."

Caroline nodded. "Most certainly."

Reznick chimed in. "I get it. My motivation is similar to yours, Ernest. I'm a patriot. And I don't believe in killing innocent Americans. Not for oil. Not for minerals. Not for anything."

Ernest said gravely, "I've read the plans you retrieved. Know what I think? The whole thing stinks. You know the comparison I would make?"

"What's that?" Caroline asked.

"There are echoes of the dilemma that Daniel Ellsberg, who also used to work at the Pentagon, faced decades ago. He worked as a military analyst at the RAND Corporation. He was a Marine, previously. But he was a true patriot in my eyes. He saw the plans. He drew up the plans. And over time he became more horrified. The lies—that's what he saw. Ellsberg realized the illegality of the operations, the widespread lies of the US administration with regard to the scope and extent of the war in Vietnam and how it was encroaching on neighboring territories."

"The Pentagon Papers, right?" Caroline said.

Steiner leaned back in his seat. "Precisely. Daniel decided to leak the Pentagon Papers via the *New York Times*. Your paper, Caroline. And the rest is history. He let the country know the truth. He let Americans know what was being done in their name."

Reznick shifted in his seat as he listened.

Steiner's eyes were sparkling. "Do you know the Supreme Court ruling was six to three? They said, and I know this from memory, 'Only a free and unrestrained press can effectively expose deception in government.' Which is interesting. The Pentagon Papers, in effect, exposed America for bombing Laos and Cambodia, while the American people were being lied to."

Caroline scrutinized Steiner. "Ernest, talk to me about the documents Jon was given. Are they genuine?"

"When I began to read what you sent me, my first reaction was that this might, on the surface, be an elaborate disinformation plot that had leaked out. That was my initial thought."

Caroline said, "Why did you think that?"

"Skepticism is an important facet of human nature. I'm in the business of analysis. It's easy to be misled. Lied to. It happens, right? Maybe a disinformation plot from Russia, China, you name it, using Stephen Leahy to propagate a hostile narrative that would discredit America. And then I got to thinking that it might be a nefarious plot by the CIA to smoke out any spies in their midst. Or maybe the purpose was to destabilize Venezuela, which they've already got in their sights, via a psyop. I couldn't rule out those possibilities, at first."

"But what did you conclude?"

Ernest shook his head. "This is quite something. I mean, seriously, the document is the real thing. Which is frightening in itself."

Reznick felt his heart tighten. "It's definitely real?"

"Oh yeah. I checked with a couple friends of mine—world-renowned experts I've worked with extensively over the years. The document was marked *SECRET/NOFORN*, meaning it is not meant to be shared with foreign countries. Even the Five Eyes—UK, Australia, Canada, and New Zealand. No one. I spoke to a close friend of mine who, once upon a time, headed up the Questioned Documents Unit of the FBI. Now he has his own consulting firm. He looked over a random sample of pages I sent over. He used ultraviolet light, microscopes, analyzed the inks on the signatures, quality of paper, watermark searches, forensic signatures analysis. He was painstaking. He was also worried that it might turn out to be like the Zinoviev letter."

"What's that?" Reznick asked.

"An MI5 forgery just before the British general election in the 1920s. Aimed at associating voting for the Labour Party with links to Communists in the Soviet Union. Pure forgery. But what you showed me is, unquestionably in my considered opinion and that of my two expert friends, completely authentic. And it's crazy."

"Can you be one hundred percent sure of that?" Reznick asked.

"I couldn't give a one hundred percent guarantee unless I'd signed off on the plans myself. But I'm telling you this: I am of the firm belief that this document is authentic."

"You know about that world, Ernest," said Caroline. "You lived it for decades. What are your thoughts? Any advice?"

"Be very careful. If what happened to Jon down in Miami is anything to go by, these guys play for keeps."

Twenty-Six

Michael Johnson's car arrived at the Hoover Building's underground parking garage. He had decided to approach the top brass of the FBI after concluding that a twin-track approach would be the best avenue to deal with Reznick. He had already ordered Edward Black to draw up new plans to delete Reznick once and for all. But he also wanted to take the legal route, determined to neutralize the serious threat Reznick posed to US national security. For that he'd need some federal muscle.

Johnson stepped out of the elevator on the seventh floor, flanked by two attorneys from the CIA and the Department of Homeland Security. He was escorted down a series of corridors into a secure conference room. Around the table, already seated and waiting for them, were the FBI's Director, the Director of Counterintelligence, and the FBI's legal counsel.

After a few brusque handshakes, Johnson and the group sat down at the large oval conference table.

Johnson carefully laid out the classified papers in front of him. He met each set of eyes around the table before launching in. "I appreciate you seeing me at such short notice. The Chairman of the Joint Chiefs of Staff has asked me to convey to you his serious concerns about this matter on national security grounds. Hence this meeting. This is a matter of the gravest concern."

Bill O'Donoghue, Director of the FBI, leaned back in his seat. "You have our ears. You have our eyes. And you have our full cooperation on any critical matters of national security."

Johnson nodded as he picked up the briefing notes that had been prepared specifically for the meeting. "Again, I'd like to express our sincere gratitude that we are having this face-to-face meeting. I know how busy the FBI is, working on multiple investigations at this moment in time. A few points, if I may, and some ground rules. There must be no contemporaneous notes taken by any person in this room." He directed this mostly at the FBI General Counsel, Fred Jiménez, who sat serenely, hands clasped. "The reasons for this are self-explanatory. This pertains to a breach of highly classified military intelligence papers concerning America's future national security. What I say here must not be discussed outside of this room. The special access program we are discussing today is known to only a few people at the Pentagon. But we now have reason to believe a catastrophic leak, threatening our plans, has occurred."

The FBI's Director of Counterintelligence, Trace Atkins, cleared his throat. "Brigadier General, I'd like to know a bit more. Are you aware how the leak happened or even the source of the leak?"

"Absolutely, on both counts."

"Do you mind me asking where this originated from? The individual, I mean."

"It's all included in the dossier I will be handing out to you in a few moments. We have reason to believe that a person who previously worked at the highest levels within the CIA, and who was party to the top-secret documentation as part of a classified Pentagon-approved planning operation, leaked this. I can't overstate how shocking this is."

A deathly silence descended on the room. Then Atkins said, "Can you give me further details? What was the motivation for the leak? Was this a foreign power pressuring this individual or a member of their family? Blackmail?"

"I will endeavor to provide this information as we move forward. All I will say is that this leak is not yet contained. Quite the opposite. And that's why I'm here today." Johnson saw that every individual around the table was locked into serious concentration. "In this dossier are the names of individuals we believe should be investigated and indicted. The charges include the unauthorized retention and disclosure of classified information pertaining directly to national security. The names we have so far include—and this list may change in the future—in no particular order, *New York Times* journalist Caroline Sullivan; Robert White, a tax attorney based in Miami; retired general Andrew Stone, previously Chairman of the Joint Chiefs of Staff; and Jon Reznick, an ex-Delta Force operator, who I believe worked for the FBI at one time."

O'Donoghue flushed crimson. "These names are unbelievable. I know Reznick. He has done work for us. I can confirm that he worked alongside retired Assistant Director Martha Meyerstein. But he never formally worked for the FBI. I want to make that clear. He was never paid by the FBI. He was used by Meyerstein for certain operations."

Johnson said, "Point taken, sir."

O'Donoghue continued. "Meyerstein is obviously no longer working here. Can you confirm if she is involved?"

"Martha Meyerstein is not on our list for a reason. The Espionage Act, as you'll recall, refers to retention and disclosure of classified information. We do not believe she has been directly involved in this. That said, we believe that Reznick has reached out to her since he arrived in DC. We have reason to believe that he may have talked to her about the plans. But we have no proof she retained or disclosed any of that information."

O'Donoghue shook his head. "We regard what you're saying with the gravest concern. I think I can confidently say on behalf of everyone around the table that this is a troubling scenario. I can reassure you, Brigadier General, that this matter will be investigated to the fullest extent. If this means shining a light on the connections Reznick had with Meyerstein while they worked together at the FBI, so be it. No stone will be left unturned."

Atkins said, "I can only reiterate what the Director has just said. We will investigate this using all the extensive tools and resources at our disposal. We will set up a hand-picked task force with the highest levels of clearance, which I will head up, and we will get to the bottom of this, you can be sure of that. However, can we back up for a few moments? The CIA officer who initially leaked this? This is intriguing. Why is his or her name not included?"

Michael Johnson's gaze wandered around the faces at the table. He had been waiting for this question. He had already prepared his scripted answer. "That's a very good question. I knew this man well. He was, at one time, the finest mind at the CIA. Highly learned, analytical, geopolitical. But this man, sadly, has had what can only be described as a catastrophic psychiatric breakdown. It's unprecedented how suddenly the illness came over him. We believe he has, in effect, lost his mind, perhaps because of his secret, heavy drug use. Cannabis, cocaine, amphetamines, and psychedelics were all found in a locked drawer in his office after a search by officers from Pentagon Force Protection Agency Criminal Investigations. But that's only scratching the surface. It is hard to comprehend, I know. But thankfully, the person has been examined, found to lack capacity, and was committed to a secure hospital not far from Washington, DC. He will also be receiving treatment for his drug addiction and withdrawal."

"Does this person have a name?" Atkins asked.

"As they are undergoing treatment, and as I'm led to believe this might take six months or more, we think it prudent as we move forward not to prosecute this individual until we can make a better assessment of their mental capacities, as well as whether they may have any accomplices or associates. We are also investigating whether a young woman who works for a foreign power has had access to this man. We have information that they had been on several dates. She's a German national, although she was born in Russia. We just don't know."

A few nods and grunts around the table.

Johnson began to weave a fictitious tale about the compromised CIA agent. "Here's what I've been told and can share at this time. We know the capabilities of Russia's Foreign Intelligence Service: highly effective and currently working heavily throughout Europe. I'm talking about the UK, Germany, and Italy in particular. In this case, we have information that the CIA officer, off duty while traveling for work, had been enjoying a meal with his new friend in Munich when he was supplied with drugs. Maybe he was initially drugged without his knowledge, then blackmailed, or maybe he started experimenting with recreational drugs to combat the stress he reported to friends and coworkers at the Agency. But, ultimately, drugs look to have contributed to his psychiatric breakdown and radically changed his behavior in the past eighteen months, leading up to his current hospitalization."

Atkins nodded gravely. "Can you tell me about this behavior?"

Johnson had consulted with a couple of behavioral psychologists prior to this meeting to gather some points he should raise. "I've learned from those within senior levels of the CIA that the man had begun frequently to scream and shout during meetings, behavior which was out of character. He began turning up to work in flip-flops and Hawaiian shirts, claiming to be on vacation."

Atkins sighed, shaking his head. "So, from this individual everything else flowed? The leak, the sharing of classified intelligence?"

"Precisely." Johnson turned to the CIA's attorney. "Phil, please distribute our dossier."

The CIA lawyer, Phil Cunningham, walked around the table rather theatrically and placed files in front of the Director, then in front of the counterintelligence chief, and lastly the FBI's legal counsel.

"Thanks, Phil," Johnson said.

Cunningham sat down and fixed his steely gaze on the FBI team opposite. "The dossier is top secret. That's a given. We know you three have the highest-level clearance. Make sure that the dossier is securely retained. Do not make copies. Is that clearly understood?"

The three senior FBI men nodded meekly, as if subordinates.

"We trust this will be investigated to the best of your abilities, Johnson said. "In our estimation, Jon Reznick and Caroline Sullivan need to be brought in for questioning. The sooner the better."

Twenty-Seven

Reznick wore sunglasses as he sat on Caroline Sullivan's terrace, discussing the ramifications of the investigation with the journalist, drinking strong coffee, eating sandwiches. "Okay, so you've had time to dig into this," he said. "We have two external verifications from experts in their fields. We've got a retired Chairman of the Joint Chiefs of Staff, General Andrew Stone. We've got Ernest Steiner, eminent former head of the CIA's Directorate of Intelligence. They have both, independently of each other, verified that this document, in their eyes, is genuine. This backs up what Stephen Leahy told me. It exists, and the plans are as real as it gets."

Caroline nodded, deep in thought.

Reznick leaned forward, hands clasped. "Caroline, talk to me. You're too quiet. Where are you at with this? Any concerns?"

"I've been reading it, the full extract, it took hours . . ."

"Me too."

"Jon, I've worked on hundreds of stories regarding national security, but this is so out of left field—how it originated from a CIA spook in a psychiatric hospital, the origin story defies belief. And that's why it worries me."

Reznick leaned forward, touching the back of her hand. "I understand."

"Do you? It's a heavy responsibility when you're trying to verify a story. I was reading a chapter of the *American Journalism Handbook*. It talks at length about the paramount importance of going back to the original source. Not only the document in this case, but also the person who leaked it verbally. There are unknowns, right?"

"Right."

"They say Leahy's lost his mind."

"Do you think he's crazy?"

"I don't know. You met with him, I didn't. I'm struggling to even wrap my head around the rationale. I write about shit like this all the time. But reading it in black and white, before the plan has happened, is scary. It really is."

"Let me ask you something. What are you going to do about this now? Are you going to write about it? At least get the wheels in motion?"

"Damn straight."

"Do you believe you can stop this? The operation, I mean."

"I don't know. But I want the American public to know about it. They have a right to know what's being done in their name. I want to expose it. It's the truth. Why shouldn't they know the truth?"

Reznick took a gulp of his coffee. "I detect a *but* coming . . ."

"But the ramifications are huge for us. Forget about me personally. I'm talking about America. And that's why I need to get this right. This is highly, highly classified shit. National fucking security. The fallout could be years of jail for me. And you. Do you understand?"

Reznick nodded as his eyes skimmed across the sun-kissed rooftops of Georgetown, all the way to the Potomac. He saw light reflecting oddly from a window on the next block.

"Are you listening to what I'm saying? You seem distracted."

"Something caught my eye. I don't know. Might be nothing."

"What do you see?"

"A glint from a window. Like metal. Maybe glass. I don't know, maybe a camera?"

Caroline analyzed the same window, a flicker of light in the sun. "Must be the window."

Reznick wasn't so sure. He knew people had been watching him. Maybe this was part of the pattern of surveillance.

"Anyway, I just don't know how to go forward with this. I'm at the stage of just taking notes, getting my thoughts down."

"Have you thought about just approaching your editors at the *New York Times* and seeing what they say?"

"I have."

"And?"

"This is not something I can do lightly. I need to be really, really sure before I give a summary to them about an article that could be so explosive. But also, even before I reach out to them, I have to have *zero* doubt."

"You're afraid that we might still be wrong, even after everything we've found out, and the verifications?"

"Damn right I am."

"A third source of verification? Would that do it for you?"

"Absolutely. A third source would nail it down."

"What you have so far, in my eyes, is pretty compelling. I'll be honest, I think you've got the story."

"I know I do. I believe it's true. I just want more. And that will take time."

"And that's something we don't have."

"I was thinking about maybe heading up to the psychiatric hospital in Maryland."

Reznick nodded. "Assuming Leahy's still there. Assuming he's still being kept as Toby Breslin."

"You don't think he'll be there?"

"I think, after what's happened, the Agency will have either moved Stephen Leahy or totally denied him access to visitors. I got lucky figuring out he was being held under a false name. Very lucky. I got in there not long after he was committed." Reznick took out his phone. "But I know a guy who can help."

"Hey Jon," Trevelle said when he picked up. "Never a dull moment with you, huh?"

"Tell me about it. Listen, you found out Stephen Leahy was being kept under the assumed name of Toby Breslin."

"Sure."

"Can you check if he's still on their records at the hospital? Is the man known as Toby Breslin still there? Or cross-check with birthdates again. Maybe Leahy is now under a new assumed name."

"I'll call you back in five minutes."

Reznick ended the call and looked over at Caroline. "If he's still there, you might be in luck. A window of opportunity."

"And what if I'm not so lucky?"

"You need to dig further."

A molten sun bathed the city. "Can I be honest, Jon?"

"Of course."

"I'm scared."

"I don't blame you. It's crazy stuff."

"I feel like I'm being suffocated. Thinking about it, overthinking it. It's like I'm stuck on a mental loop."

"You've got this, Caroline. Just keep your cool, focus, press on, don't look back."

"That's easy for you to say. The chase down in Miami, people getting shot, cars careening off the bridge? That is not my world, Jon."

"I know it's not. Your world is bleeding into mine. Or the other way around, I suppose."

"That's what's freaking me out. My area of expertise is writing books, articles, essays, meeting with contacts, taking sources to lunch. I do not get embroiled in living nightmares. I mean, when you told me about shooting at the car that was tailing you before it went off the bridge . . . Those men are dead."

"You need to get a grip. And quick. I had no choice. They blew out the rear windshield of Robert White's car. They were closing in. They were going to kill us if I didn't deal with it."

Caroline put her head in her hands. "This is so fucked up. I don't know, I've just got such a bad feeling about this. What if the Feds turn up and arrest you for what happened down in Miami?"

"I'll deal with whatever comes my way." Reznick's cell phone rang. "Hey Trevelle."

"Okay, Jon, I got an update."

"Shoot."

"Toby Breslin, the man with the same date of birth as Stephen Leahy? Jon, I don't know how to tell you this . . ."

"Spit it out. What is it?"

"Hospital records show that he committed suicide early this morning. Hung himself with a bedsheet."

Twenty-Eight

Jon and Caroline sat together on her terrace in shocked silence. Caroline's face looked haunted, her eyes still filled with tears.

"What does this mean? Surely he should have been on some sort of suicide watch."

Reznick just shook his head. It was quite possible that Leahy's cause of death had been murder, made to look like a tragic suicide. It would be easy to do in a psychiatric hospital: a psychotic, troubled man taking his own life. He remembered what Leahy had told him: *If I wind up dead, trust me, it won't be because I took my own life.* It was imprinted into Reznick's psyche.

"I'll be honest," Reznick said. "You need to consider if you want to continue with this or walk away. I wouldn't blame you if you did. Not one bit. I was thinking about it too at one stage. It feels like the whole thing is too huge and suffocating."

"Why is all this happening?"

"Why do you think? The only conclusion can be that, with state secrets too important to be leaked, the powers behind those secrets decided to silence Stephen Leahy for good. They've done that. But it's not the end. It's just beginning."

"What do you mean?"

"They have their sights on us now. Because the story needs to be buried and any trace of it needs to be deleted. And that means us."

Caroline got up and paced out her nervous energy. "I thought I was tough. I really did. I thought I was a steely investigative reporter."

Reznick nodded.

"I've interviewed powerful people. Dangerous people. Cartel lawyers down in Colombia. Nothing fazed me. But now? I'm scared."

"I don't buy that you're scared. You're tough. Tougher than you realize. Determined. But I wouldn't blame you for saying *fuck it, I'm out of here.*"

"I work on proof. I have no proof that they're killing, or attempting to kill, everyone who knows about this. That being said, I believe our government is capable of anything. And that includes killing its own people."

"You better believe it."

"But who exactly is doing this?"

"The government works in mysterious ways. Maybe people behind the scenes. Maybe contractors working for the Agency. Or the Pentagon. Maybe it was authorized by those in power who are worried that the plans have leaked. They want to snuff it out. Whatever it takes."

Caroline turned and looked at Reznick. "What should I do?"

"Do what feels right. Feels right for you. Be true to yourself."

She smiled. "Why is it that you always seem to say the right thing to me? It's like you know everything about me. But you don't."

Reznick shrugged. "Walk away if that's what's in your heart. Just do it. I'd understand. I wouldn't blame you. This is all fucked up. But know this, they won't stop. You understand? They're going to come after us."

Caroline paced the rooftop, arms folded. "I don't want to walk away. I'd feel like a fraud. Besides, I feel like I'm close. I'm building up the big picture: I've read the plans for Operation Yellow Rain, I've had two independent verifications as to authenticity. But, I don't know . . . I want to be certain."

Reznick nodded. "Makes sense. You want to go the extra mile."

"Why not? *New York Times* has scrupulous fact checkers. They verify. They check. They double-check. And then they do it all again. Three impeccable sources is better than two. Way better."

"I understand that."

Caroline's cell phone vibrated on the table and she picked it up. "That's interesting."

"What?"

"It's a text message."

"From?"

Caroline quickly scanned the message. "General Andrew Stone. He says he has what he describes as the missing piece of the jigsaw. Operational planner for the CIA Director. That would be a third source."

"Seriously?"

"I told you he had contacts. He says this guy is a really close friend of Stephen Leahy."

Reznick felt his nerve ends twitching. "That's good news, right? He can help you."

Caroline nodded, staring at the phone. "That would be incredible. Maybe the guy has an axe to grind with the Agency, I don't know. I'll have to interview him. Andrew wants us to head out to his beach house right now."

"Right now?" Reznick said.

"Right now. It's on the Eastern Shore in Maryland. Maybe a four-hour drive away. Come with me?"

Reznick's instincts were telling him it would be better if he was there. "Sure. But it's your call."

"What do you think?"

"This is your call, Caroline. Do you want the story? A third source? Operational planner? I mean, shit, that's high-level stuff."

"Dammit, I'm in!"

Caroline's SUV pulled up outside the beach home on Assateague Island. It had been a tiring journey. They had headed east to the Chesapeake Bay Bridge and then due south. "Well, here we are," she said. "I've been here a few times before, visiting friends farther along. There are three hundred wild ponies running around on this island."

"Is that right?" Reznick surveyed the house. It sat on the south side of the thirty-seven-mile-long barrier island facing the Atlantic. No other houses for miles around, a truly deserted beach hideaway.

The sounds of breakers crashing onto the nearby shore, and the distinctive squawking of gulls and terns in the night. The smell of the salty air carried in from the ocean.

Reznick felt right at home. He had been brought up beside the sea. He loved it. The sounds had a calming effect on him. He looked at the duck-egg-blue beach house, bathed in expensive exterior lighting. "Great place to spend retirement, that's for sure."

The pair got out of the vehicle and walked up to the front door.

"Now this is nice," Caroline said. "I love Madison. I love Connecticut. But this is really lovely. You ever been on the island, Jon?"

"Can't say I have."

Caroline pressed the bell. They heard heavy footsteps coming down the hallway.

The door opened.

Caroline looked surprised to see a Hispanic woman beaming at them, signaling for them to head inside. "We're here to see Andrew Stone?" Caroline said.

"Come in, come in," the woman replied. "Andrew has been expecting you."

Reznick shut the door behind him and followed them down a long corridor.

"Andrew had to head out twenty minutes ago. Medical issue."

"Is he okay?" Caroline said.

"He's perfectly fine. He apologizes profusely. He had to visit his brother Hunter who's in the hospital. His brother is not so well. Doctors phoned Mr. Stone about half an hour ago and said Hunter had taken a turn for the worse and to please come quick."

Caroline nodded. "That's too bad. Will he be long?"

"Not at all. He'll be back real soon. He had to pick up his sister-in-law and take her to the hospital to be by her husband's bedside. But he wants you to make yourselves at home."

Reznick felt as if he and Caroline were imposing on Andrew Stone at this difficult time.

The woman showed them into a spacious living room, log fire burning. "Andrew told me to tell you that after he is done at the hospital, he is picking up his friend, who lives five minutes from the hospital, and bringing him here. I believe you will interview his friend?"

Caroline nodded as she slumped down on a huge sofa. "That's good. Thank you."

"My name is Maria, by the way. I'm Andrew's housekeeper. I've worked for his family for twenty-two years. He is a fine man. Such a gentleman."

Reznick sat down on a leather Eames chair opposite Caroline. "We can come back another time, Maria," he said. "Maybe tomorrow would be more convenient under the circumstances. We understand family comes first."

The housekeeper shook her head. "Absolutely not. You've come all this way. Besides, Andrew told me to assure you both that he will be back very soon. Andrew is very close to his brother. When Hunter was young he was in and out of the hospital for months after a car accident. Hunter has always been into dangerous sports. He recently completed a marathon in the North African desert. But he took unwell shortly after he got back to America."

"That's awful," Caroline said.

"God willing, he will pull through. But we're praying he makes a recovery soon."

"I understand. How long will Andrew be gone, if you don't mind me asking?"

"No more than an hour. In the meantime, I can fix you a sandwich, a drink, perhaps?"

Reznick nodded. "Sure thing. It was a long ride. A sandwich and a coffee sounds great. I'm famished."

"Very good." Maria looked at Caroline. "And you, miss?"

"I'll have what he's having."

"No problem. I'll go and fix it for you." Maria disappeared into the kitchen. Reznick heard her singing what sounded like a Spanish lullaby as she gathered the ingredients.

Reznick leaned forward in his chair and whispered to Caroline, "I feel like I'm intruding. You know, with his brother in the hospital. Maybe we should come back tomorrow. Eat the sandwich and head out."

"I feel the same. Let's wait and see. We've come all this way."

Maria called them into the kitchen where they sat down at the table and ate the delicious sandwiches and drank their coffee. "You enjoy?"

"This is great," Reznick said, glad of the sustenance, having not eaten for hours. "I mean, this is spectacular."

Maria beamed as she began to busily wipe down the granite countertops.

"Sorry to interrupt . . ." Reznick said. "But I'm concerned that we're intruding at a delicate time."

"Yeah, I think Jon's right," Caroline agreed. "We can come back tomorrow. How does that sound?"

Maria shook her head. "Absolutely not. Andrew told me himself he is looking forward to bringing his friend over to meet you both in person. He knew you guys were on the way and didn't want to disappoint you. He won't be long. The Atlantic General Hospital is in Berlin. Twenty-minute drive away. If I know Andrew, he'll be interrogating the doctors to make sure his brother is getting the very best treatment. Very clever, thoughtful man. But he's mindful of having visitors. So you won't have to wait long. His dinner is waiting in the refrigerator, as he requested."

"Good to know. And thanks again for the food."

"My pleasure." Maria picked up a coat from the back of a chair and a tote bag. "I gotta go. Family."

Caroline looked quizzically, first at Reznick, and then at Maria. "You're going? I'm sorry, I didn't realize. We can't stay here in Andrew's house by ourselves."

"No, you're fine. Andrew said to relax, fix yourselves whatever you want. I've got my daughter home. She's been working overseas in Dubai. Family gathering. I'll be cooking for twelve! No rest!"

Caroline grimaced. "This feels really awkward. Don't disturb him any further if he's at the hospital. We'll sit tight."

Maria gave a little wave before she turned on her heel and headed down the corridor, and out the front door, shutting it quietly behind her.

Reznick shrugged. "Well, when in Rome, right?" He headed through to the front room and looked out the front window as Maria climbed into her small Honda, revved it up, and reversed out of the driveway and into the night. He headed back into the kitchen. "I guess it's just you and me, kid!"

Caroline laughed. She quickly washed the dishes, dried them, and put them away carefully in the cupboard.

They decided to sit and wait in the living room.

Reznick meandered over to the photos on the wall. A uniformed General Stone standing in his office at the Pentagon, a flag by his side. A few of Stone with past presidents. The only color photo was a besuited Stone and a young woman at what looked like a college graduation.

"I'm intrigued about this third verification of the plans," he said to Caroline. "You'll have a trio of impeccable military sources."

She sat down on the sofa. "Andrew is solid. I'm assuming this guy, if he's a CIA operational planner, will know the penalties of discussing classified operations. But maybe, as a friend of Leahy's, and hearing that he was committed to a psych ward, that moved the needle for him. Maybe that was the final straw."

"Makes sense. I don't think you can underestimate a long-lasting friendship, a bond forged over decades. So let's assume you get this third verification, what then? That's got to be the moment when you take this to your editors, right?"

Caroline looked thoughtful for a few moments. "If I have three independent experts in their own right verifying these plans, it's game on. I guess I would head straight to New York, meet up with the executive editor."

"The *Times* will get behind the story?"

"They'll have my back. At least I hope they'll have my back. I'd be working alongside the team. This will be a groundbreaking story. But we still have a long way to go."

"I'm assuming the power of the *New York Times* works as a kind of protection for you, right?"

"I guess so. Like The Pentagon Papers with Daniel Ellsberg. I thought it was interesting that Ernest Steiner saw the same parallels."

"Funny thing is my dad fought in Vietnam. It haunted him—what he saw, what he did. He returned a chronic alcoholic, clinically depressed, traumatized—a man who was never the same again. He did a job he hated when he came home."

"What was that?"

"Gutting, filleting fish, packing them in ice, then boxing them. Day in, day out. But he never went under. I loved that about him. He made sure I didn't go without."

Caroline stared at Reznick longer than he felt comfortable with. "I don't think I've ever heard you talk about your father like that."

"I loved him. He was a great man."

"Sounds like a hell of a guy."

"He was. Wasn't a great fan of hippies or beatniks or communists. But that's just the way he was. He was an American, first and foremost. And he was old-school patriotic. You fought for the flag, you died for the flag. And if you didn't like it, get lost."

Caroline sighed. "I've been thinking about what you said before. The powers that be . . . they'll come after me when this is published. Just like they did with Daniel Ellsberg."

"Distinct possibility. What happened to him exactly?"

"He was charged under the Espionage Act."

"Which is absolutely understandable."

"I get it, but it transpired that misconduct by the US government and illegal evidence-gathering resulted in the charges against Ellsberg eventually, reluctantly, being dropped."

"I believe in you. You've got this, trust me."

Caroline checked her watch. "What I've done so far is just the groundwork. I have to do a ton more before the story can be presented to the public. But it's going to be huge."

"I don't doubt it."

Caroline was quiet for a few moments. "Sometimes you've got to put your neck on the line. Stand up for what you believe in. You know—you've done it time after time. As a journalist, I believe you've got to pursue a story without fear or favor."

"I wish more of them would."

"It's a huge responsibility."

"You'll do fine. Hey, who knows, you might even win a second Pulitzer."

Caroline laughed. "One step at a time. Tonight is crucial. Assuming this guy confirms and verifies the plans are real, then I'm all in. This government, all governments, must be held accountable. I wouldn't be doing my job if I turned a blind eye to this story. It's too big."

"Good for you."

Caroline bobbed her head. "I appreciate that." She reached over to the remote control on the coffee table. She switched on CNN. "I'm a bit of a news junkie." She focused on the screen. Footage showed Iranian gunboats harassing tankers headed through the Strait of Hormuz, the narrow channel stretching between Saudi Arabia and Iran. The next item showed the US Navy and Marines carrying out an amphibious landing training exercise off the coast of Puerto Rico. "You think this might be start of the buildup? A diversion?"

"Maybe. Sending out a not-too-discreet message to governments in Latin America. In particular Venezuela. Put them on notice. Shake them up. Get them paranoid. A psychological operation."

"Not good. We've seen this move before."

Reznick got up from his seat.

"Where are you going?"

"I'm going to have a look around."

"A look around? What? You can't do that, Jon. This is Andrew's house. I feel uncomfortable with that."

"We were told to make ourselves at home."

Caroline laughed. "Seriously?"

"Just curious, that's all."

"What if he has hidden cameras and sees you snooping around?"

"You worry too much."

Caroline rolled her eyes as she looked back at the TV.

Reznick headed upstairs. He was being less than candid with Caroline. He felt something was off, but he didn't want to tell her that. He didn't want to alarm her. He couldn't wrap his head around Stone not being here and then the housekeeper disappearing. His instincts were telling him that maybe, just maybe, something was wrong. But what exactly? Had they gotten to Stone and taken him away?

Reznick went into a beach-facing room on the second floor. It appeared to be Andrew Stone's home office. There was a large wooden desk with an iMac in the center. The floor-to-ceiling bookshelves were packed with biographies of presidents: Eisenhower, JFK, Reagan. Tomes on the history of the CIA, the Second World War, and Vietnam dominated the lower shelves. History of art titles, then scores and scores of classics by Dickens, Henry James, and the full works of Shakespeare. Stone was clearly a widely read man.

Reznick noticed a hardback copy of *The Art of War* by Sun Tzu. A book he himself had read many years back. Other walls were covered in photographs of General Andrew Stone in full military uniform, shaking hands with American politicians and the current president. Other photos of Stone with what looked to be his family. He appeared to have three daughters. There were photos of each of them at their respective graduations. It reminded Reznick of Lauren's graduation from Bennington College. He couldn't have been prouder.

He looked at the other side of the room. More photos of Andrew Stone on the wall. Not one or two—dozens, of himself. A few were grainy black-and-whites.

Some seemed to show a mother and father on a farm, their son in the middle, presumably Andrew as a young boy. Reznick found it strangely touching to think that such a powerful military figure, who had reached the highest echelons of the American military, should come from such a humble farming background.

Reznick went into the room next door. A home gym. Sets of weights, cardio machines, a treadmill, a rowing machine, a TV hanging on the wall. Photos showed Stone running in the New York Marathon. It looked to Reznick like he was headed across the Pulaski Bridge into Queens. A couple of others showed him running in races in Boston, Berlin, and Tokyo. The guy was in superb shape for a man in his early sixties.

Reznick spotted a door in the corner, a key in the lock. Behind the door was a specially reinforced safe room with what looked like a nine-inch-thick steel door. In the corner, bolted to the floor, was a gun cabinet. He assumed that when shut it would be on a timer. Very elaborate security. But it made sense for a man of Stone's seniority in the American military in case of a home invasion.

Reznick saw the rationale for the safe room. He himself preferred the reassurance of a semiautomatic rifle for home defense. A good old-fashioned AR-15 would stop a small army in its tracks. His go-to home defense weapon was the LaRue SUURG, a 5.56 caliber with a pinned break the length of the suppressor. Red dots for sights.

He stepped out of the safe room, keeping the steel door open as it had been. But he shut the outer wooden door, careful to lock it again with the key.

He headed up to the third floor and looked around. Two spacious bedrooms in pastel colors. The last room was like a media room: a massive TV, half a dozen comfortable leather seats. Maybe a place for Stone to kick back and watch a ball game. Maybe a place for him to conduct Zoom meetings with the companies he advised.

Reznick headed up one final flight of stairs. He crept down a narrow corridor. A small room. The attic. Beneath sloping vaulted ceilings sat a simple chair and desk, a silver MacBook unopened, a black Anglepoise lamp. Moonlight streamed through the skylight, the window opening outward. The light cast a ghostly pale glow into the room. He imagined it would be a good place to do a bit of work. Maybe write one's memoirs.

Reznick headed back downstairs and into the living room. He slumped back down on the sofa. The TV was still on CNN. A panel of experts was discussing the tensions in the Middle East and the naval maneuvers in the Caribbean.

"Find anything interesting?" Caroline asked.

Reznick shook his head. "Like something out of *Architectural Digest*. Super tasteful."

"You shouldn't be prying," Caroline said. "It's rude."

Reznick grinned. "The housekeeper said to make ourselves at home."

"I know, but seriously?"

"Big property. I've got a small place up in Maine, tiny by comparison, overlooking a sandy cove. But this is something else. Must be worth a few million. He's doing okay for himself, clearly."

"I guess."

"You liked my place up in Rockland?"

"I liked your house and Rockland a lot. Some cool bars. What did you think of my neck of the woods?"

"Loved it. Like this place too, got to be one of the nicest beach towns. But I think I prefer your place up in Madison. Very peaceful. You've got a couple of properties, don't you?"

"I'm very fortunate. I have three homes . . . Vermont, Georgetown, and Madison."

Reznick whistled, impressed.

Caroline blushed. "Not that I need all that."

"Nonetheless, that's a nice property portfolio."

"I do use them all. Georgetown is handy when I'm working in DC. Madison is where my heart is."

"Vermont is the old family home?"

"I was thinking about selling it, actually."

"Really? Why don't you?"

"I don't know. Sentiment, I guess. Childhood home and all that. I think if I sold it, a little piece of my past would die, too. My memories of my father are there."

Reznick and Caroline made small talk on a range of topics to pass the time. The stifling August weather, the state of America, the merits of vacationing at home or abroad. It circled around to Caroline asking about Reznick's plans for the future.

"My plans? I don't really make plans."

"Not even for vacations?"

"I don't think that far ahead."

"Why not?"

"The nature of my work. I take each day as it comes. I'm an easy-come, easy-go sort of guy."

Caroline laughed, "Yeah right."

"I don't like to be on a timetable. A schedule. That kind of thing."

"You don't talk much about your daughter. Tell me, how is she? She works overseas, right?"

Reznick was reluctant to go into too much detail as Lauren was working at the CIA station in Jakarta. "I miss her. But we FaceTime once a month. She's based a long way from home and it's tough. But she's a good kid. I love her."

"I'd like to meet her one day," Caroline said.

"You will. Just never seem to find the time for us to see each other regularly. We never seem to be in the same place at the same time."

"I get it." Caroline looked at her watch. "Andrew shouldn't be long now. Ten, maybe fifteen minutes."

Reznick smiled reassuringly at her, but he sensed that it wasn't Andrew Stone they were waiting for.

Twenty-Nine

The minutes dragged and dragged. Reznick half expected CIA goons to turn up to interview Stone. He paced the living room. The fifteen or twenty minutes had long passed. He sensed something was wrong. He sensed danger.

Reznick checked his watch. "That's forty minutes after he was meant to be here. And we haven't heard a thing."

Caroline shrugged. "Andrew's brother is in the hospital, Jon. Cut him some slack. Stuff like that happens. People are delayed. Relax. He's probably just on his way to pick up the third source. I expect he'll be back any minute."

Reznick shook his head. He wasn't convinced. Stone hadn't even taken the time to send a text or call Caroline to let them know when he would return. Military men hated tardiness. He would always be on the clock. The doubt gnawed at Reznick. But he didn't dare confide his fears to Caroline.

When a further hour passed and there was still no sign of Stone, not even a text, Reznick concluded that Stone was not actually going to return home that evening, which left him questioning why they had been instructed to come in the first place.

"This is bullshit," he said. "Something's wrong. Why don't you call his number? Otherwise, we should get out of here."

"I feel awkward."

"Do you want me to do it?"

Caroline picked up her cell phone and called Stone's cell. She left a message saying she and Reznick were at Andrew's house and that she hoped his brother was doing okay. She ended the message with "Give me a call when you're on your way."

Reznick felt agitated. "I think we should get out of here and come back tomorrow. Check in at a nearby hotel. Let's do that."

"Just be patient. You've met Andrew. He's a good guy. He'll turn up." But she began to look anxious. "We're safe in his house. What could happen to us?"

Reznick's gaze wandered around the beautiful living room of this beachfront home. He needed to come clean about his fears. "We need to get out of here."

"What's gotten into you?"

"I think we should leave. Text him and say we'll be back tomorrow."

Caroline looked at Reznick. "We came all this way."

Reznick shook his head.

"You seem uptight all of a sudden. Wound up."

Reznick tried to brush off her concerns. "I tend to get caught up in my work. Assignments. Overseas stuff."

Caroline shrugged. "So where have you been?"

"Here, there, everywhere. Europe, Middle East. Jumping around."

"Give me something."

"What?"

"A snippet of what you were doing. I won't tell."

"Classified."

"Give me something, Jon. Come on."

"This is off the record, right?"

"No notes. Cross my heart."

"Stephen Leahy's father was best friends with a guy called William Crenshaw."

"I remember reading about Crenshaw. Some accident in Bahrain or something."

Reznick nodded. "*Or something* . . . is more accurate."

"I see. You were involved in that?"

"And a good friend of mine from Scotland. William Crenshaw was Stephen Leahy's godfather. Stephen's father was tight with Crenshaw: family friend."

"How do you know?"

"Leahy told me in the hospital. He knew that Crenshaw had been, shall we say, neutralized."

"How did he feel about that?"

"He understood the rationale. Crenshaw was a traitor."

Caroline was quiet, thoughtful.

"Don't even go there."

"What?"

"I can hear the cogs in your brain turning."

"It's interesting."

Reznick looked at his watch for the umpteenth time. "I'm sick of this. How long have we been sitting here? It's ridiculous. Let's move."

"Three hours twenty-one minutes. What do you suggest?"

"I say we head to a nearby hotel, have a drink, and then come back in the morning. Andrew will hopefully be back by then."

Caroline glanced back out the window. "That does make more sense. The problem is that he said he'd be here. He's a military guy, like you. I hope nothing happened to his brother."

"Even under those circumstances, I would have imagined that Andrew would have called or had someone call on his behalf. He has your number. He could have texted you to say he was running very late, apologized, that kind of thing. Maybe arrange a different day to meet up."

"The maid explained that he had to rush out at short notice."

Reznick's stomach tightened. He was wired. He pulled out his cell phone.

"What are you doing?"

"I'm going to call Andrew at the hospital."

"I think this is a bit intrusive. Jon, please, I'm not sure that's a good idea."

"We're in his goddamn house. He isn't home. You can't get much more intrusive than that."

Reznick's mind was racing. He knew in his bones something was wrong. The whole thing seemed off. He dialed the number for the hospital switchboard.

"Atlantic General Hospital, how may I direct your call?" A cheery woman's voice.

"Good evening," Reznick said. "I'm trying to find out what room Hunter Stone is in. I'm trying to contact his brother, Andrew Stone, who's there visiting Hunter. It's an urgent matter."

"Hold please . . ."

Caroline said, "Jon, I feel really uncomfortable with this."

The switchboard lady came back on the line. "Did you say Hunter Stone? Standard spelling?"

"Correct."

"We have nobody by that name being treated in the hospital."

"Hang on, no one by that name? Are you sure? No one at all called Stone in the hospital?"

"Positive. We have no patient registered under that name in our hospital. No record of him."

"Could you please check again. Has he maybe been transferred?"

The sound of tapping on a keyboard. "No, I'm sorry, sir. I'm also not showing any transfers from the past seventy-two hours for anyone under that name. Do you want me to page someone over the intercom?”

Reznick felt the room lurch. He now had confirmation that something was very wrong. “Thank you, I appreciate your time.” He ended the call. “This is not good.”

Caroline shook her head. “Maybe he’s been transferred to another hospital.”

“No, she checked.”

“I don’t know, maybe patient confidentiality? Maybe he was listed under a false name, just like Stephen Leahy. Besides, the maid was clear that Andrew had gone to the hospital with his sister-in-law.”

Reznick called Trevelle.

“Hey, Jon, hanging out at the beach, huh? Very romantic.”

Reznick ignored the banter. “Can you track a number for me? It’s urgent.”

“Sure.”

Reznick gave him General Stone’s cell phone number and the details about his brother. “I don’t know if Hunter has been transferred to a different hospital, if they’re not allowed to share such information. I’m guessing that’s what’s happened.”

There was a pause as Trevelle trawled the hospital databases. “He’s definitely not at Atlantic General.”

“I know. What about hospitals in DC?”

“Nothing for the name Hunter Stone has come up so far. Drawing a blank.” Then: “That’s strange.”

“What is?”

“I’ve got Stone’s file at the Department of Defense up on my screen. This is really fucking strange.”

“Spit it out!”

“There is no Hunter Stone. Andrew Stone is an only child.”

“Stepbrother maybe?”

"Nope."

Reznick got to his feet and relayed the news to Caroline. "Okay Trevelle, listen carefully, here's what I want you to do. First, try and get a GPS fix on Andrew Stone's cellphone. Real-time location."

He waited while Trevelle did his thing.

"Got it."

"Where is he?"

"Andrew Stone, according to his cell phone, is in Poland."

"Are you fucking with me?"

"Nope. He's visiting a NATO missile defense site in Redzikowo."

"Andrew Stone? Same date of birth, Andrew Stone?"

"I've checked, I've verified. I also just checked surveillance footage at the base. Facial recognition confirms it's him. And yes, he has his personal cell phone with him. One more thing. The woman you thought was the housekeeper?"

"What about her?"

"She's an imposter. I ran a photo from Stone's internal home surveillance system through facial recognition. Her real name is Carmen Riaz—intelligence operative who works for a shadowy Arlington-based private security firm with links to the CIA."

It was happening. Red flags everywhere. This was a trap. Reznick cursed that he had gotten suckered. But first he needed to figure out what to do. *Shit!*

"Jon, what the hell is going on?"

"I don't know, but I'm sure as hell going to find out."

Reznick ended the call.

"Jon, what's happening?"

"We've got a problem. Listen, General Stone told you to come here, right?"

"He texted me before we left."

Reznick squinted out the windows toward the ocean. He could see what was going on, clear as day. A fake text. *They* must have known Stone was out of the country.

He focused on the here and now. He switched off the living room lights.

"What are you doing, Jon? You're scaring me."

"Give me a minute."

Reznick bounded up the stairs, fueled by adrenaline. He crept into a dark, upstairs back bedroom and peered out the small circular window. The moonlight cast a pale glow on the huge rear garden.

His eye caught a glint from the woods that fringed the property. The light from the moon had caught the slight movement of a rifle.

Reznick stared and stared. Then he saw them. Silhouetted men crouched in the woods, armed, watching and waiting. But what were they waiting for?

Thirty

Edward Black sat in a command vehicle four hundred yards to the rear of the beachfront property, in a clearing in the woods, watching a monitor. Operatives using night-vision goggles—including Chico, whose brother had been killed in Miami—were positioned farther forward, within striking distance of the house, watching and waiting for his order. The algae-green footage showed the house lights being turned off, plunging it into darkness.

John Crespo, a wingman for Black, was watching the same monitor, headphones on, shaking his head. "Fuck."

Black turned to him. "What do you think?"

"Either Reznick has decided to have an early night with his author friend, or he knows something's wrong. Maybe he has a visual on our guys and he's cloaking the house in darkness to make it difficult."

Black seethed. "There isn't a fucking light on anywhere in the house. Nothing. I think he figured it out."

"You going to call it?" Crespo said.

Black looked at the monitor. "Tango-Delta-Echo-Papa." The call sign.

"It's a go," Crespo said, rubbing his hands. "We've got him in the kill zone."

Thirty-One

Reznick bounded down the stairs and into the living room. "On the ground!" he hissed to Caroline. "Keep low."

Caroline complied, lying flat on her stomach. "What's going on?"

"Don't move! We've got company." He prowled around the dark first floor of Stone's home, locking and bolting all the doors to the front and rear of the house. Then he returned to the living room.

"Jon, what's going on? Who's there?"

"Just listen to me. We've been set up. There's a team outside. But we'll figure this out."

Caroline began to shake. "What are you talking about? What does that mean?"

"It means you need to do exactly what I tell you."

"I'm scared."

"It's okay, this is what I do. In the meantime, you need to focus. Got it?"

"Yes, got it."

Reznick grabbed her hand and they ran upstairs. He headed straight for the safe room where the locked gun cabinet was located. "Shine your cell phone light on the lock."

It was a standard-issue mortise lock, nothing special. It might have been twenty or thirty years old.

Caroline shone the light so Reznick could get a better look. "That's good, thanks."

Reznick took a Swiss Army knife out of his back pocket. He pulled out the smallest and thinnest blade. It was as thin as a wire. He inserted the tiny knife into the keyhole, crouched low, and pressed his ear to the safe's door. He closed his eyes, twisting, listening for a sound in the locking region. He twisted to the right. He felt some resistance. He turned the knife counterclockwise. There was the sound of a faint click. He pulled the gun cabinet open.

Inside were four semiautomatic rifles. He grabbed two and handed one to Caroline. Then he grabbed two boxes of ammo, one for each of them. He inserted a fresh magazine into his rifle. Locked and loaded.

Caroline did the same. He knew she was experienced handling firearms. She'd told him when they first met that her father had taught her how to shoot. She expertly slid in the magazine in a matter of seconds. "What's the plan?"

"You'll be fine in here. It will be on a timer lock when it's shut."

Caroline shone the light of her phone around the safe room. It had a bed, a chair, and a desk, and was stocked with a flashlight, blankets, a first-aid kit, water, packaged food, and a simple portable toilet. "Are you kidding me? No way!"

Reznick grabbed the flashlight and handed it to her.

"Jon, I'm not going to be locked in a safe room."

"Yes, you are. Do not argue." He grabbed her arm and firmly led her to the opposite side of the room.

"Are you going to leave me here?"

"If you want to survive then shut up and do what you're told!"

"Jon, please don't! I'm scared. Why are you doing this?"

"When I shut the door behind you, it will be on a timer. You've got your phone. You've got the rifle. I know how these things work. Reinforced steel. One-hour minimum when it's shut."

"Jon, I'm scared of enclosed spaces. Besides, what if they blast it open?"

"You're armed."

"They've been sent to kill us?"

Outside, the sound of a branch cracking. "Inside! Now!" he hissed.

Caroline stepped farther into the darkened room, clutching the rifle, flashlight in hand, beginning to sob. "Jon, don't leave me!"

"You will be safer in here. Trust me."

"Jon, please."

"Just do it!"

"What about you?"

"Forget about me. We've walked into a trap. We need to think. We need to be brave now."

"Jon . . ."

"What?"

"Don't leave me here."

"Just trust me. I promise, I'll come back for you." Then Reznick pulled the door shut, the locking mechanism clicking loudly. She was inside. Safe. At least for now.

Reznick's head had been awash with strategies to deal with this situation. A plan was already forming in his head. He headed up the wrought-iron staircase to the attic and locked the door behind him. Pale moonlight streamed through the skylight. He texted Trevelle. *Emergency! Call 911. Say there's a home invasion underway at Andrew Stone's address. Now!!!*

Reznick stood and listened. His gaze drawn to the skylight. He put away his phone. He was armed. He was ready. His mind had switched to kill mode.

Thirty-Two

Edward Black had joined the western flank of the group crouched in the woods. Armed with semiautomatics, positioned maybe one hundred yards from the rear of the house, the group were mostly still hidden by the trees and bushes. He watched as one of the masked operatives moved a few yards forward, stopped, crouched, and aimed his M39 rifle at a first-floor window. A couple of muffled shots rang out.

He watched as the incendiary ammo bullets crashed through the glass, exploding on impact. Flames ignited, quickly engulfing the kitchen and spreading to the living room. A series of mini-explosions erupted across the first floor and more windows blew out.

Chico raked the back doors with rapid-fire shots. The fire spread quickly, consuming the corners of the building's first floor, the last of the windows exploding as the flames took serious hold.

Black watched and waited, plotting out what the reaction would be. He had Reznick and Sullivan cornered. He had expected that they would try to make a run for it as the smoke overpowered them. Otherwise they would be burned alive, slowly. He figured Reznick would want to go down guns blazing. He wasn't the type of man to go quietly.

Black felt relaxed. His mood was strangely euphoric. He finally had the fucker. He had suckered the bastard, luring him to Stone's beachfront home. His men had them surrounded. There was no way out. At least not alive.

He watched as the operative with the M39 rifle took aim again and laid down a fresh burst of incendiary fire. The second-floor windows were now blown out, fires erupting, trapping the occupants. He knew his team was being methodical. He had his targets in a viselike grip. And he wasn't going to let them go. A slow death would be payback for the deaths of his three operatives, and the serious injuries sustained by two of his men in the diner bathroom.

Reznick was going to pay with his life.

Black watched as more fires erupted upstairs, windows cracking and then exploding as the inferno consumed the property. The whole of the first and second floors was engulfed in a firestorm. More flames ate the exterior, spreading thick, black smoke.

Black signaled for the launch of phase two. Tear-gas grenades were fired in through the broken windows. His men had pulled on their gas masks, night-vision goggles, and fireproof clothing. He signaled for them to advance out of the woods and head through the expansive rear garden. Choking black smoke, fire, and tear gas were now spreading through the house. He could only imagine the hellish death Reznick and the journalist would experience.

Black afforded himself a smile at the thought.

The seconds ticked by. The flames were exploding through the upper windows now, licking the ivy at the side of the house, incinerating everything in their path.

Black and the support team watched and waited for Reznick to emerge from the inferno.

Thirty-Three

The smoke filled the upper reaches of the house, wafting underneath every closed door. Reznick, choking and coughing, dragged the table and chair across the floor of the attic. He placed them directly beneath the skylight.

He screwed up his eyes as smoke stung them. He stepped onto the chair and then up onto the table. His semiautomatic rifle, locked and loaded, was strapped across his shoulder. Black smoke seeped through the floorboards and under the door. He knew there would inevitably be an air filtration system in the safe room, but he prayed Caroline would be able to hold on. *Fuck.*

He looked up at the skylight.

He wasn't panicking. Quite the opposite. He felt strangely calm. He knew the importance of focus, of making the right decision. *Slow is smooth, smooth is fast.* The Marines dictum, drilled into him.

He looked up at the skylight and jumped, grabbing hold of the wooden frame. He pulled himself up and squeezed himself out of the narrow window.

Reznick crouched and moved slowly across the sloping roof. He crawled to the left side, the modernist sloping design shielding him from sight of the rear garden. Black smoke and the acrid smell of tear gas drifted out of the open skylight into the sultry night air.

He suppressed the urge to cough and retch. He lay on his belly and carefully crawled up the steep incline, a mental picture in his head of the layout of the back garden and the rear of the building. The gas wafted toward him, stinging his eyes, burning his throat. He felt the heavy weight of responsibility knowing that Caroline was hunkered down in the safe room. He needed to figure this out. And fast.

He gritted his teeth, resisting the temptation to turn back. His eyes watered as he peered over the highest point of the roof.

He spotted two, six-man teams clad in black, wearing gas masks and goggles, emerging from either side of the woods, closing in on the back of the house.

Reznick ducked down and crawled farther across the far side of the roof, rifle tight against his shoulder. He needed a better line of sight. He was maybe ten yards away from the skylight. He pulled himself up the steep roof and peered over the edge again, one final time. The masked men had stopped, assessing the situation.

Reznick adjusted his position. He lay spreadeagled on the roof, peering through the scope. The men were in the crosshairs. He felt his finger on the trigger. Held his breath. Then he opened fire, raking the group on the right with rapid gunfire, wiping out the six men in seconds. Gunfire pinged across the roof. Someone had spotted him. Hand signals pointed in his direction. *Fuck.*

He fast-crawled farther along the other side of the roof and peered over from twenty feet away in the other direction.

He had the other group in his crosshairs now. He watched the lead operative in the group run toward the house. He shot him through the chest. The rest of the group began to run as well, panicking. He opened fire again. The five scattered but were mown down in seconds.

Twelve down, how many more to go?

Bullets whizzed by his head. It wasn't over.

Reznick sized up how many more he would have to deal with. He commando-crawled farther to his left, peeking through the thick, black smoke billowing from the windows of the house.

A four-man formation emerged from the woods at the side.

Reznick quickly headed back to the other end of the roof. He clambered down a drainpipe, concealed by the black smoke as well as the thick bushes and shrubbery.

Reznick stayed low before laying himself flat. He spotted a trio of men in the garden. They emerged through a thicket, firing wildly up at the roof. He composed himself, smoke filling his view. He squeezed the trigger. One-two-three! All dead. Blood seeped into the grass, streaming onto the concrete patio. Smoke and flames erupted from a nearby window.

Reznick dashed through a side gate at a crouch, keeping low. A spectral, silhouetted figure stood on the edge of the woods. A solitary figure, rifle in hand.

He watched and waited. In the distance, he heard the sound of a woman's screaming. It was Caroline.

Reznick pushed the thought to one side. He remained vigilant, waiting for the figure to make a move. None came. It was just the man. Alone.

"You're fucked, Reznick!" the man shouted. "Totally fucked. Give up while you still can."

Reznick peered through the crosshairs. The silhouetted figure was clad in black, a ski mask covering his face.

"You're surrounded. Just surrender! Do you hear me?"

Reznick aligned the reticles in the eyepiece. He took aim and fired a shot straight through the man's chest. The man staggered forward. He tried to raise his rifle.

Reznick drilled a second shot through the man's head. He collapsed, twitching for a few moments before he went lifeless.

Reznick remained crouched, hidden from sight, as he waited for others to take aim.

He surveyed the scene. Multiple bodies strewn all over the garden. He heard his heart beating. He was breathing hard.

In the distance, more screaming. Caroline.

Reznick wanted to break cover. But he stayed focused. The sound of sirens. Smoke spilling from the house. In his peripheral vision he saw movement. He spun around. Five cops approached, shotguns drawn.

"Police! Drop your weapon!"

Reznick complied as smoke billowed through the windows, doors, and roof of General Stone's house, out the skylight, into the inky-black moonlit sky.

The cops fanned out. "Hands on your head, motherfucker!"

Reznick placed his hands on his head. "Don't shoot."

A crew of firefighters wearing breathing masks and holding water hoses came into sight with ladders, axes, and flashlights.

Reznick shouted, "There is a woman in a second-floor safe room. Timer activated. Get her out of there, now!"

A cop walked toward him, long gun drawn. "On your knees!"

Reznick dropped to his knees. "Did you hear what I said?"

The cop signaled for a fire chief and directed him and his men back around the front of the house, away from the carnage at the rear.

"You need to find her!" Reznick shouted above the sirens. "Get her out!"

A couple of firefighters with axes burst through the ground-floor rear door, while three others smashed their way through a bullet-peppered patio door as the water hoses burst into life. The men disappeared through the thick black smoke still billowing out, flames bursting from the second-floor windows.

He shouted up at the cop. "There's a woman still in there! You need to get her out!"

"Fire crews are going in after her." The cop looked around at the group of dead operatives, dressed in black. "What the actual fuck? What happened here tonight?"

Reznick coughed and spat out some black gunge which had clogged up his lungs. "Shit."

"Who are those guys?"

"I don't actually know."

"Who are you?"

"Reznick. Jon Reznick."

"Did you do all this?"

Reznick shook his head, reluctant to get into a big discussion at that moment. He just wanted Caroline Sullivan safe.

A gruff shout from inside. "Control panel located. Safe room timer deactivated."

The cop shook his head. "What the fuck did you do? You kill them all?"

Reznick bowed his head as water lines were brought around to the rear of the property. The high-pressure hoses blasted water through the windows, up onto the burning roof, eventually dousing the fires.

"You need to find her! She's in there!"

The cop trained his gun close to Reznick. "Who is she? Your girlfriend?"

"She's a friend."

"Who do you work for?"

Reznick bowed his head, hoping and praying to see Caroline Sullivan alive. The seconds dragged by. Then a few excruciating minutes elapsed. Still nothing.

Suddenly, a flurry of activity.

She came out of the house with a couple of firefighters, her face blackened, coughing uncontrollably, sobbing, but having escaped from the smoking ruins. She fell to her knees beside Reznick and sobbed. "Jon, you bastard!"

"I'm sorry."

Caroline was coughing and spluttering, on her knees, struggling to breathe.

"Don't ever do that again!" she snarled. "You hear me?"

"I hear you."

"Please don't leave me again. I was scared."

Reznick hugged her tight. "I won't leave you. I'm here. It's over."

The cop with the gun trained on them shook his head. He turned and looked around the garden. At the dead bodies of more than a dozen men clad in military fatigues and masks lying in the huge back garden, and at the fringes of the woods, drenched in blood. "What happened here? Can someone please answer me?"

Reznick hugged Caroline tight as she sobbed and coughed, holding onto him as if for dear life.

Thirty-Four

The hours that followed were surreal. Reznick and Caroline were handcuffed, and placed in the back of a cop car.

Caroline was still coughing up black phlegm, spluttering and struggling to breathe. "You bastard. Why did you lock me in there?"

"It was the choice I made. I'm glad you're alive."

The police officer in the passenger seat turned and faced her. "You okay?"

"No, I'm not okay."

"Sorry, just asking."

Caroline coughed for a few more minutes, hacking up more black sludge, spitting on the floor of the car. The cop unscrewed a small bottle of water and handed it to her. "Drink that. You're suffering from acute smoke inhalation, lady."

Caroline grabbed the bottle with a shaky left hand and gulped down the water. She coughed and spluttered for a few more moments before she finally seemed to breathe easier. She handed the empty plastic bottle back to the officer. "Appreciate that, thanks."

The cop faced the front as they accelerated away from the beachfront house.

Reznick said, "I'm sorry about everything, Caroline. I'm sorry for reaching out to you. I never wanted any of this for you."

Caroline blinked away tears. "And you decided to lock me in a safe room behind a thick steel door? While the place burned down around me? It was like you wanted to get rid of me."

"Don't be so dramatic. It was either that or you would have been up on the roof. I got lucky, I didn't get hit. But trust me, that was no picnic either."

"You think it was a piece of cake being stuck in that room as smoke seeped in, inch by inch, even with a filtration system? I'm lucky to be alive."

"We made it out."

"Are you for real, Jon?"

"What can I tell you? Just another day at the office, right?"

Caroline bowed her head and began to sob. "I can't believe what just happened."

The cop turned around and focused on Reznick. "So who are you, man? You military? Ex-military?"

Reznick shrugged, not wanting to get drawn into conversation.

"You kill all those guys yourself? I mean, it couldn't have been anyone else. There was only you."

Reznick gazed out of the rear window.

"I asked you a question, son."

Reznick turned and looked at the cop, who was chewing gum, giggling like crazy.

"I know you did. I need to see a lawyer. And so does my friend."

"Before you see a lawyer, tough guy, you both need to get checked out by a doctor."

The hospital did a series of heart and lung function tests before Reznick was given the all-clear. Caroline Sullivan's condition presented more concern for the doctors. The oxygen levels in her blood had plummeted. A mask was placed over her mouth and nose and the doctors administered drugs to help her.

Reznick was still handcuffed as he sat at her bedside, cops flanking him, prepared in case he tried to make a run for it. He remained by her side, occasionally holding her blackened hand. He squeezed it three times. She never reciprocated.

He felt helpless as the doctors monitored her levels. Then she fell into a deep sleep.

Reznick was handed a cup of coffee by one of the officers.

The cop said, "You mind me asking you a question, Reznick?"

"What?"

"Why were you in the house?"

Reznick shook his head. "It's a long story, pal."

"Do you know whose house that is? Is the owner a friend of yours?"

Reznick sipped his scalding hot coffee, glad to get some caffeine in his system. "He's not a friend. But I know him."

"Do you work for the homeowner? Are you his security?"

Reznick said nothing.

The cop didn't push it any further. His radio crackled to life telling him that Forensics had arrived at the beachfront scene. "We're going to leave your friend Ms. Sullivan to recover here in the hospital. You, my friend, are going for a ride." He uncuffed Reznick.

Reznick got to his feet and finished his coffee before he was escorted outside. Three SUVs were waiting. Reznick was bunded into the back of a US Marshals Service truck. Then he was transferred to Chesapeake detention facility. He was booked in and placed in solitary confinement.

The cell door clanked shut. Reznick was alone in the six-by-nine. With only his thoughts to distract him, he began pacing the room, head raging with the blizzard of events from the night before.

Thirty-Five

The hours dragged, then turned into days. It dawned on Reznick that he wasn't going to see the outside world for a while. Night moved into day. Day became night again. He needed to know how Caroline was doing. He hoped and prayed she was recovering. But the smoke inhalation had been bad. He got no updates, only an occasional meal.

Reznick's mood was low. He figured he was just going to have to get used to this. He was locked up twenty-three hours a day. He got one hour of regulated exercise in a yard, all by himself. He exercised furiously with weights, medicine balls, and laps on an outdoor track. Sweating and straining every sinew as he used his time to stay fit, sharp. And all the while, armed guards watched him.

When he was returned to his windowless cell, Reznick did hundreds and hundreds of push-ups to keep himself strong and alert. Day after day, he asked repeatedly for a lawyer. But none came.

Reznick knew that isolation was just a basic psychological strategy to enhance the feeling of powerlessness. He knew all that stuff. He had been trained in all forms of warfare. But then again, maybe they were just trying to figure out what the hell to do with him.

Six long days later, just before dawn, the warden arrived outside his cell flanked by four guards.

"FBI are waiting for you."

"What do they want?"

"I don't give a shit. You're out of here."

The interrogation room was on the first floor of the FBI headquarters in DC, the Hoover Building. Two agents—a man and a woman—sat opposite him, smiling. The man wore a well-cut navy suit, white shirt, pale blue tie, shiny black Oxfords. The woman wore a dark brown pantsuit, pale pink blouse, low heels. The agents had legal pads, pens, and folders stuffed with documents.

The woman looked up from her papers. "My name is FBI Special Agent Fiona Carrington," she said. "You are Jon Reznick?"

"I am."

"Before we start, can we get you anything, Jon? Tea, coffee, sandwiches?"

"I'm good. Thanks."

The male Fed introduced himself. "My name is Mark Cortez. I'm a special agent at the FBI's National Security Branch. Primarily concerned with counterintelligence along with Ms. Carrington."

Reznick nodded.

"Do you understand what I just said?" Cortez said.

"I do."

Carrington said, "I will be taking contemporaneous notes throughout."

Reznick laughed quietly.

"I'm sorry. Do you find that funny, Mr. Reznick?"

He knew the drill. He understood the pointless, petty little techniques and strategies deployed by the FBI. "Not particularly."

Carrington wrote down the date, time, and location of the interview.

Cortez cleared his throat. "You don't have any problems with us taking notes?"

"None at all," Reznick said. "Special Agents Cortez and Carrington, I respectfully request to see a lawyer to represent me."

"All in good time," Cortez said. "I believe that an eminent national security attorney, based here in DC, is already in the building."

Reznick shrugged. "I wonder how that happened so quickly?"

"I believe an associate of yours reached out to them. So you will be well represented."

Reznick knew it had to be Trevelle looking out for him. "I'd like to talk to my lawyer now, before we proceed. If that's alright with you guys. Unless that's a problem?"

Carrington gave a patronizing smirk. "Not a problem at all, Jon. But all in good time. You don't mind me calling you Jon, do you?"

Reznick realized he was about to be put through the mill. He wouldn't be seeing his lawyer for a while. "Whatever works for you."

Carrington said, "I want to talk about your nighttime visit to a beachfront property in Maryland. Quite an evening. So, we have some pressing questions we need to ask you. I'm assuming you'll answer a few simple questions for us?"

"I'm listening."

"Do you know whose home it was that you illegally broke into on the beach? Were you aware of the identity of the owner?"

Reznick thinned his lips at her.

Carrington scribbled a *no comment*.

"Agent Carrington, I never said *no comment*. I never said anything. Your notes are inaccurate already."

Carrington flushed the color of her blouse. "You have refused to comment so that is *no comment*."

"That's misleading. With respect, a third party might assume I said *no comment*."

Carrington took a few moments to compose herself. "I think you're being pedantic."

"I'm asking for accuracy."

"Getting back to the question," she said, deftly changing the subject, "I see I'm going to have to ask you again. So, let's start over. Do you know who owns the property?"

Reznick sat in silence.

Carrington again wrote down *no comment*.

"You keep on reinforcing those inaccuracies, Carrington. False narratives."

Cortez was holding his pen tight, angry and riled up already. "What if I told you that a retired general lived there?"

Reznick shifted in his seat.

Carrington again wrote *no comment*.

Reznick shook his head. "I'm pointing out, once again, that Special Agent Carrington's notes are inaccurate and prone to misinterpretation. But you must know that, right?"

"We're the FBI," Carrington said. "This is how we do things."

Reznick grinned and shook his head.

"This is not a comedy show, Jon. People died at that property. We need answers."

"Are you recording this?"

"No, we are not. We take contemporaneous notes."

Reznick shook his head again.

"Can I ask why you're shaking your head, Mr. Reznick?"

"Your so-called notetaking provides a potentially false narrative. The same discredited techniques used as far back as the J. Edgar Hoover days, right?"

Cortez fizzed with fury, eyes dark, smoldering. "You're being obstructionist."

Reznick said nothing.

Carrington said, "I think we've gotten off on the wrong foot. I just want to say that we want to try and understand what happened out at the beach house. It's been nearly a week since the events."

"What took you so long? Why not interview me in the hours after it happened?"

Cortez gave him a tight smile. "We've been doing some preparation. That takes time."

Reznick folded his arms.

"Jon, can you try and be helpful? We're asking simple questions. What were you doing out there? Did you break in? Were you invited in? Who invited you in?"

"With respect, I'm asking, one more time, to see my lawyer."

Cortez slammed his hand on the desk, making Carrington wince. "Men are dead. Killed by you. You need to cut the bullshit and start answering questions."

Reznick sighed. "Here we go."

"You are in deep, deep trouble, Jon," Carrington said, "in case you hadn't realized that. National security issues were front and center in our preliminary discussions once we reached out to the wider US intelligence community. We believe, in addition to these unexplained killings at the home of a retired official within the Pentagon, that you have committed multiple felonies under the Espionage Act. And we want answers. The ramifications can't be overstated. So, you need to get with the program and tell us what the hell happened. If you don't, we can't help you."

Reznick sat in silence.

Cortez leaned forward, teeth clenched. "The act is written so that obtaining or transmitting information pertaining to national defense, if it could help a foreign nation, constitutes a criminal offense. So, let's cut the bull and you can explain to us the meeting you had at a hospital in Maryland. A meeting with a former CIA officer. You want to talk about that?"

Reznick chuckled.

"You think this is a laughing matter?" Cortez said. "Do you deny you were there?"

Reznick said nothing.

"You need to be upfront with us and let us know how this whole situation began and developed. Maybe we can help you. I can't make any promises. But you need to start cooperating. You have failed to do so far. And I don't know for the life of me why. We're trying to understand what happened."

Carrington took out a grainy black-and-white photo and placed it front of Reznick. It showed Reznick meeting up with Martha Meyerstein in Lafayette Square in Washington, DC. "This was taken a couple of weeks ago. Help me understand what this photo relates to. Tell me about your meeting with this woman. I believe you know her very well."

Reznick remained silent.

Carrington said, "Let me help you out, Jon. Former Deputy Director of the FBI. Is she in on this scheme too? And if you're waiting to speak to your lawyer, don't hold your breath. We sent him away."

Reznick shrugged.

"So it's just us, trying to figure things out," Carrington said. "You worked with her for many years, Jon. Strange relationship between a man like you, a trained killer, and an ex-deputy director of the FBI. No one seems to understand what that relationship was. Was there a sexual element?"

Reznick said nothing.

"I've heard anecdotally that there was a lot of discontent within the FBI's upper echelons about your unconventional friendship. You need to decide if you want to obstruct this investigation or help it. Were you working for her? We can help you, Jon. But you need to be upfront with us."

Cortez wrote down the words *remains silent in his seat*. He reached into a folder and pulled out another black-and-white photograph, sliding it in front of Reznick. It showed Reznick sitting on the terrace in Georgetown alongside Caroline Sullivan and General Andrew Stone. "Do you know this man?"

Reznick cleared his throat.

"Is Andrew Stone part of this illegal activity? He would know as well as anyone on the planet the repercussions of violating the Espionage Act. How long have you known him? Has he been leaking intelligence to you and Sullivan? Was he also having a relationship with Meyerstein?"

Reznick shifted in his seat.

Carrington interjected. "Cat got your tongue, Jon? This photograph of the three of you was taken by a drone, if you were wondering. You wouldn't have noticed. Miniature drone, most powerful in America. We caught you, Jon. All three of you together. Conspiring. You are in a heap of trouble. You keep up this silent act, and we won't be able to help you."

Cortez pointed his finger at the photo of Reznick with Meyerstein. He then jabbed his finger toward the photo of Reznick with Stone and Caroline on the terrace. "I'm going to cut to the chase. You need to start answering our questions. Who are you spying for? Have you been contracted by a foreign power? Maybe in the Middle East?"

"I might be able to help you," Reznick said.

Carrington clapped. "Now we're getting somewhere."

"Just as soon as I see my lawyer."

Cortez's eyes became hooded. "You turn up at the door of General Andrew Stone, out on the beach, yes or no? Simple question."

Reznick remained silent.

"Why aren't you answering, Jon? Were you told by your handlers to stay quiet? Tough it out? We'll find out, Jon. We'll trawl through your life. The lives of your friends. The lives of anyone you know."

Reznick zoned out.

"You broke in with your journalist pal Caroline Sullivan. Why would you do that, Jon? I can't get that to make sense. And what were you going to do? Were you going to share more intel with Andrew Stone? Were you planning to put pressure on him? Blackmail him? Were you going to kill him? Maybe that's what it was."

Reznick compartmentalized the barrage of questions. He flexed and unflexed his hands, releasing the tension. They'd been trained to interrogate; he'd been trained to evade.

Carrington sighed. "Help us out, Jon. Don't do the silent thing. This is way too serious. You see, Jon, a few hours after you broke in, there were dead guys all over the lawn. You gunned them down in cold blood. You'll go down for the rest of your natural life. If you're lucky. But we can help you help yourself. Just talk to us. You know what the supermax penitentiaries are like? Not good, let me tell you."

Reznick folded his arms.

"Who sent you to that property?"

Reznick shrugged, relishing the irritation on their faces.

Cortez leaned forward. "I believe you're working for a foreign government. Why on earth else would you be sharing classified intel? The Espionage Act was used to prosecute Edward Snowden. Then he fled to Russia. Is that what this is about, Jon? Are you a Russian spy? You work for Venezuela? Cuba? How much did they pay you, Jon?"

Reznick felt his blood boil, the accusations outrageous and disgusting. He knew they were intended to provoke him to say something. Incriminate himself. But instead of responding, he just sat and stared at the pair of red-faced agents, working themselves up into a synthetic anger.

Carrington jabbed his finger in Reznick's face. "The lawyer is not coming to help you, Jon. No one is coming to help you. You'll have to help yourself. Tell us who you're working for. We just need an explanation, that's all we're looking for."

Cortez said, "I never imagined you as a spy, Jon. How did it come to this?"

Reznick shifted again in his seat. The barbs, the accusations, were beyond hurtful. He was many things, but he was no traitor. He loved his country. He had fought for his country. And he would die for his country.

"You know the name Aldrich Ames, Jon? Name mean something to you? I bet it does. He used to work at the highest levels of the CIA. But we got him in the end, spying for the KGB. We always track them down. You'll be no exception. Everyone leaves a digital trail these days. You'll be no different. I can't believe you stooped so low, Jon. A common traitor."

Reznick felt himself getting closer to snapping. His one real weakness was being accused of things which were patently untrue. The theory that he was working for a foreign government, and especially the Russian government, was insulting. He wasn't a traitor. He was a patriot. To his bones.

Carrington seemed to sense Reznick's bristling anger. "Was this ideological, Jon? Did you decide that you wanted to help the Russians? Maybe it was money. We've been looking at your bank balances and they are very, very healthy. Where did all that money come from?"

Reznick speculated how long they were going to go down this path. It was endlessly irritating. But that was the point, after all. To get underneath his skin.

Cortez said, "Aldrich Ames . . . he ratted out CIA agents in Russia. Many were killed. Drugged and killed. Know his motivation? Money. His financial situation spiraled out of control and he needed money. Lots of money. Some interesting parallels. We figure you're a Russian spy. You want to be put on trial for being a spy?"

Reznick beamed. "I love that vivid imagination. You should take up writing novels."

"Cut the smartass comments," Cortez said. He fished out six color photos from a folder. They showed Reznick with tax attorney Robert White getting picked up in his car in Miami. "So, this was the conduit, wasn't it? Robert White, son-in-law of Michael Leahy, who had been passed the intel by Stephen Leahy, who you met up with in a hospital, remember? And you shot up a car that was tailing you, killing the three occupants. I'm guessing your Russian handlers were delighted. We're going to be speaking to Robert soon. I don't think he's as strong as you, Jon. I suspect he'll fold very quickly under pressure."

Reznick leaned back in his seat, arms still folded.

"That's a rampage. And it got me thinking. Is it possible maybe you're not of sound mind? Maybe *you* need to be in a psychiatric hospital. Just like Stephen Leahy. Maybe we need to have you examined. Would you have any objections to that, Jon?"

Cortez let the threat of Reznick's detention in a psychiatric hospital sink in, allowing the threat to burrow deep into the darkest recesses of his mind.

"We're trying to reach out to you, Jon," Carrington said. "Help us help you, Jon. Meet us halfway."

Reznick sighed.

"If you give us the name of your handler here in the States, we'll consider taking a more favorable look at what you've done. How does that sound?"

Reznick felt himself detaching himself from the conversation. It was a self-preservation thing. A way of operating without getting unduly emotionally involved. His eyes traveled around the room. They took in the blank, white walls, antiquated AC vents. He spared a thought for the men who had installed them in the Hoover Building all those years ago. Where were they now? Were they even still alive?

The pair of Feds continued to fire a barrage of questions and veiled threats at Reznick. Hour after hour, he tuned out the accusations that he was a spy. The question of who was he working for. The suggestion that maybe he needed to be in a hospital to be evaluated.

Reznick lost track of time. That was the point. It was ultimately an irritant to Reznick. No big deal.

Eventually, Cortez, looking puffy with red eyes, checked his watch. "I say we call it a day. Whole new ball game tomorrow. We'll ship you across town for tonight."

"Where are you taking me?"

"The Central Detention Facility. Get a good night's sleep, Jon. You're going to need it."

Thirty-Six

Reznick rose after a sleepless, disturbed night. The shouts and screams from other prisoners had echoed around the jail the whole time. Calling out, demanding to be seen. He showered. Put on his clothes. He sat down to a breakfast of lukewarm black coffee and buttered toast before being taken on the short journey to the Hoover Building. The same windowless room. It was day two of the interrogation.

Reznick saw the same two FBI agents from the National Security Branch, already behind the desk, looking fresh-faced, papers in front of them.

He sat down without being asked.

Special Agent Carrington smiled. "I hope you slept well."

"Like a log," Reznick lied.

Cortez put on a soothing voice. "I'm looking to start afresh today, what do you say?"

"What's on your mind?"

"I found it rather frustrating, Jon. We were trying to be open and hoped that you would reciprocate."

"You got a question?"

Carrington reached into a folder and took out a black-and-white photo. It showed a familiar face. Reznick's heart nearly stopped.

He studied the surveillance photograph of his daughter. He read between the lines of the game they were playing.

"I assume you know who this is."

"What do you want?"

"We want the truth, Jon," Cortez said. "We believe in being frank with those we interview. We prefer to lay our cards on the table."

Reznick seethed. Lauren was a red line in the sand. If they thought that bringing her into the conversation would move the needle, they were wrong. He felt his heartrate rise a notch.

Carrington said, "We know a lot about you: your black-ops background, time in the military, then at the CIA. Very, very impressive. I was reading about your months in Fallujah. Tough place, right?"

Reznick wanted to knock someone out cold.

Cortez continued, "But we also know a lot about your daughter. Lauren, isn't it? She is giving us serious cause for concern. Is she involved in this conspiracy you're involved in? Is she working for the Russians too? I can't disentangle what's what. Therefore, we have to assume there's a link unless told otherwise. We will have to investigate her, her contacts, everything about her. We'll have to trawl through her bank accounts. Does she receive money too?"

"Leave my family out of this. You got any problems with me, you speak to me."

Carrington scribbled on her legal pad something he couldn't make out, while the grinning agent opened a buff-colored file in front of him. "That's what I'm trying to do. I want to speak to you." Carrington flicked through the file. "Let me see now . . . So, Lauren Reznick—extremely bright, highly ambitious, is indeed an Agency employee. Stellar qualifications, résumé, best grades, top of her class. And I can read for you the numerous commendations on her performance from the station chief in Jakarta. Very well liked, respected, superb analyst. As a father, you must be very proud."

Reznick knew they were getting to him. Like pulling at a loose thread on an old sweater. But this was not just any thread. It was the blood thread. His family. "This is all very interesting. But what the hell has this got to do with my questioning?"

Cortez showed him a grainy image of Lauren, backpack slung over her shoulder, walking through what looked like an airport. "You know where and when this was taken?"

"How the hell would I know that?"

"Jakarta International Airport, two days ago. She flew back to DC. Bet you didn't know that?"

Reznick took in the photo. He chewed over how far they were going to push him, and what he would do when he got there.

"Here's the deal, Jon. We can make this go away. We can make it all go away. And that means we can take Lauren out of the equation. She doesn't need to be part of this discussion. But you need to accept responsibility. You need to admit that you shared highly classified top-secret intel. Tell us all about it. Who is involved? Take it on the chin and we won't need to interview your daughter."

Reznick laughed.

"What's so funny?" Cortez said.

"You. Is that your shakedown? Is that your Hoover Building shakedown? *You sign this confession, Jon, and your daughter gets away scot-free?* A patriotic young woman who serves her country with distinction each and every day. Is that how you treat her? Let me tell you something, you piece of shit, I asked for a lawyer and I haven't gotten one. Write that down! But here's the thing. My daughter is as tough, smart, and resourceful as they come. She doesn't need me to fight her battles for her. She'll know how to handle any interviews with you lame fuckers."

Cortez picked up the photo of Lauren and took a few moments, nodding his head as if admiring it. "Such a shame. Such a pretty girl."

Reznick reached over and grabbed him by the throat. "Don't ever talk about my daughter like that, you fat fuck!"

Cortez screwed up his eyes as Carrington sat rooted to the spot. "Let me go!"

Reznick growled as he pressed his thumb tighter against Cortez's carotid artery. "Do you hear me?"

Cortez was breathing hard, knowing Reznick could kill him in a second. His face began to redden. "I hear you. Now let me go!"

Reznick slowly released his grip.

Cortez's face flushed bright red; his eyes watered. He took a few moments to compose himself. He cleared his throat. "That will be duly noted. Attack on FBI Special Agent, National Security Branch. Manual strangulation."

Reznick's face went back to placid, pleasant even. "You enjoy that?"

Carrington said, "Do you think that helped your case?"

Reznick folded his arms, fixing his gaze on her.

"You need to wise the fuck up, Jon. You are in serious, serious shit. You just assaulted an FBI agent. I witnessed it. But that's the least of your worries. You are facing life in prison if this goes to court and you're found guilty. Lauren will never, ever see you again outside the walls of an institution. Think long and hard about that."

Reznick tilted his head at Carrington, shaking it.

She showed him a color photo this time—Lauren arriving at Dulles International Airport. "You know why she's back in DC?"

"No, I do not. That's her business. She operates on a need-to-know basis. But you already know that, right?"

Do you know where she is at this precise moment?"

Reznick said nothing.

"She seems to be cooperating, you'll be glad to know."

He let their remarks land and rolled with it.

"She has agreed to a full interrogation, interview—call it what you like—as we try to figure out who knows what about this leaking of classified intel. Have you told Lauren details of the plan? Have you messaged her about it? Does her story line up with yours? We'll find out if you did. But it would be easier if you just confessed everything now. For her sake."

Cortez smirked. "Did you call her about it, Jon? We have a court order to search all of her devices. She will be subject to intense scrutiny about what she does or doesn't know. She's on our radar. And that's never a good thing. Did she meet up with the Russian military attaché in Jakarta? We're going to find out everything. We've got all the time in the world."

Reznick felt sick to the pit of his stomach. But his face remained impassive.

"No one is above the law, Jon, not even you. Or your daughter. You could have allowed her to return to her job unscathed. I half expected you to take the fall."

"For what?"

"But you've chosen to let your daughter sink or swim. I'm not sure I would have taken the same course, Jon."

"She's well trained. Well schooled. Besides, that emotional leverage bullshit that you pull? That stuff might've worked on General Michael Flynn. Remember him?"

Carrington flushed pink again, eyes cold.

"You pressured him to take the fall, admit his guilt, so his son's business interests wouldn't be investigated. A murky, murky deal. Well, let me tell you something, I ain't no Michael Flynn. But I know why he might have felt pressured to accept the deal, right?"

Cortez scribbled note after note.

"I don't crumble. I don't walk away. Neither does my daughter. You don't scare me, you lying sack of shit."

Thirty-Seven

The days rolled into one another.

Reznick got grilled and grilled. He was interrogated for nine long hours every day. The same questions, the same recalcitrant attitude. The same two Feds. They were trying to wear him down. But without success. It was more irritating than soul-destroying.

And all this time, he still hadn't seen a lawyer. He reminded them that he wanted to see the lawyer Trevelle had arranged. But all they could say was "all in good time." Then the cycle continued.

Reznick wanted to know how Caroline was doing. He hoped she was out of hospital. He hoped she had been released and had secured a good lawyer. But he sensed that she'd be getting the same treatment.

Reznick was held for twelve days and twelve nights. The same tactics, yielding nothing. But finally, on the twelfth day, he was allowed to see his lawyer.

Reznick was escorted into a narrow side room adjacent to where he had been interrogated. His lawyer was waiting and stood up to introduce himself.

"I'm Bernie Krugman. I've been trying to get to you since you were brought in. Before anything else, how are you?"

"I'm fine."

"You don't look fine. Do you want a doctor?"

Reznick shook his head. "I'm fine. When did you become my lawyer, Bernie?"

Krugman paused. "When Trevelle Williams called me on your behalf."

"What did Trevelle say exactly?"

The lawyer gave a low rumble of a laugh. "He said you would ask that. He said to tell you that he told you he had a bad feeling about this, but he also said that he always says that."

Reznick nodded. "That sounds like Trevelle. Guess you're my lawyer. So, what's happening, Bernie?"

"I'm afraid to say that they're tightening the screws. You are going to be indicted. As will Caroline Sullivan."

"Are you kidding me?"

Krugman shook his head. "They're throwing the book at you, son. They want to make an example of you. Also, I would not recommend meeting up with Caroline until after the trial. I'm concerned they'll bug her house or her phone and get proof of a conspiracy. Do you understand what I'm saying?"

"That's a bit draconian."

"What can I tell you? It's in your interests to keep your distance from her. There is one ray of light."

"There is?"

Krugman smiled. "You are about to be released. They have a court order. You just need to sign a release document, declaring that you won't flee the country. And you have to hand in your passport."

Reznick felt himself grimace. "A lot of my work is abroad."

"They know that. But that's what you're dealing with. It's a take-it-or-leave-it deal."

"I guess that's the best I can expect, right?"

"Pretty much. But we need to focus. We need to prepare for trial, assuming the district attorney follows through."

Reznick shook his head. "What about my daughter? She's the most important thing to me. They said they were going to interview her. They said if I accepted a guilty plea, they would let her go. I need to know she's going to be okay."

Krugman beamed. "I've got good news on that front. Your daughter isn't far, Jon. In fact, she's waiting for you."

"She is? What about Caroline?"

"My colleague is representing her. She's back home at her townhouse in Georgetown."

Reznick was shown a twelve-page document, which he signed.

"Take care, Jon. And under no circumstances try and flee the country. I can't help you then."

"Got it. So where exactly is my daughter?"

"Come with me."

Reznick went with Krugman out of the Hoover Building into the bright sunlight. He put on his sunglasses as we walked alongside his lawyer. It was a couple of blocks to Krugman's car. He got in the passenger seat and Krugman drove Reznick to his firm's nearby offices. He followed Krugman into an elevator and rode up to the ninth floor.

The lawyer opened a door into a conference room.

Lauren was sitting, beaming. "What took you so long?"

Reznick thought his heart was going to burst. He walked forward and hugged her tight. "You okay, honey?"

"I'm good, Dad. I was worried about you."

Krugman cleared his throat. "I'll leave you to catch up. I'll be in my office across the hall if you need me."

Then he shut the door behind him.

Reznick hugged his daughter tighter than he ever had. "I'm sorry for getting you involved," he said. "I had no idea it would lead to this."

"Dad, don't sweat it."

"How long did they interview you for?"

"Twelve hours."

Reznick felt enraged. "Seriously? How did you cope?"

"How do you think? With ease. Don't forget, you taught me how to deal with bureaucratic bullshit, right?"

Reznick laughed. "That's my girl. What did they want to know?"

"They asked question after question about what I knew. Did I know Stephen Leahy? Did I know about classified operations in South America?"

"And what did you say?"

"I'm taking the fifth. Get me a lawyer. Now!"

Reznick hugged her tight. "Smart girl. I can't believe they flew you halfway around the world. I was worried sick."

"Look on the bright side, Dad. I got a trip home, right? I'm seeing you."

"I love that. My God, Lauren, it's so good to see you."

Lauren touched his scraggy beard, grown in the time he had been taken into custody. "Dad, you need to shave. You look like a bum."

Reznick laughed. "Yeah, you got that right."

"I knew the game they were playing, Dad. What about you?"

"What about me?" Reznick said.

"What's going to happen?"

"They've forced me to give up my passport. I am going to be prosecuted. I'm assuming you're not."

"That's terrible, Dad."

"What about your passport? You still have yours?"

"Still got it. I'm in the clear."

Reznick clasped her hands in his. "I didn't want any of this for you. But I'm proud of how you dealt with this. You showed backbone. And you never wavered. You're one tough cookie."

"I learned from the best."

Reznick hugged her again. "I love you."

"I love you too, Dad."

"Listen, and this is important. Did the FBI ask you to stay away from me or anyone else? Did they threaten you with losing your job?"

"No, they did not."

"I suppose we should be grateful for small mercies."

"All they said at the end of the interrogation was *we thank you for your time*."

Reznick shook his head. "Glad you made it through. Listen, there's another person who was interviewed by the Feds. A journalist. A national security expert: Caroline Sullivan."

"I'd love to meet her."

"I'm not allowed to see her. Maybe we can see her another time when this is all over. In the meantime, it's been a while since you were last back home in Rockland."

"I know. Too long."

"What do you say we head back home?"

Thirty-Eight

When he arrived back in Rockland, after a much-delayed flight from Dulles, Reznick felt his mood lift. He was back at his home by the sea. The familiar sights and sounds. And his daughter was there with him. "You hungry?"

"Starving."

Reznick fixed her a meal of Sicilian-style meatballs in a thick tomato sauce, with a blizzard of parmesan and roasted garlic and parsley. He poured them each a large glass of Rioja, put on some jazz and raised his glass. He clinked it against hers. "Here's to family."

Lauren took a small sip of her wine. "That's good."

They ate in companiable silence as a Bill Evans jazz album, *Sunday at the Village Vanguard*, played quietly in the background.

Reznick looked at his beautiful daughter, forging her way in the world. Tough, resilient, and smart. He loved that. It reminded him of the combination of qualities his wife Elisabeth had. Nothing ever seemed to faze her. And Lauren was the same. A chip off the old block.

"What's this music? I've never heard it before."

"It was one of your grandfather's favorites. He introduced me to the record. Bill Evans. Apparently he met him once in a bar in

New York. One of the greatest jazz pianists in history. Played with the best, including Miles Davis."

"Wow. Dad, I'm shocked."

"About what?"

"I didn't know you were into stuff like that."

"What's wrong with that?"

"Nothing, Dad, relax. I just always think of you as the hunting, fishing guy who loves guns and disappears abroad for months at a time."

Reznick sipped some wine. "This is nice. It's been a long time, Lauren."

"It's good to be back."

"How's the job? How's Jakarta?"

"Long hours, sleep deprivation, stinking heat. Station chief driving me nuts."

Reznick laughed. "That's pretty much every job I've been on. You get used to it."

"I don't think I'll get used to being away for such long periods. I was thinking about coming home again."

Reznick remembered she had been homesick a couple years back. "That's your choice to make."

"I know. And I've made it."

"Good for you. Your room is always here. Haven't changed a thing."

"That won't be necessary, Dad."

"Why not?"

"I've got a new job. Back home in the States."

"You got a new job? You kidding me? Where?"

"I'll be working as an NSA contractor. Intelligence analyst for a private company: Rooz Chern. Applied two months ago. Interviewed via Zoom."

Reznick clapped. "So this trip home wasn't for nothing."

"Quite the opposite. It was actually good timing."

"Honey, all I can say is I'm glad you're home. I'm thrilled you're coming back."

"I think I've done my stint abroad."

Reznick raised his glass and clinked it against hers. "To family."

Lauren raised her glass, taking another small sip of wine. "Amen to that."

Thirty-Nine

It was the dead of night at Reznick's isolated home on the shore. He sat in the kitchen, nursing a glass of single malt, still awake, buzzing on adrenaline, listening to Miles Davis playing low on the speaker, Dexedrine flowing through his bloodstream. Lauren was asleep upstairs. He felt desperately sad, thinking of Stephen Leahy and his tragic death. Leahy's demise had probably already been signed off when he reached out to his father in Florida, who reached out to his lawyer in DC, who contacted Reznick. Now all three were dead. It was inexplicable that three such tragic incidents should befall the three men. But they had been no accidents. It was a pattern.

It was conceivable that Leahy, tormented by what had happened, had indeed hanged himself because of psychological issues. That was the official narrative, but it was one Reznick didn't believe. A brilliant man, a patriot, hidden away in a psychiatric hospital, kept under a false name. Before he was neutralized. His days had been numbered the moment *they* knew he had leaked the plans.

His cell phone vibrated in his pocket, snapping him out of his introspection.

Reznick took a sip of Scotch and pulled out his phone. No caller ID. "Yeah, who's this?" he said.

"Hey Jon, glad you're finally home. I was worried about you." The voice of Trevelle Williams.

Reznick felt relief wash over him. "Good to hear your voice, man."

"Yours too. I mean, what the hell just happened down in DC?"

"Don't worry about it. I was more concerned about them dragging Lauren into the whole thing."

"Me too. How is she?"

"Lauren? Sound asleep upstairs in her old bed. It's good to have her back."

Trevelle sighed. "Man, what a trip you've been on. Jon, I thought I'd never see you again."

Reznick snorted. He'd heard that before, more times than he could count.

"There's something I thought you'd want to know, Jon."

"What?"

"What Stephen told you about. The plans."

"I was trying to forget all about that."

"Turn on CNN. Right now. I'll stay on the line."

Reznick picked up his remote and switched on the small TV sitting on his countertop and flipped to CNN. He stared at the screen. He felt numb.

It had begun just as Leahy had predicted.

The live footage showed huge explosions rocking offshore American oil installations in Guyana, helpfully filmed by unknown sources. Then the footage switched. There were gunmen running amok in gated communities used by American oil workers, sparking gun battles in the streets. People fleeing into the night. Bodies lying in alleys. Tanks on the move. Buildings ablaze.

"What have we done, Jon? It's happening. It's all happening. This is what Stephen was talking about, right?"

Reznick knocked back the rest of his whisky, which warmed his insides. He felt heartsick watching the footage, all of it predicted by Stephen.

The news report showed a British reporter on the scene, wearing a bulletproof vest with *PRESS* emblazoned in yellow, standing in front of a burning building, rioting raging in the background. Armed police firing live bullets. "Intelligence sources are telling us that mercenaries and powerful drug cartels, working on behalf of the government of Venezuela, are responsible for the bombings, which have murdered scores and scores of American workers and their families. It is believed to be a reprisal for attacks on boats used by the cartels to transport drugs up to the United States. The latest reports from my colleagues say that four separate offshore oil and gas drilling rigs are in flames, with secondary explosions destroying the facilities, costing the lives of countless oil workers, many of them American. A gated community two miles from where I'm standing has been attacked by a mob of masked terrorists, known to be mercenaries working for Venezuela. This has been confirmed by multiple sources within the State Department, the CIA, and members of the Senate Intelligence Committee. Caracas has laid claim to the Essequibo Region administered by Guyana."

Reznick muted the sound, staring at the horrific footage coming in.

"It's happening. Just like Leahy said. They kept you and Caroline out of the way until it all started."

Reznick poured himself another large Scotch and swirled it around the glass before knocking it back in one. He gawked at the screen as CNN switched to a live press conference from the White House. He couldn't stop it now even if he and Caroline tried. It was too late. Way too late.

The President approached the lectern and turned his eyes coldly to the camera. "Fellow Americans, the killings in Guyana are an attack on the United States. Make no mistake. The American people are demanding we take action. I have just ordered our military to take whatever steps they deem necessary. This will not go unpunished. It is a monstrous, savage, unprovoked attack not only on our people, but on our energy security and our vital national security interests across Guyana and Central and South America. This is the work of the communist government of Venezuela. A rogue state."

Reznick observed the screen, numb.

"I have just been informed," the President continued, "by the Central Intelligence Agency and the Joint Chiefs of Staff at the Pentagon, that their latest analysis shows the attacks to be the work of the leaders of the failed socialist narco-terrorist state of Venezuela. A country whose citizens are rising up day after day, year after year, against this despicable government. But make no mistake, the corrupt leadership of Venezuela is backed by its military ally, Russia. They tried to make a land grab in Guyana, to seize vital oil and gas installations, destabilizing the whole of Latin America. They might have started this, but it will be the United States of America that finishes it, so help me God."

Reznick closed his eyes.

"I want to tell the nation, my fellow Americans, that the government in Venezuela will pay the price and will be brought to justice. They will pay like they've never paid before. The full might of the American military, its incredible power and its incredible warriors, will be unleashed on the regime in Caracas. The nightmare of socialism will end. We will end it. And we will crush them. God bless our brave troops headed to Venezuela and Guyana to deal with these terrorists. God bless our people. And God bless the United States of America."

Reznick switched off the TV. Still on the call with Trevelle, he picked up the bottle of Scotch and his glass, and headed out to his deck, overlooking Penobscot Bay. He poured himself a large drink and sat down, staring out over the dark waters.

He thought of the lives lost. The hundreds of lives: innocents. And then he thought of the countless more lives that would be lost in the coming days, weeks, and months. Then he thought back to Stephen Leahy, who had predicted it all.

"I don't know what to say, Jon," Trevelle said.

Reznick peered into the dead of night. "Nothing to say."

He ended the call, put his phone on the table, next to the bottle of Scotch, and leaned back in his seat, closing his eyes, tumbler in hand. His mind flashed with images of the bodies lying in the street, gas rigs exploding, gated communities being overrun.

All that was left to do was pray.

Epilogue

Three months later, Reznick was among the mourners under a gray sky in Cypress Grove Cemetery in New Orleans. He watched the coffin of Ray LeBlanc, draped in the Stars and Stripes, being slowly lowered into his grave. His friend had finally succumbed to the cancer. Reznick consoled Ray's widow, trying to soothe her, talking about Ray in the old days. But she was consumed by grief, wailing and crying.

Later, he turned and walked out of the cemetery with a handful of mourners, family and friends. Then he caught a cab back to the French Quarter.

Reznick felt like drowning his sorrows. He walked into The Abbey in lower Decatur. He pulled up a stool, sat at the bar, ordered a drink.

Reznick sipped from his bottle of beer, remembering the old days. Ray had been a reconnaissance expert who specialized in high-value targets. A man Reznick had trusted, like every one of the men who had served alongside him, thousands of miles from home.

He snapped out of his reverie when a familiar, stunningly attractive woman walked into the bar.

Reznick caught Caroline Sullivan's eye, signaled her over, and she sat down beside him.

"Long time no see, stranger," she said.

Reznick was taken aback. He ordered a couple of beers for them both. "Well, this is unexpected. How've you been?"

"Not so good, if you must know. I've been struggling to deal with everything."

The bartender handed over the cold beers. "Enjoy!"

Reznick picked up his bottle of German lager, clinking his against Caroline's. "To old friends." He took a long swig. "How did you find me?"

"Trevelle mentioned you were coming down here. I hope you don't mind me joining you. I know you were at a funeral earlier."

"I'm pleased to have the company, trust me. The funeral was rough. His widow broke down at the graveside. My friend suffered for too long. Not very pretty."

"I'm sorry."

Reznick shrugged. "He's at peace now. For that, I'm grateful. What about you?"

"I'm not sleeping well. I'm having nightmares, actually. I'm on medication, too. Therapy."

Reznick felt guilty, knowing he was responsible, having contacted her in the first place and then locked her in the safe room. "I get it. Traumatic events . . . was it the night at Stone's house? I'm sorry for that decision. I can only imagine the trauma of being locked in there."

"It is what it is. I survived. But I've also been thinking about the chain of events. Jon, one of the reasons I wanted to speak to you in person is, I'm still scared."

"What are you frightened of? It's over. Besides, it's out of your control—what's happening down in Venezuela and Guyana."

"I'm not talking about that. I'm getting calls in the dead of night. Terrible calls: threats to kill me, to decapitate my nieces."

Reznick reached over and held her hand. "I'm so sorry. I'll find out who's making the calls. I'll make sure you never get another phone call again."

Caroline shook her head. "No need. They quite openly say they're working on behalf of the American government."

"Shit."

"They've also been watching me at my home in Madison. Or they say they have. At my house, walking on the beach. Photographs of me walking alone, sent to my home. They know me. They know everything about me. I feel like I'm being watched night and day. Maybe I am."

Reznick felt his heart sink.

Caroline continued. "The calls said that if any article, or story, or book discussing Venezuela or Guyana were to appear . . . I'd be buried alive."

"I think we need to find out who's doing this."

Caroline sipped her beer, shaking her head. "No way. I just want it to end."

"They want to silence you."

"Yeah, well, they've silenced me alright. I thought I was a brave journalist. But I'm not so brave after all." Her eyes filled with tears. "It's such a disappointment. That I don't have the guts to tell this story."

"I think it'll come out one way or another—maybe in a few months, maybe a few years."

"I have the story. I should have the guts to tell it."

"Have you reached out to the *Times*?"

"Yeah."

"What did they say?"

"They're starting some background. It looks promising. And I would lead on it. But . . ."

"But what?"

"I'm thinking about my life. My nieces' lives. Does that make me selfish?"

"Makes you human."

"I want to do it. I've started writing."

"Good for you. You've got to figure out the motivation for what you're doing. What's your purpose?"

"Speaking truth to power. Telling people the true story. The real story. Not the fabricated narrative."

Reznick pulled her close. "Do what you have to do."

"I'm reluctant after the threats."

"I don't blame you. It's natural."

"But if I don't get the story out there, what was it all for? Finding out about the operation. Watching the whole hellish spectacle unfold on live TV. And to be struck dumb? With fear? It's not very heroic."

"Caroline, I've known many, many tough, brave, and honorable men reduced to mental rubble from trauma. From fear. You need to heal yourself. Go away for a while, take some time."

"You think I should move away?"

Reznick nodded. "Under the circumstances you've described, I think that would be a prudent move. Sell all your homes and disappear. I could help you. I know people."

"They would find me, wouldn't they?"

"Not if you do it right."

"How would I do that? And where would I go?"

"Where do you want to go?"

"I don't know. I don't want to run away."

"They know where you live, right? What if they change their mind and neutralize you to remove the potential threat?"

"Maybe I should just go to the FBI."

"I wouldn't trust the Feds to keep you safe."

Caroline closed her eyes, clenched her teeth. "Jon, I'm scared as it is. But I think you're right. I don't think they could protect me."

"Let's get out of here. I'm staying at the Four Seasons on Canal. We can continue the discussion there. What do you say?"

"I dropped my luggage off there an hour ago."

"You staying there, too?"

"Great minds and all that."

"The bar in the lobby, the Chandelier, is a nice place to hang out. What do you say we have a nightcap or two?"

Caroline kissed him on the cheek. "Thanks."

"For what?"

"For making me feel like less of a fraud."

Reznick smiled. He held her hand and they headed outside into the night, where he hailed a cab. Five minutes later they were sitting at the bar of the Four Seasons, knocking back a Mojito and a single malt.

Reznick took a sip of his Scotch, warming his belly. "They might carry it out even if you *don't* write the story."

"What if I get a new identity? New passport? I know that can be done."

Reznick nodded.

"I can work from anywhere. Maybe if I wrote under a pseudonym."

"You want to do it, don't you?"

Caroline shrugged. "My head is telling me no. But my heart is telling me yes. If you were in my shoes, what would you do?"

"I can't answer that. You've got to figure it out for yourself."

A couple of hours later, Reznick escorted a tipsy Caroline to her room.

"You want a final nightcap, Jon?"

"No thanks. Got an early start in the morning."

Caroline smiled, her eyes heavy. She kissed him on the cheek. "Goodnight, Jon."

"Goodnight." Reznick waited until she was locked safely inside before he headed back to his room up on the eighth floor. He showered and put a towel around himself.

Half an hour later, there were a couple of knocks on the door.

Reznick instinctively reached for his gun before he peered through the peephole. It was Caroline, red-eyed, crying. He opened the door and let her in. "What is it? What's wrong?"

She handed him a large envelope. Inside were four black-and-white photos: images of Reznick and Caroline at The Abbey. A piece of paper inside was scribbled with the words: *We'll be watching you. We'll always be watching you. You need to forget all about this. If not . . . you die.*

"They're going to kill me, aren't they, Jon?"

Reznick held her close as she began to sob; he realized she was in the middle of a never-ending nightmare.

Dawn, the following morning. The sun peeked over the headstones in Cypress Grove Cemetery. Reznick had been up for hours. He stood again at the graveside of Ray LeBlanc, not quite twenty-four hours after his funeral. He was due to fly out later in the morning to DC with Caroline, before catching a flight back up to Maine. But he thought he'd take a few minutes to himself with Ray. He touched the alabaster stone and the inscription, *The Lord is my Shepherd, I Shall Not Want.* The latest member of the Delta cadre to have passed.

Reznick bowed his head. "So long, Ray. Next time I'm back in town, I'll come visit. Glad you're finally at peace, bro."

He stood, lost in his thoughts. Thinking back to Ray in Iraq. The pair of them together.

Reznick suddenly sensed he was being watched. He turned around and saw a stranger approach from behind the headstones.

The man wore a St. Louis Cardinals baseball cap, sunglasses on, long coat, Glock gun pointing at Reznick. It was Tom Steele, the lawyer.

Reznick noticed Steele was wearing forensic gloves. He realized in a split second that they were going to try to make it look like Reznick had taken his own life, yards from the grave of his friend. It was brilliant. And it was diabolical.

His mind raced. He debated reaching for the Beretta in his waistband. He fixed his gaze on the man's gun.

"Can we talk, Jon?"

Reznick considered if this guy was for real. He shook his head. "Put down the gun."

"I just want to talk."

"So talk. You following me?"

"No, I'm not."

Reznick thought he sounded drugged. "You sure? How did you find me? And what's with the gun? I thought you were a lawyer."

"They told me you were here."

Reznick stood still as Steele stopped about ten feet away, gun still pointed at Reznick's chest. "This doesn't have to go down like this. Drop the gun."

Steele shook his head. "They told me you were here."

"Who's *they*?"

"I can explain. Two minutes, Jon, that's all. I just want to talk."

Reznick needed to keep him talking. He needed to focus. He took a step forward. "Take it easy, man. What is it? I thought we were done?"

"They wanted me to talk to you. Again."

Reznick stepped forward.

"Freeze! Not one more step."

Reznick stood rooted to the spot. "Tom, what are you doing?"

"They wanted you to know something."

"What?"

"They're going to kill me if I don't kill you."

Reznick knew that already. He locked onto the gun. "Who is they?"

"The people who hired me. I get calls every day saying they're going to kill me. They said they know how this can all go away. They talked about investigating my firm. Billable hours . . . we fucked up a couple years back, IRS on our back. Money problems. I thought I had it figured out."

"You need to go to the cops. The Feds. I'll help you."

Steele shook his head. "Do you know why they're going to kill me?"

Reznick shook his head.

"They said you're a threat to the country, Jon."

Reznick saw that Steele was beginning to shake. He took in the tall, athletic man. He couldn't believe what he was hearing. Steele took off his sunglasses with his left hand, his right hand still holding the gun trained on Reznick. "They say I know too much. They say the only way for me to live is to come down here and kill you. They knew you would be back in New Orleans for the funeral. They waited and waited. They wanted me to do it after the funeral yesterday. Then last night at your hotel. But I refused."

Reznick saw it was classic plausible deniability. The CIA or the government didn't have to kill Reznick if they could get some poor schmuck to take the fall. "What changed?"

Steele blinked away tears. "They visited me in the middle of the night. I drove around with them. We parked near your hotel."

Reznick pondered the extent of the CIA cover-up operation still ongoing, all following the plans.

"Turn to your right. Out on Canal Street, other side of the road, there's a black Suburban. Do you see it?"

Reznick's gaze wandered around the cemetery and across the street. A black Suburban had pulled up, a white guy standing beside it, cell phone pressed to his ear.

"They're watching me. Right now. You see them?"

Reznick's mind could see the brilliance of the setup. He hadn't walked away. Now they were going to neutralize him . . . except *they* wouldn't be pulling the trigger.

He needed to keep Steele talking. "Is that them?"

"They told me to come here, introduce myself again, engage you in conversation, then kill you."

Reznick nodded at Steele. "Do you know who they are?"

"They said they work for the government. The gun is government-issue, no serial number. Untraceable, they said. I don't know anything about it. But they're telling me to do it. No way out, Jon. You see how it is?"

"I see exactly." Reznick now wanted to rush him. He sensed he had to. But something inside him cautioned against being rash. He had to try to get inside Steele's head. Build whatever rapport he could. "Are you going to kill me, Tom? It's just me and you. I'm not threatening you, am I?"

Steele shook his head, tears spilling down his cheeks. "If I don't do it, they'll kill me."

"I understand." Reznick glanced around again, over toward Canal. The Suburban was just idling, engine on, the man watching from afar, like some kind of ghoul.

"They're watching me, aren't they? They're watching and waiting for me to kill you."

Reznick put out his hand. "Give me the gun. Nice and easy. And we can figure this out."

Steele took a step back. "If I don't kill you, they're going to frame you for killing me. You're the fall guy. Don't you get it?"

"I get it, Tom. I see the setup." Reznick looked deep into Steele's dark, hooded eyes. "Just gimme the gun, man. Don't do anything stupid. You're not a stupid man. Don't start now."

Steele shook his head. "I'm sorry. I can't think of a way out. Please forgive me." He pressed the gun into his mouth and blew his brains out. The muffled *phut* sound of the gunshot scattered the birds in the trees across the graveyard.

Steele collapsed to the ground, eyes open, the back of his head blown off.

Reznick felt sick as he looked down at the body. The whole thing had played out like a slow-motion film. It had been a setup. He stood motionless. He felt the shock reverberate around his body. Steele had decided to take his own life rather than become the patsy.

He looked down at the blood pooling around Steele's head. He looked over toward Canal. The Suburban was gone. The poor bastard. What had he gotten himself into? The problem now was that Reznick was in the frame. It was a brilliant setup. That's how *they* would have wanted it. Reznick or Steele dead—either way, Reznick was fucked.

He took a few moments to process the catastrophic events. He could see it now—if he stayed, and called 911, Reznick would be incriminating himself. He'd be back in a cell, and perhaps they'd follow through on the threat of committing him to a psychiatric hospital this time.

He needed to think. *Think, goddamn it.*

Steele was dead. Reznick couldn't help him. But he could help himself.

Reznick turned away from the bloody body on the ground, walked out of the cemetery, headed along South Bernadotte, and moved swiftly down the weed-strewn side streets away from the cemetery, shaded by live oaks.

He walked for miles, back to his hotel. He showered again.

Reznick and Caroline met up in the hotel lobby and caught a cab together to the airport.

"Where were you this morning?" she said. "I was hoping you'd join me for breakfast."

"Just getting some air and stretching my legs before the flight home."

"You okay, Jon?"

"I'm fine, why?"

"You seem distracted."

Reznick was more than distracted. He stared out at the passing streets, at a single cop car, lights on, cruising down Basin Street. "Just looking forward to getting home."

Caroline reached across and held his hand, squeezing tight. "Me too."

The cop car passed by. The officer in the passenger seat wore shades, had his tattooed arm out of the window.

Reznick closed his eyes, thinking of the body of Tom Steele lying in the cemetery, only yards from the grave of his friend Ray LeBlanc. He said a silent prayer, knowing he was lucky to be getting out of New Orleans alive.

Acknowledgements

I would like to thank my editor, Maisie Lawrence, and everyone at Amazon Publishing for their enthusiasm, hard work, and belief in the bestselling Jon Reznick thriller series. Thanks also to Faith Black Ross for her terrific work on this book, and Randall Klein, who looked over an early draft.

I would also like to give my heartfelt thanks to Kevin Heller, an international-law professor at the University of Copenhagen.

Thanks also to Todd Hodnett, long-range shooting expert, founder of Accuracy 1st, who has trained military groups around the world for the past twenty years.

Special thanks to my agent, Mitch Hoffman, of the Aaron M. Priest Literary Agency, New York.

Last, but by no means least, my family and friends for their encouragement and support. None more so than my wife, Susan.

If your heart was pounding as Reznick raced to solve the case, then you'll absolutely love *Hard Road* by J. B. Turner. Don't miss the book where it all began for Reznick . . .

When you work outside the law, the only person who can protect you—is you.

Jon Reznick is a "ghost": a black-ops specialist who takes his orders from shadowy handlers, and his salary from the US government. Still mourning the loss of his beloved wife on 9/11, he's dispatched to carry out a high-level hit. Reznick knows only that it must look like suicide. It's textbook. But the target is not the man Reznick expected. The whole setup is wrong.

When Reznick's young daughter becomes a pawn in the game, he has to use more than his military training to stay one step ahead of those responsible. Meanwhile, he is the only person who knows the true extent of the threat to national security—and has the stealth and determination to stop it.

An utterly gripping action thriller that will have your pulse racing as you fly through the pages! Available now or keep reading for an exclusive extract . . .

One

The call came from a man he knew only as Maddox.

Jon Reznick was sitting on his freezing deck as darkness fell over Maine, nursing a bottle of beer, staring out over the ocean. He let his cell phone ring a few times, knowing what lay ahead.

It had been ten long weeks. He pulled his jacket tight and watched his breath turn to vapor. He sighed long and hard before he picked up the phone.

"We got a delivery problem in Washington," Maddox said.

Down below in the cove, the Atlantic breakers crashed with a deafening roar, sending salt water into the winter air. The silhouettes of the tall oaks and maples shorn of their leaves—trees his late father had planted in the garden when he was a boy—bent and creaked in the wind. Away in the distance, out in Penobscot Bay, Reznick could see the lights of the lobster boats as they headed back to Rockland with the day's catch.

Maddox finally broke the silence. "They want to know if you can ensure the safe transfer of a consignment."

"When?"

"You must leave tonight."

Reznick said nothing.

"Is this inconvenient for you?"

"Kinda short notice."

"Are you available?"

"Tell me, how's the weather where you are?"

A long pause. "It's wet."

The word "wet" said it all.

"Someone must want this delivery real bad."

"Will you do it?"

Reznick was silent again.

"This has got to happen. This is an important customer."

He let out a long sigh. "Tell them I'm in."

"Smart move, Reznick. Pick up your tickets at the airport."

"Where am I going?"

"You'll see."

The line went dead.

Reznick's plane landed at Dulles just before midnight. He wore a black leather jacket, a gray T-shirt, dark blue Levi jeans, and scuffed cowboy boots. He slung his overnight bag over his shoulder and headed over to the Avis lot. There he picked up a black Chevy Camaro. In the trunk was an envelope with a fake credit card and two thousand dollars in cash alongside a reservation receipt for three nights at the Omni Shoreham Hotel in northwest Washington.

Reznick knew the city well. He headed onto the airport toll road and drove due east on Interstate 66, over the Roosevelt Bridge, then exited onto Constitution Avenue. The traffic was still heavy, despite the late hour. His mind flashed back to the time he first visited the city with his father. It had been the winter of 1982, the first of many trips to see the Vietnam Veterans Memorial. He remembered his father in the rental car, cursing the snarled-up traffic. But most of all he remembered what his father wore: a dark suit, white shirt, Marine Corps tie, and black shoes polished to a glassy shine. On every visit, without fail, his father had touched the names of the young men carved into the black granite wall the moment he arrived. Reznick would stand in silence, arms by his side, as his father fought back the tears.

The blaring siren of a fire truck in the distance snapped him out of his reverie as he drove over the historic Taft Bridge, past the imposing concrete lions guarding each side. He took a left onto Calvert Street, the hotel up ahead. He pulled up outside the traditional, eight-story building and tipped the valet ten dollars.

Reznick walked through the grand, sprawling lobby. Marble floor, ornate columns, chandeliers. A young man at the front desk took his details as he signed in under a false name: Ron Dixon.

"Three nights. Good to have you with us, Mr. Dixon. Do you mind me asking if you're in town for business or pleasure, sir?"

Reznick managed a smile. "A bit of both."

"Excellent. Can we help you with any bags?"

"No, you're OK, thanks."

His fake credit card was swiped and he took the elevator to the sixth floor. Reznick used the keycard to open his door and flicked on the lights. He hung a "Do Not Disturb" sign outside before locking the room.

It was too warm, but it was spacious. A huge TV was on one wall, a welcome message on the screen. The decor was the "classic" look—green, floral-patterned carpet, and a king-size bed with a couple of rosewood dressers. The drapes matched the carpet.

Reznick peered out the window over the upscale Woodley Park neighborhood: a good base, well away from downtown. He turned down the climate control switch to "Cool," showered, and wrapped himself in a white terry bathrobe. Then he lay down on the bed and stared at the ceiling, waiting for the phone to ring.

The next morning, Reznick ordered a freshly squeezed orange juice and a black coffee from room service, before getting changed into his jogging gear—navy T-shirt and sweatpants with well-worn Nike running shoes. He walked over to Rock Creek Park under the flawless winter sky for his daily run. When he arrived at the water-powered Peirce Mill near the entrance, he did some stretching and warm-up moves, the temperature in the low thirties. A handful of runners were already pounding the snowy trails.

He switched on his iPod, blocking out the outside world, helping him focus on the task at hand. The thunderous riffs and beats of a Led Zeppelin song got his blood flowing. Reznick checked his watch: 8:48 a.m. precisely. He headed north on the Western Ridge Trail, a smell of pine trees in the mid-December air.

After about a mile, he passed a young woman sitting on the curb of a parking lot near Broad Branch Road. She grimaced as she rubbed her knee.

Reznick ran on by. No need to engage in unnecessary conversation with a stranger. Being anonymous was best. He knew the rules—the list was endless. Do not wear loud clothes, talk too much, appear distracted or lost; in fact anything that meant you were no longer blending in. Appearance is crucial: grays, navy tracksuits, and business suits are good; black shoes, also. But you have to fit in to the surrounding environment.

The way you speak, the way you carry yourself, your accent, dialect—they all give off signals. The moment a concierge thinks your luggage looks too flashy or too beaten-up, it all paints a picture. If you're in a top-end hotel, wear top-end clothes and carry smart cases.

The small things matter. Be attentive. Logos are easy to remember—better without them. The trick is to be anonymous. But don't try too hard. Don't shun eye contact. That in itself will attract attention. *What has he got to hide?*

The senses have to work overtime. And tactics have to be changed, depending on the circumstances. Move to another hotel, change into new clothes, ditch the car and get a different model.

He headed along Beach Drive as he ran through the park. Heart rate steady. Deeper and deeper into this verdant urban sanctuary in America's capital city.

Reznick's mind began to feel clearer. Slowly, he felt his senses sharpen as the sun flickered through the branches of the leafless trees. On and on he ran.

Up a hill and down a ravine, and back onto the main trail, passing a small stone police substation in the center of the park, two officers leaning against a cruiser, drinking coffee. He gave a polite nod and they nodded back.

Heart pumping harder as his head cleared. This was his routine ahead of every job and it passed the time. Kept him focused.

Up in the northern section of the park, he passed Rolling Meadow Bridge and doubled back along a trail by the public golf course. On past the amphitheater and across Bluff Bridge to where he'd started.

He checked his pulse. Only slightly raised.

Ten minutes later, Reznick was doing some cool-down stretching exercises against a park bench when the cell phone in his pocket vibrated. He switched off his iPod and saw the familiar caller ID.

"How you feeling today?" It was Maddox.

"I'm fine."

"So, any questions?"

Reznick wiped some sweat off his brow with the back of his hand. "You got a name?"

A beat. "All I know is that he's an American. OK?"

"On home soil? How come?"

A long pause. "Look, they wanted to keep it in-house. That's all I can say. This is a sensitive one."

"Tell me, where's the subject now?"

"Walking the National Mall with his son."

"What kind of monitoring?"

"Electronic. Far safer."

Reznick stayed quiet, knowing Maddox was right.

"How about we speak later today?"

"When?"

"I don't know. But stay close to your hotel."

Reznick shielded his eyes against the sun. "Why?"

"Why what?"

"Why stay close to the hotel?"

Maddox sighed. "Look, I've not had any confirmation, but I've heard from someone higher up the chain that we might have to move very quickly on this particular delivery."

"Timescale?"

"Sooner rather than later. Bear that in mind."

The rest of the morning dragged as Reznick waited for Maddox to call.

It could be a matter of hours. He dialed "12" and ordered a brunch of scrambled eggs, black coffee, buttered toast, and more freshly squeezed orange juice. After a warm shower, he channel hopped between CNN, Fox News, and the Weather Channel.

Bombings across Kabul and Helmand province, as the Taliban launched a coordinated series of attacks to destabilize the Afghan government and instill fear in the population. He could see the way the wind was blowing there and it was all bad.

Early evening, he ordered a club sandwich and a Coke from room service. Afterward, he went for a walk, keeping within six blocks of the hotel. He returned to his room, lay down on the bed, and fell into a fitful sleep.

When he woke, he checked the time. It was 8:09 p.m., and still Maddox hadn't called. Had there been a delay? Perhaps a lastminute change of plan?

The thought of delays depressed him. He'd been asked to do a job; he wanted to get it over with. Then move on. He couldn't abide the drawn-out ones.

Feeling groggy, Reznick headed down to reception, bought a pair of swimming shorts, and swam forty lengths of the empty pool, leaving his phone on his towel on top of a lounger.

He headed back upstairs and changed into a fresh T-shirt and jeans. He paced the room, stopping occasionally to do push-ups and sit-ups, trying to keep sharp, not knowing when the call would come—if it would come at any moment.

Eventually, he slumped in the room's easy chair and turned on an old black-and-white Jimmy Cagney film with the sound down.

His cell phone vibrated in the chest pocket of his T-shirt.

"You're on the move." The voice of Maddox.

"Where?"

"Go to the Park America garage, one three zero one K Street Northwest, and leave your car on Level Two."

Reznick made a mental note.

"Proceed to Level Five, where you'll find a black BMW convertible.

Your key fob can electronically open it. Proceed to the St. Regis hotel, and book in under the name Lionel Fairchild. New ID and documents are in the glove compartment, and a brown Louis Vuitton travel bag with overnight essentials is in the trunk."

"What's in the bag?"

"The usual kit. Laptop, delivery equipment—it's all there. After you check in, head straight to your room, which has already been allocated, and await final instructions."

Reznick did exactly as he was told.

First, he checked out of the Omni, taking time to thank them for such a pleasant stay but he was sorry, he had to cut short his visit for family reasons. He picked up his car from the valet and drove to the nearby parking garage as instructed. He left the vehicle on Level 2 and climbed the stairs. A rather smart BMW with tinted windows was parked at the far end of Level 5. He popped open the trunk—the monogrammed men's travel bag was inside. He picked it up, got into the car, and clicked the fob to centrally lock the doors before he unzipped the bag.

Inside was a thirteen-inch metallic MacBook Pro, a specially modified cell phone, a pair of night-vision binoculars, a 9mm Beretta handgun and sufficient ammo to kill a small town, a high-tech fob that opened all cars and jammed any surveillance, a sleeping drug in a nasal spray, a military-issue Taser, a powerful muscle relaxant in a syringe disguised as a ballpoint pen, and five thousand dollars in cash.

Reznick zipped up the bag and slid it under the passenger seat. Then he drove straight to the deluxe hotel in downtown Washington to await final instructions.

Two

The St. Regis on 16th Street was known as one of Washington's smartest hotels. Two blocks north of the White House, its impressive limestone facade was festooned with Christmas lights, only hinting at the grandeur inside.

Reznick pulled up shortly after 10 p.m. and handed his keys over to the valet, careful to take the Louis Vuitton bag.

A concierge opened the door and he strode into the lobby. It was like some Italian Renaissance dream—chandeliers hanging from coffered ceilings, gilt-framed paintings, oriental rugs on the marble floor, dark wood furniture.

Reznick handed over the new fake driver's license and credit card to a young woman behind the desk. "Good evening," she said.

"Nice to have you at the St. Regis, sir." She brought up his details on the computer. "Is this your first time with us?"

"Yeah."

"Well, we hope you enjoy your stay." She handed over a swipe card as a smiling, uniformed bellhop approached. "This is Andy. You need anything, don't hesitate to ask."

Reznick smiled and was escorted to the sixth floor by Andy, tipping him twenty dollars. "I'll get it from here."

"Are you sure, sir?"

"Absolutely."

The bellhop gave a polite nod and headed back to the elevator. Reznick waited until the guy was out of sight before he carefully swiped the keycard. Inside, the large room was decidedly upscale. A king-size bed, large flat-screen TV, an antique-style writing desk, chair and sofa, and a minibar stuffed with Krug and Rolling Rock beer. Original artwork on the walls and chandeliers set the scene. The bathroom featured brass fittings and earth-toned mosaic tiles, a large mirror that doubled as a fifteen-inch "intelligent" TV, two marble sinks, and a fluffy white St. Regis bathrobe hanging behind the door.

The first thing he did after looking around was hang a "Do Not Disturb" sign outside his room and lock the door. Satisfied he wasn't going to be interrupted, he unzipped the Louis Vuitton bag and placed the pre-configured MacBook on the desk. He opened it, and within a matter of seconds it was up and running.

Reznick sat down, punched in his allotted password—*coldbracelet1*—and brought up his inbox. A soft beep, and there was one encrypted message with an attachment.

He clicked on "Decrypt Message" to view the file and was prompted to confirm two unique passwords. He keyed in *OfwaihhbTn*, initials from the first line of the Lord's Prayer, followed by *DNalKcOr*, his hometown spelled backward. Then three personal questions: his grandmother on his father's side's maiden name—Levitz; his father's birthplace—Bangor; his blood group—Rh negative.

He typed in the answers and the email displayed on the screen. He clicked on the "Reply" button and the attachment was downloaded securely.

A two-page dossier and six black-and-white photos appeared before his eyes. The man he'd been sent to kill.

Reznick's stomach knotted as he scanned the screen. Tom Powell, aged fifty-nine, described as an "imminent security risk." Powell lived with his second wife and their two school-age children in a quiet cul-de-sac in Frederick, Maryland; his oldest son was away at university. According to the file, he had checked into the St. Regis the previous evening—room 674, three doors down. It didn't say exactly why he should be neutralized.

Reznick pondered on that. Usually when he did a hit, the reason was made quite clear. It could be spying, terrorism, or one of a whole host of threats to the country. Invariably, they had an explanation.

So why not now?

Reznick read on. The file said Powell had to be a "suicide." No other options.

This was the first time that Reznick had been asked to kill an American citizen on American soil. He knew that it would have been impossible if he were still a part of Delta Force because of the Posse Comitatus Act, which under federal law prohibited the military being used in operations within the United States. But he was no longer constrained.

In the past he'd taken out a Saudi military attaché in New York, a billionaire banker in London who was funding Hezbollah, a Russian spy in Vienna, a host of jihadists across the Middle East, and a smattering of Islamic fundamentalists living and working in America.

It was business. Realpolitik. The stone-cold reality of politics based on facts and material needs.

He studied the pictures of the man—including one of him playing football in a local park in Frederick with his eldest son, John, a law student at George Washington University. The son was a good-looking kid: clean-cut, short hair, preppy clothes.

He looked at the photos of Powell until he could remember the smallest details. The dime-sized mole on his left cheek, the graying sideburns, the bushy eyebrows, and the small scar above his right eyebrow caused, according to the file, by a schoolyard fight.

Reznick's training at "The Farm" in Virginia, all those years ago, had stressed the importance of knowing the subject inside out. This enabled an appropriate plan to be drawn up and executed.

Maddox and his team would have explored Powell's lifestyle and habits. His sleeping patterns and any health problems. The file noted that he was a keen golfer, not on prescription medication, and led a clean life—a glass or two of expensive French red wine at dinner on a Friday or Saturday evening was his only vice.

Reznick finished reading the dossier, shut down the computer, and waited for Maddox to call. The waiting was always the worst part of the job. Endless hours spent hanging around motels, hotels, safe houses, halfway houses, flophouses, apartments—a myriad of places—before the final phase.

The endgame.

Reznick was not the judge. Nor the jury. He was the executioner. Except he didn't sit in on the trial, because there was no trial. This was summary justice, as practiced by every government in the world. Sometimes the dirty work was subcontracted to a foreign intelligence agency or their associates. But this was in-house.

Just after midnight, Reznick's cell phone vibrated in his pocket. He switched on the TV, which was showing highlights of a Redskins game, to drown out his voice.

"Are you in place?" Maddox asked.

"Yes."

"This is a wet delivery. Do you understand?"

"Absolutely."

"OK, run-through time. Our guy is a creature of habit. He's in his room, fast asleep."

"How do you know?"

"GPS on his BlackBerry and a bug in his room's smoke detector. Hold back until five minutes *after* zero two hundred hours, when the video camera in the corridor will be remotely switched off until zero three hundred and the lights dimmed. You have a copy of his swipe card. Assume you have fifty-five minutes to make this delivery."

It was enough time.

"Do good," Maddox said.

"Count on it."

"Your room will be cleaned as soon as this delivery has been made. A maintenance uniform is hanging in your closet." A long pause elapsed. "Sit tight. Then it's just you and him."

With less than one hour to go, Reznick was sitting in his darkened hotel room, primed to carry out the delivery. He had changed into a pale blue, short-sleeved work shirt and black pants, gold wire-rimmed glasses, and shiny black shoes. There was a metallic nametag on his lapel—*Alex Goddard, Service Engineer*—and a bag at his feet. He pushed a tiny audio device into his right ear for communication; the nametag concealed a hidden microphone.

Everything in place. No diversions. No TV, radio, music, magazines, or newspapers to sidetrack him. The way he always worked during the crucial last hour.

The LCD display on his digital watch showed 01:21. Not long now.

Reznick's earpiece buzzed and he tensed up.

"Reznick, do you copy?" Maddox's voice was a whisper.

"Reznick?"

"What?"

A small sigh. "OK, we have two room-service types—a guy and a woman—one dropping newspapers outside doors, the other pushing a trolley with food and drinks. They're in the elevator, and they're heading your way."

Reznick could hear his heart beating.

"OK," Maddox whispered, "now they're on the sixth."

On cue, the ding of the elevator doors opening and dull footsteps padding down the carpeted corridor. The faint tinkling of metal against glass, accompanied by a low male voice. Thuds as the papers were left outside each room. The sound of a door opening.

Three long minutes later, they were gone.

"OK, buddy, sorry about that. You all set?"

"How's our guy?"

"Sleeping like a baby. Slam dunk, Reznick. You've got a clear run."

The line went dead at 1:23 a.m.

When it hit 02:05, he peered out of the peephole. No movement or sound. He lay flat down on the floor and pressed his left ear—the one without the earpiece—to the carpet, listening for elevator vibrations, footsteps, sudden noises . . . anything.

He heard the faint sound of water pipes creaking. Perhaps the merest hint of laughter somewhere below.

Apart from that, all quiet.

Reznick got up and stood, picking up the bag. He took half a dozen slow, deep breaths.

Just breathe.

His breathing even, he was ready.

Slowly he turned the handle, stuck his head out of the door, and peered down the dimly lit hallway.

Not a soul.

Slow is smooth, smooth is fast.

The military dictum of the Marines kicked in. It meant moving fast or rushing in was reckless, and could get you killed. If you move slowly, you are less likely to put yourself at risk.

He edged out and closed the door as softly as he could. The metallic locking system sounded to him like a rifle reloading.

Reznick looked around and took the short walk to Powell's door. Carefully, he swiped the card, the metallic clicking noticeably softer. He cracked the door. The sound of deep snoring.

He kept the door ajar for a few moments as his eyes adjusted to the semi-darkness. The room smelled of stale sweat and old shoes. Underneath the window, the crumpled silhouette of the man lying in bed, facing the wall, duvet on. Reznick shut the door softly, and it barely made a noise as it clicked into place.

He crept toward the sleeping man. Closer and closer, careful not to trip on any objects lying around.

Standing over him, Reznick saw the dime-sized mole on his left cheek. Suddenly the man groaned and turned over onto his back. The springs of the bed creaked.

Reznick froze, not daring to breathe. A deep silence opened up for a few moments as he wondered if the man was really awake. He stood still and waited.

One beat. Two beats. Three beats.

Eventually, on the fourth beat, the snoring continued as before, rhythmic and deep. Reznick exhaled slowly. Then he reached into his pants pocket and pulled out a lipstick-sized Taser. He leaned over and pressed the metal device hard against the man's temple. Electric currents provoked convulsions for three long seconds. Powell's eyes rolled back in his head. The sound of gurgling and groaning. Then nothing.

Unconscious.

A standard first-step procedure. Eight minutes, maybe ten, before the man came to.

Reznick rummaged in the bag and produced the auto-injecting syringe disguised as a ballpoint pen, containing succinylcholine chloride, which he knew as "Sux." The drug was a skeletal-muscle relaxant used as an adjunct to surgical anesthesia and had been employed as a paralyzing agent for executions by lethal injection. A twist of the nib and a quick stab into the man's skin would deliver seven milligrams of the drug. But only five milligrams was necessary for death.

The victim would be paralyzed within thirty seconds. The muscles, including the diaphragm, would shut down, with the exception of the heart. He would be unable to speak or move, although his brain would still be working. Then he had three minutes until his breathing ceased, unable to scream out for help.

The beauty of the drug for assassinations was that enzymes in the body begin to break down the drug almost immediately, making it virtually impossible to detect.

Powell was to be injected in the buttocks, as—in the absence of evidence of foul play—most medical examiners would suspect a heart attack as the natural cause of death.

Reznick pulled back the duvet and switched on his penlight, examining the paunchy, unconscious man lying before him. He wore pale blue pajamas with a white tank top underneath. He had on a cheap watch with a frayed, brown leather strap. The last moments in his life, and the poor bastard didn't know anything about it. Reznick never usually felt anything when he had to kill a foreign terrorist or one of the billionaires who bankrolled them. But in this case it did feel strange, knowing that this was an American.

The penlight picked out something around the man's neck, tucked inside his tank. Reznick looked closer, and thought it looked like an aluminum dog tag. He held it in his hand, turned it over,

and saw an inscription in Hebrew—the name Benjamin Luntz—
and a seven-digit identification number.

Israeli Defense Forces.

He stared at the dog tag for a few moments.

Why the fuck had Tom Powell got the dog tag of an Israeli
soldier around his neck? It didn't make any sense.

The doubts began to set in. He needed certainty.

He had to wait more than eight minutes before Powell came to
with a low groan. Reznick pressed the Beretta to the guy's forehead.
Powell gazed up, confused and scared.

"Shut up and listen," Reznick snarled, hand covering his mouth.

The man nodded.

"Any sound, and you die. Got it?"

He nodded again.

Reznick removed his hand. "All right," he said in a low voice.
"Gimme your name, and date and place of birth. Right now."

The man gulped hard. "Please, take whatever you want."

Reznick pressed the gun tighter to his skin, making a small
indentation as the guy began to tremble. "This is the second time
I'll ask. I don't ask a third time. Now, give me your name, date and
place of birth. Failure to comply will result in the maids cleaning
your brains off this wall in six hours' time. Got it?"

"My name is Frank Luntz, born New York City, October
twelve, 1953."

Reznick's mind went into free fall for a split second. The target's name was Powell. Something was badly wrong.

"Tell me about the dog tag around your neck."

"It's my son's."

"What's his name?"

"Benjamin Luntz."

Reznick wondered whether to believe the man or not.
Something wasn't adding up. Was he being played?

"Are you Israeli?"

"No. My son emigrated. He had joint citizenship."

"What do you mean *had*?"

"He was . . . he was blown up by a suicide bomber at a checkpoint in the West Bank three years ago."

The man made a sudden movement and Reznick pushed him back down into the pillow. "Don't even think about it."

"I want to prove it to you."

He reached under his pillow and pulled out a silver photo pendant. A faded color picture of a young man in combat fatigues, rifle slung over his shoulder, sitting atop a Merkava tank.

The man pointed to the bedside cabinet. "The top drawer. Check my wallet if you don't believe me."

Reznick reached over and opened the top drawer. Empty. No driver's license or credit cards to establish the man's true identity.

"There's nothing there, you lying bastard."

"That's impossible. Perhaps Connelly has it next door."

Reznick was tempted to kill the fucker there and then. "Who's Connelly?"

The man began to cry.

"Answer me. Who's Connelly?"

"He's a Fed. He's in the adjoining room. He's looking after me."

Reznick's stomach knotted. "What the hell are you talking about?"

"He has the adjoining room to this." The guy pointed a shaking finger in the direction of a door next to the dresser.

"Are you lying to me—because if you are, you die, here and now."

He began sobbing. Reznick placed a huge hand over his mouth to muffle the sound.

"One more peep out of you and I'll rip out your wiring. Do you understand?"

The man nodded, tears spilling down his cheeks.

"Hands on your head."

He complied. Reznick pulled a sock out of the dresser and stuffed it into his mouth, before tearing up strips of the bedsheet and tying it around his head to secure the sock. Then he tied the man's wrists and ankles to the four corners of the wooden bed, crucifixion style.

Reznick shone the penlight directly into his eyes. "Don't even think about fucking moving."

He nodded quickly. Reznick walked across to the door and pressed his ear up against it, listening for several seconds for any sounds. Creaks. Groans. But he heard nothing.

Slowly, he turned the handle and opened the door. His eyes scanned the room. The bed was made, the wooden blinds and curtains shut, as if awaiting the next hotel guest. Perfect order. Empty.

Or so it seemed. The hint of sandalwood in the air told another story. The room had been occupied.

Reznick sensed something was wrong. He shone the penlight toward the bathroom and opened the door. Opulent white marble sinks, bath, and floor. White towels neatly stacked on a metal rack above the bath. A slight smell of damp pervaded the air, as if from a recent shower.

Again, that didn't add up to an unoccupied room.

Reznick went back into the bedroom as the penlight raked the high-quality carpet beside the huge closet. His gaze wandered around the room, past a small flaxen sofa, until he fixed on a white louver door. He saw it wasn't shut properly. Perhaps half an inch ajar.

He moved closer. Kneeling down, he shone the light through the slatted openings. Inside, he saw what looked like tousled blond hair.

He held his breath. Then he reached out and felt the wooden handle, before yanking open the door.

Reznick's heart jolted as the penlight picked out the crumpled, semi-naked body of a blond-haired man. Telltale purple bruises around the neck and throat, hemorrhaging around the dead eyes.

Reznick had seen this sort of thing before. Many times. The man had been manually strangled.

This was so fucked up it wasn't real.

His mind was racing when he returned to the first room. He leaned down beside the man strapped and gagged to the bed. The guy stared up at Reznick like a terrified child, afraid of his fate.

Reznick untied the strips of bedsheet around the man's mouth and pulled out the sock. Then he pressed his face right up against the other man's, smelling the sweat and fear. "Who the fuck are you?"

"I already told you."

"Why do people want you dead? Who do you work for?"

"I work for the government. Look, please tell me who you are. What've you done to Connelly?"

"Forget about him. Forget about me. What about you? What exactly do you do?"

"I told you, I work for the government."

"Doing what?"

The man closed his eyes and shook his head.

"Answer me."

"I'm a government scientist."

Reznick stuffed the sock back into the guy's mouth. He walked over to the window and buzzed Maddox on his lapel microphone, giving him the lowdown. The discovery of the murdered man's body—perhaps a Fed—and the possibility that they had the wrong guy.

Maddox listened in silence before he said, "Gimme two minutes and I'll get back to you."

In less than a minute, the earpiece buzzed into life.

"The subject is to be protected and brought in. Make your way with the subject to a motel, the Clarence Suites, six blocks away on N Street Northwest, due northeast, and sit tight. Room seven eight seven. You're booked in under Ronald D Withers. He's your brother, Simon Withers. Clear?"

"Then what?"

"We're sending two of our guys, Bowman and Price. They'll take him off your hands."

About the Author

Photo © Robbie Bald 2024

J. B. Turner is a former journalist and the author of the Jon Reznick series of political thrillers (*Hard Road, Hard Kill, Hard Wired, Hard Way, Hard Fall, Hard Hit, Hard Shot, Hard Target, Hard Vengeance, Hard Fire, Hard Exit, Hard Power, Hard Duty, Hard Lights,* and *Hard Sun*), the American Ghost series of black-ops thrillers (*Rogue, Reckoning, and Requiem*), the Jack McNeal Thriller series (*No Way Back and Long Way Home*), and the Deborah Jones crime thrillers (*Miami Requiem and Dark Waters*). He has a keen interest in geopolitics. He lives in Edinburgh, Scotland, with his wife and two sons.

Follow the Author on Amazon

If you enjoyed this book, follow J. B. Turner on Amazon to be notified when the author releases a new book!
To do this, please follow these instructions:

Desktop:

1) Search for the author's name on Amazon or in the Amazon App.
2) Click on the author's name to arrive on their Amazon page.
3) Click the "Follow" button.

Mobile and Tablet:

1) Search for the author's name on Amazon or in the Amazon App.
2) Click on one of the author's books.
3) Click on the author's name to arrive on their Amazon page.
4) Click the "Follow" button.

Kindle eReader and Kindle App:

If you enjoyed this book on a Kindle eReader or in the Kindle App, you will find the author "Follow" button after the last page.